NEW YORK REVIEW BOOKS
CLASSICS

LAMENT FOR JULIA

SUSAN TAUBES (1928–1969), born Judit Zsuzsanna Feldmann in Budapest, was the daughter of a psychoanalyst and the granddaughter of a rabbi. She and her father emigrated to the United States in 1939, settling in Rochester, New York. She attended Bryn Mawr as an undergraduate, and in 1949 married the rabbinically trained scholar Jacob Taubes. Taubes studied philosophy and religion in Jerusalem, at the Sorbonne, and at Radcliffe, where she wrote her dissertation on Simone Weil. She and her husband had a son and a daughter, in 1953 and 1957, and in 1960 she began teaching at Columbia University, where she was the curator of the Bush Collection of Religion and Culture. During the 1960s, Taubes was a member of the experimental Open Theater ensemble; edited volumes of Native American and African folktales; published a dozen short stories; and wrote two novels, *Divorcing* and *Lament for Julia*. Her suicide came shortly after the publication of *Divorcing*, in November 1969. Two collections of Taubes's extensive correspondence with Jacob while they lived apart in the early 1950s were published in Germany in 2014; the letters appear in their original English with German annotation.

FRANCESCA WADE is the author of *Square Haunting: Five Women, Freedom and London Between the Wars*. She has written for the *London Review of Books*, *The Paris Review*, *The New York Times*, and other publications, and has held fellowships from the Leon Levy Center for Biography and the Dorothy and Lewis B. Cullman Center for Scholars and Writers.

LAMENT FOR JULIA

and Other Stories

SUSAN TAUBES

Introduction by
FRANCESCA WADE

NEW YORK REVIEW BOOKS

 nyrb

New York

THIS IS A NEW YORK REVIEW BOOK
PUBLISHED BY THE NEW YORK REVIEW OF BOOKS
207 East 32nd Street, New York, NY 10016
www.nyrb.com

Library of Congress Cataloging-in-Publication Data
Names: Taubes, Susan, author.
Title: Lament for Julia / by Susan Taubes.
Description: New York: New York Review Books, [2023] | Series: New York
  Review Books classics | Identifiers: LCCN 2022022472 (print) |
  LCCN 2022022473 (ebook) | ISBN 9781681376943 (paperback) |
  ISBN 9781681376950 (ebook)
Subjects: LCGFT: Novels.
Classification: LCC PS3570.A88 L36 2023 (print) | LCC PS3570.A88 (ebook) |
  DDC 813/.54—dc23
LC record available at https://lccn.loc.gov/2022022472
LC ebook record available at https://lccn.loc.gov/2022022473

ISBN 978-1-68137-694-3
Available as an electronic book; ISBN 978-1-68137-695-0

Printed in the United States of America on acid-free paper.
10 9 8 7 6 5 4 3 2 1

CONTENTS

INTRODUCTION

In SEPTEMBER 1969, Susan Taubes returned to Budapest, the city where she had lived until the age of eleven. Standing outside her childhood home amid the bustle of the late-afternoon rush hour—the veranda bright with plants, the bushes still filled with berries, the wrought-iron gate closed—Taubes was overcome by a feeling of "beauty and grief, unbearable." "Intolerable," she wrote in her diary, "that I should stand here as another, denied access to the house; intolerable to stand here after thirty years of disembodied rootless wandering." Confronted with the ghostlike vestiges of a former self, Taubes found herself impelled to turn away: "A frozen memory now thaws suddenly into live, raging, devouring monster of time."

Taubes's fiction is suffused with such moments of disorientation, her characters caught between past and present, fantasy and reality, dreaming and waking. From childhood, Taubes had questioned "the commonplace assumption that a person has a self, soul, or core of some sort which he is born with and carries with him from cradle to the grave." Having moved from one country—and language—to another at a formative age, she was convinced that an individual is not one singular entity but a "fleeting changing multiplicity." *Lament for Julia*, an extraordinary novel that Taubes described as "about the bafflement of an angel or merely an exalted consciousness, incarnated in a woman," takes this idea to a darkly comic extreme. Its disembodied narrator, a "celestial spark" of sorts, who envisions himself as a "very thin gentleman in black with a cane," yet whose destiny has been entangled with that of a woman named Julia Klopps since her birth, attempts to tell the story of Julia's life, in a futile effort to make sense of their shared, yet split, identity. Despite his privileged vantage point—sometimes by Julia's side or watching over her from above, sometimes lurking inside her body or attached to her forehead "like a miner's lamp"—his understanding is flawed, his ability to reconstruct her personal history fallible: a working title for the novel was *Remembering Wrong*.

Lament for Julia opens with a howl of anguish, like that of a betrayed lover: Julia has vanished, and the narrator is, almost literally, rent asunder. Trying on her skirts, dwindling into nothing, this "princely parasite" is forced to confront the question that drives his account of her troubled childhood, adolescence, and adulthood: "what was I without her?" At first, the narrator's voyeuristic fascination with Julia's body, his prurient anxiety over her burgeoning sexuality, and his simultaneous adulation of her as a virgin and bride recalls Vladimir Nabokov's Humbert Humbert, or the predatory pursuer of Anna Kavan's *Ice*. The narrator considers Julia his "prisoner," his "creation"; by turns he plays father, husband, and pimp, while she remains elusive, the subject of his fascination, disapproval, bemusement, and, increasingly, envy. But as the narrative progresses and their relationship becomes clearer, the dynamics shift. By leaving, Julia has coolly stepped beyond his clutches, putting an end to his attempts at control. "I fancy she is my puppet," he ruefully admits, "when in fact Julia leads me by the nose." In Gnostic tradition, the creator of the universe was a potentially malevolent demiurge who trapped a "divine spark" within human beings; Julia's failure to apprehend her spiritual essence blocks off her path to self-knowledge and condemns her—and the spirit—to the miserable materialism of the earthly realm. His desperate attempts to redeem her mirror a sense of moral urgency felt by many thinkers of Taubes's generation to transcend the hypocrisy, conformity, and violence of the postwar, postnuclear world. Yet if the spirit represents Julia's ideal ego—the perfect self to which Freud considered the narcissist aspires—his inability to save her from a meaningless life of bourgeois frustration marks a crushing failure that undercuts the novel's commedia dell'arte surface.

Like Taubes's groundbreaking novel *Divorcing*, *Lament for Julia* lays bare the arbitrary forces that shape the direction a life can take. Its prevailing tension lies in the conflict between the narrator's expectations for Julia—that "she was made to belong to a man, to adorn him like a jewel"—and Julia's own desires. The stories collected alongside *Julia* in this volume also often depict women who are desperate to reject the roles ascribed to them and radically remake themselves. Julia's dissatisfaction in her marriage to a man who likes to drink her breast milk and declares himself "addicted to work" is echoed in "The Gold Chain" by Rosalie's strident wish to become pregnant by someone other than her ineffectual husband, and in "Easter Visit"—a gemlike piece whose poignancy belies its shock value—by the illicit lovers carving out a space to confess and act out fantasies far removed from the drudgery of their ordinary lives. In *Beyond the Pleasure Principle*, Freud articulated his idea that our lives are governed by the competing drives of Eros and Thanatos. Whether fantasizing about being eaten alive so as to mingle with a lover in a hawk's belly, committing infanticide in a wedding dress, or pledging marriage to Death himself, Taubes's heroines exemplify her own belief, as expressed in a letter to her husband in 1950, that "human passions are dark dark things."

Readers of *Divorcing* will be familiar with the contours of Taubes's life, which can be traced, in fragments, throughout her fiction. Born in Budapest in 1928, she moved to the United States in 1939 with her father, Sandor Feldmann, the author of Freud-inflected studies on sexual pathology, mannerisms of speech, and nervous disorders, while her mother remained behind in Hungary with her new husband. Several of Taubes's stories feature absent mothers and domineering psychoanalyst fathers: Dr. Rombach, who attributes his teenage daughter's coldness to "a compensatory mechanism in overcoming your strong oedipal attachment to me," or Dr. Sigismund in "Swan," who commits his patients one by one to an asylum, for fear of their seducing his daughter. Finding a language and beginning to write, in these stories, is often associated with the fraught transition to adulthood:

For Marianna Rombach, who can "spend hours just paging through the dictionary," words help her stay grounded in reality, while Griselda Sigismund's eerie fictions—written on scraps torn from her father's prescription pad—presage the uncanny events that follow.

Simone Weil, a lodestar for Taubes, wrote that "to be rooted is perhaps the most important and least recognized need of the human soul." Taubes experienced her "continuous estrangement" from the home and family of her childhood—many of her Jewish relatives did not survive the war—as a "malnutrition or nervous disease." As a child, she wrote epic poems in Hungarian, and later reflected that she had never truly felt at home in English. That estrangement became her major preoccupation across her life and work. It is manifest in her academic interest in atheism, particularly Weil's profound religious experience of the absence of God; in her refusal to engage with organized religion (despite her husband's devout Judaism, she was suspicious of "any mass belief and tradition," and preferred to "build my own altar"); and in her fictional explorations of states of limbo, where time is suspended and fairy-tale logic reigns. Taubes considered surrealism "the true realistic novel of this generation." Just as *Divorcing* cuts between everyday scenes, historical experience, and dream images, her short fiction shifts registers with relish, often fragmenting into hallucinatory endings that leave the reader unmoored.

Taubes later claimed that she had begun writing "sporadically, clandestinely, and with a bad conscience." Her father "regarded writing as a sickness"; her husband, the philosopher Jacob Taubes, "disapproved on religious grounds." She married Jacob when she was twenty-one and spent the subsequent decade moving between Europe and America, pursuing a doctorate in philosophy and bringing up two children. Her first, unpublished novel, *Downgoing*, drew on their short courtship and portrayed a young couple's tense negotiations over the place of religion in their marriage; she also compiled two anthologies of Native American and African myths and folklore, an interest that sprang from her work as a curator at the Bush Collection of religious artifacts at Columbia University. In 1961, living alone in New York and with her marriage falling apart, Taubes joined a circle of women writers led by her close friend Susan Sontag, whom she had met while living in Boston, and the Cuban playwright (and Sontag's lover) María Irene Fornés, who met regularly in one another's apartments to share work in progress. These women were the first readers of *Lament for Julia*; their invigorating exchange confirmed Taubes's decision to leave her job (teaching comparative mythology and religion at Barnard College) and reinvent herself, to create the conditions that would allow her, finally, to devote herself to writing. When asked by an agent to compose a biographical note to accompany the manuscript, Taubes listed her studies at Bryn Mawr, Geneva, Paris, Jerusalem, and Harvard; her essays on Genet, Heidegger, and Camus; a dissertation titled "The Mystical Atheism of Simone Weil"; and four years on the faculty of Columbia University. The final line read: "Left New York and husband to live in Paris with my children. And write." A handwritten postscript added: "Probably better not stress my academic career. Anyway it's over."

From the autumn of 1962, Taubes continued to revise the novel in Paris, where she spent most of the next two years, immersed in New Wave cinema, electronic music, and voracious reading. "In N.Y. I am a mess, a misfit," she wrote to Jacob, but "here one can cultivate one's eccentricity creatively." Her attempts to find a publisher for *Lament for Julia* were frustrated: Éditions de Minuit offered to publish a French translation, galvanized by a recommendation from Samuel Beckett, who called her "an authentic talent without doubt," but American publishers were wary, and the only house that expressed interest promptly closed down. "It seems undefined, implied central European settings make editors uneasy," she wrote to a friend in frustration. Over the 1960s Taubes reignited her interest in drama, taking classes with the French mime Étienne Decroux and working with Joseph Chaikin's avant-garde Open Theater. She completed *Lament for Julia*, wrote several short stories, and began *Divorcing* at the Radcliffe Institute, while on a fellowship specifically aimed at women writers whose work was stymied by family or economic constraints. Among her application materials is a letter of recommendation from Sontag, calling Taubes "an extremely gifted writer, and a person of exceptional depth and seriousness...she needs encouragement badly." Taubes was found dead on November 6, 1969, a few days after the publication of *Divorcing*. A few years later, Sontag dissected Taubes's last months in a story, "Debriefing," about a neurotic friend who shocks and infuriates those around her by committing suicide. Her name, tellingly, is Julia.

Though *Divorcing* is Taubes's most overtly personal work, *Lament for Julia* played a crucial role in her formation as a writer. It prepared her to write about her childhood, and set her thinking about the possibilities of first-person narration (a note from 1965 plays with the idea of a book to be called "The Real Life of Susan Taubes by Julia Brody"). The outpouring of accolades *Divorcing* received on its republication in 2020—favorable comparisons with the best work of Ingeborg Bachmann, Elizabeth Hardwick, and Renata Adler; claims for Taubes's status as a precursor to contemporary autofiction—are testament to how fresh her writing feels. This new publication invites readers deeper into Taubes's grotesque worlds, where nothing is quite as it seems: doubles proliferate, taxidermies watch on while waxen fathers smoke plastic cigars, and Death, a "shy and gentle lover," waits under the crystal chandelier, ready to doff his mask and devour his bride.

—FRANCESCA WADE

LAMENT FOR JULIA

Prologue

SHE IS gone. Julia has left me. For good now, I think. She went silently under the cover of night. It was the only way she could leave without being followed. I think of her going out into the night, going out like a candle, going down perhaps. I will never know where. I will never know how long ago. This used to be Julia's room. She left skirts hanging in the closet, the many skirts I bought her, flared, pleated and scalloped. I try them on one after another. Sometimes I wear several skirts at a time. Skirts of different colors, full of her fragrance, her mysteries, skirts embroidered with flowers and butterflies and little fishes flitting through seaweed. Her skirts subdue and appease me. Whenever I am about to smash the windows or put fire to the house, her skirts rustling against my legs plead with me. Small, naked and violent I go sheltered under her gently swaying skirts.

I am dwindling, changing shape. I feel my bones grow soft as if I were being boiled in a caldron, then suddenly turn brittle. As I diminish, let her increase. We shall change roles, I no longer lord it over her, entangle her in my web, dangle her like a puppet. No, I am old and dry and she shall be my bride of freshness, she shall warm me like the twenty virgins swarming around old King Solomon, or I will be her little child, I will cling to her skirts, better hide under them. Yes. She shall hide me under her skirts, she won't mind, she won't notice, she is kind. She shall encompass me, I shall be diffused through her, annulled in her.

No. She has taken them with her, the skirts, the beads, the fringed shawls, everything. This is no longer Julia's room.

How did I come by her? What had we to do with each other? She was my constant nagging pain. My shame and despair. I wanted to get rid of Julia. But what was I without her? I would have to do something about Julia, make something out of Julia. Make Julia out of Julia. Before I knew it I had staked everything on Julia.

For years I have worked on her, trained her for one role, then another. The hours we have spent trying on dresses, experimenting with different hairdos. Sometimes I wonder what she would be like left to herself. I try to remember her as she was when I found her, before I spoke to her, when she belonged to God. Oh, that blessed state! The calamity of our encounter, whereby I usurped her being. Yet all my pains were toward preparing her for God.

Why was she ever joined to me—Oh, miserable corruption—if I was not to restore her to innocence?

Though she was content to live from moment to moment I was troubled continually for her salvation. Julia did not care. While her hands were busy scraping carrots, tying shoelaces, caressing the cheek or thigh of one or another, her heart sang, My kingdom come carelessly on the shower of the years; or, All grief is of the same measure in the small space of the heart.

But I had the care of her soul. How shall she dress on Judgment Day? As a child or a maiden? If mistress, then whose? Judgment Day! How sweet those words sound. Or used to in the days when I was grooming Julia for God's mansions. I made every day in Julia's life Judgment Day. I had her stand before God's judgment seat as other women stand before the mirror. And vanity it was.

Long periods when I abandoned my work, I would relinquish her, let her go. I left her to drift. I followed driven by the impossible passion to possess Julia as she might be without me. To behold her as she is or might truly be in herself unbeheld by me.

Julia shall lie in the hands of God, she shall be a gift as gratuitous as a grasshopper, as justified as a blade of grass. But what about me? My clandestine labor? My ugly intrigues? How shall I be blotted out?

No one shall know about me. No one suspect that we live together. It shall remain a secret between Julia and myself, and even Julia will be in the dark about our pact.

I shall remain hidden behind Julia, invisible as the artist behind his work, more so for my creation is not of wood or stone, but a living thing.

I shall remain unknown that Julia alone may be known. Julia who was born a little child and chased down the green slope, Julia who laughed at the moon when she lay down in the grass with her lover. It is she who shall stand before God's judgment seat while I cover my face, metaphorically speaking, for I have no face. It is with Julia's face I cover myself. It is Julia's face that shall be bared to death, Julia whom I want to be known, to be remembered, to be. Until I have put her on the ground perfect and entire I remain unatoned.

She sleeps, she drifts, she is absent. She is prisoner. Past and future hold her dismembered in their many rooms. I shall use others to deliver her, things and people, lovers, husband and children. She must have a brood of them. And because so much of her still remains captive, I will see to it that she shall have more lovers to discover her. I would have her opened like a fan, unraveled like a clue, exploded like a firecracker. I shall not relinquish any part of her. I shall not rest until she is bound as fast as a brush stroke to its pigment. The moment her portrait is finished she shall pass into the canvas.

———

Yet how am I to understand my part in this grave farce? Shall I say I am an intelligence of a sort? At times I have fancied myself as a celestial spark. A fallen angel if you like; without, however, inquiring into the particulars as to whence fallen, how or why or fabulate on the celestial home of which I must still be a member. For if fallen, that crash has altogether blunted my memory; so trying to steer clear of that mythological bog, a spark, a gnat, a ghosting strand of thought, call it what you like, set, searching now for the most neutral metaphor —though at times it seems this consciousness has been struck in the flesh like a nail, or merely attached to the forehead like a miner's lamp, or planted like a seed to shoot root and branch, a creature within a creature or perched on the shoulder like a chained hawk, not the right image—therefore let us leave it at set, put, garrisoned in a body and a woman's body it was to be to heighten the scandal; cavernous, a thin partition wall of live membrane communicating with the wilderness, at moontimes reimmersed in the sea of blood. My part then will appear in the course of the struggle as I exert a counterweight, hang on to the ledge while she storms and snaps and pounds about me like a rabid sea; keep my wits about me counting each second of lucidity preserved a battle won. I shall improvise the other by virtue of which she who is eternally the same shall be just that. I will be endlessly variable, assume contrary parts, eventually I will disappear and leave her to her own devices, of which nothing will ever be known.

———

Mine was the peculiar sense of accomplishment of the Japanese actor trained from earliest childhood to be a female impersonator. With Julia I have always felt like a child actor playing a female role. Was it to please others? What I wanted was of course to accomplish the act of deception. Yet not primarily to deceive others. This was simply a necessity. I had to present a face. No, I wanted to play a woman, it was my pleasure. I was most daring in my improvisations when we were alone.

The fact that Julia was born a girl, that I graft my phantom woman on her flesh, requires an added subtlety as there is a greater danger of confusion. In my lustful fascination with the carnality of woman I have at times stopped in the middle of my act of make-believe to take a real bite out of the flesh-and-blood Julia. At such moments Julia seems to take possession of me, erupt in me. But I cannot be certain whether it is Julia who gets out of control or whether it is not rather I. No sooner have I created my illusion than I want to luxuriate in the reality.

———

Sometimes Julia vanishes altogether. I rear my head. Yes, what of me behind the masks of Julia? I grow, it's almost as if I took on shape and face. I feel my bony butt, my stiff joints, the bitter taste in my mouth. Julia in her bodily image becomes a penumbra of disassociated sensations. I am real and she mere appearance. Julia a sham devised solely for the public. They required of us a show. I have her twirl like a figure on a music box. A demure Julia, a seductive Julia, a maternal Julia. There comes the moment of revulsion when I pounce on my puppet; and when I'm done stamping on it, kick it in a corner.

———

If she were simply a body and I simply a mind. If only it were as simple as that. But we are a jumble of odd bits and between us we do not even make up a person. Something is missing. Or perhaps I am in the way. Unless it's Julia's fault. For all that her coat flutters in the wind, she has never been quite real. She doesn't care, however. My sense of her is less of a person than of things, places and seasons.

———

If I could simply go along with Julia such as she is in whatever she does. Be this Julia and that Julia. Julia here and Julia there. Julia now, Julia then. It's simple. Julia is so simple. She yields as simply to Peter today as she will yield to Paul tomorrow as she has yielded to Bruno yesterday. She is simply a different Julia from one occasion to the next; or the same Julia for all I know and Julia is yielding as the grass. It may be simple but is it not madness? Could Julia so much as get through the day on her own without my having to tell her and remind her and decide for her? Would she so much as try? Leave her to herself and she thinks she is on a holiday. I can't even trust her to get up in the morning without my prodding. And even supposing that she did, that some bodily need or the lure of a sunny day eventually induced her to leave her bed, would she know what to do, where to go, or would she spend the hours doing nothing, wandering about aimlessly, intent on nothing, absorbed by anything, street noises, a dim craving, the tiles of the bathroom floor arranging themselves in different patterns, or worse than doing nothing, doing some foolish thing, going on a ride with anyone anywhere because she cannot refuse. Oh, it is a fearful thing to be Julia, to give in to Julia all the way, a thing from which I would save myself, save Julia, save myself the better to save Julia.

I'll say we're two then. I'll limit it to two, for all that Julia is legion, I shall count her as one. For to give her a different name for every phase, every humor, to make her into a pantheon would be to ease her predicament when she is monstrous.

———

I did not make her hair grow down her shoulders or shape her breasts just so. It is not I shall fret her brow or turn her hair white, or stop her heart. When her time comes I shall be there, beside her, but I will lower my eyes respectfully. I shall not peer. Perhaps we shall go down swiftly together, united in the last struggle for breath, one cry, one distress, crying with the single voice of the flesh as we came. But where will I be going? Julia shall be at ease in the dust. But what will become of me? They will not let me go with her, they will not let me in.

I will howl outside the walls of a bubble of air. I will beat my fists against a grain of dust. Somewhere else. Nowhere. Outside of the world.

———

When did I begin? It must have begun at one point. Suddenly I found myself in the center of the stage. No, not the center. I didn't know where I was. Say my predicament dates from the moment I began thinking in the first person; seriously, that is. It started out as an experiment. Let us assume that it is I who speaks, I proposed to myself, let us drag the hidden author on the stage, uncombed, in his nightclothes, and turn the spotlight on him as he blinks and stammers, chewing his pencil. We will have done with the dashing buskined actors, the queens, clowns, the beauties in period costumes. We shall not permit him to hide behind his creatures, henceforth he himself will have to show himself on the stage. I dare you, I order you, I said, without reflecting at the time to whom the pronouns I and you referred, but with the secret conviction that the experiment would be his undoing, his ruin. From now on I shall simply say, my undoing. I will go through with it saying I, to be through with myself once and for all, rid of the I.

———

I was there when Julia was born; suspended in the opal jelly of her eye. What did I make of it? After the interminable night of battle, after the bloodbath, the cheery hospital room with immaculate walls, flowers, greeting cards, the red screaming terror wrapped in lace. I turned my face to the wall. But I am reconstructing from Julia's later experience. The moment of her conception is unimaginable. No, I have imagined it, and sickened at the thought. Would that the priest who shall come to her deathbed to administer the last unction had been present at her conception. Or that God would not have allowed it to happen. Not that way. Better that she had never been brought forth into the light, that no fisherman's net had hauled her up. And she would have gone on winding through the dark waters, unseen, unknown, there in her own element, pushing ahead the darkness, her path traceless, silently, unknown and unknowing, feeding on the abundance of the sea, until in time she in turn enriched the waters with her decay.

But now she is out, she is in the daylight. There is no turning back.

———

Speak only of Julia. How shall I speak of Julia? Haven't I said I am done with it; done with these compound anomalies, selves, ensouled bodies, bodied soul. Having abandoned the idea of the person, I would rediscover the names of the gods, ghouls, ogres without number who would henceforth wear the human face like a rubber mask. The totem pole made up of voracious ancestors would be her true portrait. I shall put you together out of your miscellanies, matchsticks, candle drippings, the rusty viscera of boilers, pitch, gull feathers and fishbones that discolor in the wind.

———

Her life was to be as pure and constrained as a fairy tale. Having failed at this, can I say at what point the plot began to waver, blur, split off in several directions and tell the story up to that point—if only it had ended there...

I try to picture her. The child Julia. Julia the woman. How did she make that jump? Where is the connecting link? Am I the connecting link? I? Did I lose her then, or earlier still, the years we played together in the attic and I dressed her in fables, did I sacrifice the child Julia to my dreams? Was she there or was I alone in the attic, alone as I am now, always alone?

There never was a Julia, only her memory. No, I will not say this. I would not have gone on but for Julia. Julia looking out the window at the graying sky. She did not seem to notice me at all; she was in another world, her world of fresh mornings. The sound of her feet running down the stairs assured me that I was nothing. She ties a kerchief around her head and I follow her out into the wet morning, follow her like a child, like a lover. Or was that also a fiction?

———

I turn in vain to her several ages; the child Julia already harboring the spider. There, hidden, eminent in my seat between her eyes, or at the pit of her brain, or deeper still, in the most secret chamber of her heart, I toiled secretly, spun the mesh of her life. I or another I. My ancestor, grandfather I, old, cunning and sinister. And never having seen the spider, did she suspect? Did she try to imagine him, and endow him with the most delicate legs?

I shall never know. I was not there in the beginning. One never is, one always has to make it up. That's why there must be so many different accounts. The world supported on the back of a turtle. That makes sense. Or belched out by a one-eyed lizard. That's even better.

———

Her life cannot be told. She would not suffer it. Nor I. Imagine Augustine writing his confessions if God had passed him by. If he had missed his moment of grace in the garden when God so turned his soul that in an instant all his life unfolded new from its true center, its true beginning. Yet could that life have made sense of itself along the way in the wilderness? Could the groping in the dark be told before God's gift of faith retroactively redeemed it? But then could he have written a confession at all? There would be no one to tell it to, for who would bare himself, his secret sores, unless to God, shrouded in prayer? And there would be no one to tell it, for the soul is not of a piece unless God's image is mirrored in it.

I keep harking back to the early years as if the key to Julia's life lay hidden there. But how do I know it's buried with her toys in the trunks of the attic rather than by the gates of the convent garden, or in the rooms where she walked as wife, mistress and mother; or who knows if the true center of her life is not locked in some future event, with people and places still to come and only time can tell and it will be then and only then that her life can be told.

Whichever way the center lies, I cannot hope to find it except by going on. If I do not find it today, I must go back again tomorrow, keep going back till the day I shall stand before the right door. Keep going forward and backward, or try to stand still; for every step forward multiplies the steps behind me that I shall have to retrace.

I, not Julia. Julia goes on wherever the road leads, while I trace circles. She is not caught in my web. She is somewhere else. Walking by the sea, or through the fields, or along the streets. I don't know where. She is not down here with me. Down where nothing changes. I say down, when it may be in between, when it is outside of the world. Hell is nowhere. I'll say it's down and Julia walks above in the sunlight. I see her cross the meadow trailing a brood of children hand in hand, they twine about her like a flower chain opening and closing. I lie. No. It may be so. I don't know. In the dark I try to remember Julia.

Part One

I

HAVE I made too much of Julia? How could I take her so seriously? Didn't her skirts, her graces, her soft ways, gall on me? All this fuss about a mere girl! Yet how was I to judge whether to take her lightly or in earnest, not knowing how long, in what manner and to what end we two were thus joined. Have I made a fool of myself exalting a frivolous child? Have I played the cynic when it was a matter of salvation or perdition? But I rode both horses, the tragic and the comic. I have alternately worshiped and mocked her.

Shall I be blamed for my devotion to Julia? I who was nothing had been brought unto the day in the shape of this child. Flesh and bones! I leaped like a shade of the dead when the libation of blood is poured in the trench. Made human that eyes might break on my brow, eyes open to my carnality and woman to make it the more fleshbound.

So it had to be Julia. Julia my one and only one. Is this certain? No one before Julia? I must confess the idea of reincarnation never appealed to me. I am aware of the merits of the oriental doctrine: it's less of a gamble; all is not staked on one throw. I concede it is a wise and soothing doctrine to progress by stages along a gentle slope, not that steep ascent. Move on, or slide back, small difference. The fall is not bottomless or final. A temporary demotion from bird to fish, at the very worst to the last rung of the ladder, with an eternity to resume the climb to the top. But where did I get this passion for the once and only once; now or never in all eternity? Unless it's simply my short temper, my impatience to be done with it once and for all. Because I never had a doubt that it was now or never. This Julia or nothing.

Yet in case I should be mistaken and I have in fact enjoyed a former existence of which no trace is left, I strongly suspect that I must have smoldered in some pale scholar, a brooding seminarist, most likely. Perhaps I even attained some stature as a heretical monk. The idea appeals to me: yes, I was a great and terrible ghost at that time and drove entire monasteries to despair, madness, excesses of self-flagellation, libertinism, apostasy, and now is my time to redeem myself. What could be more probable than that I have been put in Julia's body for scorning the flesh; and for my improvement? Whatever I possess in the way of piety I owe to Julia. This would explain my great concern for her salvation; why the convent seemed the natural solution; also my strict views on marriage. Who shall say? I have been left without instruction on the matter.

One thing seems certain, I was never in a woman's body before; or it would not be so new, so strange. Perhaps I was in the wind, a flying insect, a creeping thing. A spider, most likely. No, a gnat. Never in a beast of any considerable size beside the human, that's certain. The great mammals impress me, but I have never felt any kinship with them. No, I was tiny, a mere speck.

But this does not help me now with Julia, for it is with Julia I have been charged. Charged myself, who shall say it was otherwise, yes, entirely on my own, without endorsement from on high, plunged into my self-appointed role. I braced myself against the void and made the leap into Julia. It was not quite like that. One must allow for time and the force of gravity. The lights are dimmed on the opening of that first scene; the curtain rises while the stage is still shrouded in darkness. Not until somewhere toward the end of the first act or the beginning of the second act, did it dawn on me with a certain uneasiness that a play was going on.

2

Was I at all aware of her existence? Faded snapshots of children squatting in the sandbox, tumbling over a snowbank. She was there among others. Her presence must have been a source of embarrassment for I dimly recall trying to ignore Julia. I pretended I did not know her. When Julia's nose ran I did not bother to wipe it. I looked out the window or up at the sky when they were talking about Julia. Perhaps I hoped that if I continued to take no notice of her she would eventually disappear. Time passed; Julia stubbornly adhered. Shall I say she seduced me? Moved me to compassion? Or that I was flattered by her stubborn attachment to me? Because time came I resigned myself to the fact of Julia, that I existed with and through Julia, mysteriously grafted on Julia, a parasite, if you will, on Julia.

It will be said that I have tried to make the best of a distasteful reality and gone too far. At the time the task of mastering my new responsibilities was too demanding to allow me to perceive the absurdity of my situation. I became a child with Julia.

3

How shall I describe the house where we spent our best years? Which house shall I speak of first, the house I built for Julia, or the other, the Klopps house with its strange folk, as unlikely as my fabled world. But what is the aim of description? To transcribe from one slate to another? Transmute from one substance into another as the meat of a rabbit is changed into the flesh of a cobra? Or to seize experience, yes, take it by the ears and slap it on both cheeks?

In all my attempts to reconstruct the Klopps household in its physical layout, daily routine, the number and status of the personages belonging to it, I have failed to arrive at a coherent picture. Memory is not necessarily at fault here. No, my experience of the Klopps household at the time, as I distinctly recall, consisted of impressions with as little logical connection as in a dream. I must therefore insist that the various facets and angles of the Klopps household did not make up a consistent object, whether due to my distorted or partial perception at the time or in fact full of gaps and contradictions. I will concede either possibility, or both: errors of perception and flaws in the texture of things. I need mention only a few of the discrepancies which bothered me at the time.

Viewed from the garden, the Klopps house was of clearly assessable shape and magnitude: a somewhat gray stone construction, three stories high with a central doorway; the top floor or attic narrowed with the slant of the roof. When we were inside the house, however, I had the impression of several wings, connected by meandering passageways; there were entire sections of the house with rooms we never entered. How is this possible?

Did Julia have a nurse? Several nurses? The incompetence of the nurse was a constant topic of discussion with the Kloppses. Nurses were continually being dismissed; or they left without notice. Yet it is a fact that after one of the servants, sometimes the maid, sometimes the old cook, sometimes the arthritic butler, dressed her, Julia was left on her own for the day.

The exact location of the Kloppses' living room remains a mystery. I distinctly remember it being on the same floor as Julia's bedroom. Yet on many occasions I had to reach it by descending a wide, circular marble staircase.

I never saw the Kloppses except in the living room. But were the Kloppses always in the living room? Or were we at times alone there? Difficult to ascertain. There were moments I fancied we were alone. It was so silent and still. We stole glass cherries from a crystal bowl; a bright feather from the tail of a stuffed pheasant. Nobody seemed to be watching. But I may be deceived. Father and Mother Klopps could maintain a rigid posture for hours like wax dummies, impervious to the patter of Julia's feet, insensible to such unpleasant noises as Julia passing a stick over the metal grate of the heating. When in this paralytic stupor they seemed as much part of the still life of the interior as the stuffed heads of moose, grizzly bear, rhinoceros and entire specimens of smaller game mounted along the wall and decorating the mantelpiece. I recall Julia staring with equal fascination at the stuffed arctic fox on top of the piano and the flabby bulk of Mother Klopps propped up by pillows on the divan, equally fearful of touching either, in time more fearful of touching the latter, which she had learned could at times quite unpredictably come to life and blink. Mother Klopps had a bloated look. Her natural snail-gray pallor would yield to pink, purple and blue at progressive stages of suffocation in the course of her asthmatic attacks. Gray-white fuzz covered her large head, extending somewhat more sparsely down her cheeks, across her many chins and over her thick upper lip. She had round blue eyes, a round head, round little hands; but the roundest thing about Mother Klopps was her smile. When Mother Klopps smiled her lips did not form a crescent like most people's, but produced a full circle.

Father Klopps's jaw was fixed in a tight grin, or some expression between a grin and a snarl, although it may not have been expressive of any emotion at all: lips pulled away from the teeth, cigar clamped between two rows of teeth which never parted, thus accounting for the partial unintelligibility of his speech. Father Klopps always sat in a leather armchair clutching a tumbler of whiskey in his stiff, outstretched arm. His pale, glassy, protruding eyes scarcely ever blinked. When Julia walked in and saw him sitting thus, it was hard to tell whether he was dead or alive, especially when his plastic ersatz cigar was stuck in his mouth.

Father Klopps and Mother Klopps resembled each other in appearance, notwithstanding the fact that Father Klopps was hard, gnarled and knobby, while Mother Klopps was soft, smooth and flabby. They had the same shape and shade of glassy blue eyes not very different from that of the stuffed arctic fox, although theirs occasionally blinked. Their teeth were also similar although Father Klopps's were a shade browner and longer and his grin was fixed in the shape of a rectangle, whereas Mother Klopps's smile was in the form of a circle.

They could in fact have been sister and brother. Perhaps they were.

Even before she became aware of these distinguishing marks, Julia had no difficulty in telling them apart. Not that she ever felt the need to tell them apart. She did not. In fact, she often took them for one and the same person and even after she perceived that they were two, she still regarded Father Klopps as a duplication of Mother Klopps or Mother Klopps as a duplication of Father Klopps, quite indiscriminately. But after a while a distinction naturally dawned upon her, owing to the fact that Mother Klopps was always lying on the divan, while Father Klopps was always seated, most of him hidden in a deep leather armchair by the hearth. Finally, Julia like most girl children grew to prefer her father. Father Klopps had an endearing weakness: he was ticklish. When Julia tickled his chin with a feather his mouth twitched and he was seized by little spasms resembling giggles. I suspect Julia had a genuine fondness for her gnarled, knobby, bristly haired, talcum- and tobacco-smelling Daddy. But this, as I have noted, is natural in girl children. Had it been the other way, had Father Klopps been soft, fat and flabby and Mother Klopps been hard, gnarled and knobby, would Julia still have preferred her Daddy to her Mummy, or would she not have preferred her Mummy who was in fact more Daddylike, that is, hard, gnarled and knobby, than her Daddy who was more Mummylike?

Such questions preoccupied me at the time.

4

I did not love her at first; not for a long time. She did not suit me at all, this fidgety, freckle-faced, thumbsucking, bedwetting Julia. She was too plump and tart for my taste; already as a tot she loitered around the servants' quarters on the lookout for the maid's lovers. And the way she threw herself about wantonly in the presence of any male! I was ashamed of Julia.

My situation appeared near hopeless at the start. Julia was indiscriminate, credulous, moody, perverse; prone to break out in prolonged fits of giggles and tears; now riotous, now listless, as the humor had her. She accepted candy from every stranger and would have followed him to the ends of the earth if he would but have her.

Julia's appearance was a constant source of irritation. I found her particularly ridiculously dressed up in her bulky little white fur coat, fur hat, fur-lined boots and white leggings complete with a little fur muff. She reminded me of a polar bear. And how silly she looked with that big white bow pinned on one side of her hair. The many times I tore it off and flung it in the mud or among the bushes.

Was that Julia? No, the Klopps girl I'll call her. When was Julia born? Shall I confess to my ancient crime? For years that shapeless, whining, woebegone thing had been following me around: one day I took the Klopps girl, that reproach to God, and stuffed it down the laundry chute together with the dirty bibs, socks and panties. In its stead I would create Julia. For the time being I took its place. No one noticed. All the changes were for the better. For a while I almost believed I had succeeded, the dry stick blossomed. No, I did not think of it as my success. It was Julia. It was a miracle. Julia was the real child. The other, the Klopps girl, the changeling.

5

Her parents were a trial, and of course I had to live with them too.

Father Klopps and Mother Klopps like most parents took an avid interest in their child. The Kloppses more so than most, Julia being the child of their old age and their only child. Moreover, retired as they were from the world and their failing health forbidding any activity more strenuous than a light conversation now and then, with long rests in between, the topic of Julia was actually their sole diversion.

Did they name her Julia? I cannot help but wonder because they never called her Julia or any other proper name for that matter. Father and Mother Klopps always referred to their child as Baby Klopps. What could be more natural? For them she always was and would always remain Baby Klopps. When speaking of their child, they inevitably contracted a slight lisp.

Mother and Father Klopps had the curious habit of talking about Julia's cunning little ways in Julia's presence while quite ignoring

Julia. And whether Julia curtsied as she should, or pulled down her pants and stuck out her tongue as she should not, whether she cried or laughed, and when she said or did the most ordinary thing, they invariably found her the cutest thing alive.

More curious still was the fact that while they would endlessly discuss Julia, it never occurred to them to speak to Julia. And even when it would have been most natural and imperative for them to address Julia because Julia was making so great a nuisance of herself, they preferred to sit back and watch the little scene as if they were in the loges of a theater. In the worst case Mother Klopps might remark to Father Klopps, Don't you wish Baby Klopps would stop banging on the piano like that? Or Father Klopps might say to Mother Klopps, My, my, there goes Baby Klopps breaking the last of our Ming china. But ordinarily Mother Klopps and Father Klopps would exclaim with glee, Just look at Baby Klopps making wee wee on the rug!

Fortunately, whenever Julia was at the point of jumping out the window or knocking the chandeliers down on her head, a servant promptly appeared on the scene, and like a deus ex machina intervened to avert disaster.

The Kloppses never enjoyed Julia's little oddities so much as when they thought it reflected a family trait. Her tantrums were Aunt Etta all over, according to Father Klopps. Her *pseudologia phantastica* was Uncle Gundolf *redivivus*, Mother Klopps would observe with delight. Prematurely oversexed, just like Grandmother Klopps, Father Klopps often remarked fondly. And a little hysterical, too, like Grandmother Fuchs, Mother Klopps would add. Her stubbornness, they both agreed, was a slice of Uncle Bobbie who stayed in bed for twenty-five years because his mother wouldn't let him ride a horse.

The Kloppses made these observations with mounting glee, tickled to find traits of their dear deceased in Baby Klopps. The conversation took a less amiable tone as soon as Mother Klopps would propose that Baby Klopps's phlegmatism was inherited from Father Klopps, or Father Klopps propose that in her bedwetting Baby Klopps takes after her mother. Such allegations would plunge them in the bitterest wrangles, Baby Klopps soon forgotten in the heat of accusations and counteraccusations, Mother Klopps's eyes bulging, Father Klopps's Adam's apple riding up and down; as Mother Klopps eventually succumbed to an attack of asthma, Father Klopps usually had the last word: But dear, you were a bedwetter when I first met you! I'm not referring to the time you had inflammation of the bladder, but, don't you remember, during our honeymoon—?

The Kloppses' genealogical obsession was not confined to the behavioral syndrome but extended to every detail of her physiognomy. They could never agree whether her nostrils were Aunt Heda's or Uncle Gustav's, whether in general her face was Klopps rather than Fuchs, or Fuchs rather than Klopps, Father Klopps arguing that Baby Klopps resembled him rather than Mother Klopps, while Mother Klopps maintained that Baby Klopps resembled her rather than Father Klopps. If only they had agreed either way the discussing might have been closed once and for all.

In my opinion Julia did not bear the slightest resemblance to either of her parents. Is it possible that she was an adopted child? But wouldn't they have discussed that too in all their talk? But no, they always said, when the stork brought our little panda; or, it's been five years now since the postman brought us our little package of sweets. Could these remarks be interpreted as evidence for the fact that Julia was adopted? Strictly speaking, no. A much more likely possibility is that they were not her parents but her grandparents. And the parents? Blotted out of memory for they were never mentioned. It happens sometimes that a generation gets lost like that.

6

I stood by helpless while the maid following the parents' instructions forced her into a starched petticoat and pulled the pink taffeta dress over her head. The cook was there too, the two women fumbling with the tiny ribbons in the puffed sleeves, telling her to stand still. Perhaps Julia saw me frown when they tied the big pink bow in the back. She reached behind her to touch the bow. The nurse slapped her hand.

I think that is when I threw my first fit. Several windowpanes were broken, a flowerpot smashed, a bottle of ink poured over Julia's new dress. They thought she had a devil. Why was I so outraged? I would have the moment my charge was hung with the emblems of her sex accompanied by ceremonies as violent and arbitrary as the act of investment. Or perhaps it was simply my constitutional aversion to the color pink?

7

But was I there at all, distinct from Julia, fully emerged as I am now? Was I not buried in Julia, a mere grub, just beginning to work myself out? Comfortably nestled in Julia I dozed like an infant hanging on its mother's neck while Julia went about her child's business. For I remember moments of Julia's summers as though they were mine. Julia's pleasure in her own heartbeat racing down the slope, a handful of wild berries. Mine and yet not mine. How can I be sure, for I have only a pack of faded images, picture postcards of distant lands that I shuffle and reshuffle. I decked her with feathers, hung her with gaudy beads, wrapped her in lion skins, the treasures of black kingdoms, plundered by Julia's great-grandfather.

Only if I possessed the past without recourse to memory as only God can possess it could I possess Julia. For she was always lost to me, her moments ground up in the mills of my day-to-day revisions. But I exaggerate. Haven't I fixed roadmarks? Yes, at some crucial juncture I codified the past, set down the canon for good, a final version. As the need arose I issued special bulls and emendations. So I managed in part, in my desperate effort to salvage Julia's life. But I could never abide by my own rules. I will probe, pry behind the text, pick it apart, blacken the margin with variant readings. Once more I piece together one of those fictions, my lives of Julia. In the hope of stumbling upon a hidden detail. Or because it's my only way of being with Julia. Or to purge myself of Julia. Raise one more phantom from the sealed shrine of her present.

Her childhood then. The childhood I made up for her, one of the many robes in which I dressed her. If there is another I have only glimpses of it, a snag in my fabric, and odd thread, a patch of another weave.

8

Ours was a kind of child marriage. Homeless, I attached myself to her, usurped all her hours. Was it not clear from the beginning? I was sent to the Klopps house to save Julia. One day we simply eloped.

We hid in closets and behind drapes; we played under the cellar stairs, but we were found. We crouched in the tall grass where the wasps harassed us. Till one day I climbed up the crooked stairs leading to the attic, turned the rusty knob and found myself in a forgotten storage room. A shroud of dust, hoary in the thin morning light, lay over the furniture. I held my breath, enamored by the stillness, the dust that was the visible seal of stillness. Was I in a dream? For I felt I had been here before. Or Julia, one of the many times she lost her way roaming through the house. Before I discovered its treasures I felt it had always been mine.

I installed myself in the attic with Julia, my foundling, my abducted bride. We had all the props for games of adventure and high romance. General Klopps's collection of ancient weapons, sabers, daggers and pistols. And snarling fiercely from their mounts, a gallery of stuffed animals Julia's great-grandfather Wilhelm Fuchs shot a century ago in the jungles of the Amazon and the arctic wastes. Crates of books, encyclopedias, grammars, lexicons, manuals of science and theology, the library of Julia's great-uncle, Gundolf Klopps. What more could be desired? I could not have imagined a more perfect setting. High above the town with a view over the small forest and stretches of grassy dunes sloping down to the sea.

Up in our attic room we rehearsed sounds of passion, love scenes and death scenes. I call this our romantic period. I made believe her garments were removed by others, played attendant women, combed her hair, lined her eyes. Her confidante, page boy and minister, I buckled her shoes, whispered the last instructions in her ear.

Was I her servant or her master then? Parent, lover or friend? All. My imagination knew no bounds when I sought to impress and delight Julia. I tried out every role; took on the guise of her illustrious ancestors. Soldier, adventurer, alchemist, I strutted about in hunting boots, a black cape, cracked a whip. On high occasions I wore a headdress plucked from the sacred guacamaya bird. And Julia? Did she appear on the landing in faded velvet or brocade? But I was so infatuated with my diverse roles at the time that I do not even have a clear physical image of Julia. Strange, that the imaginary wizard's high conic hat inlaid with stars, General Wilhelm Klopps's fancied moustachio, a bushy red, and my picture of pale Gundolf Klopps brooding over hieroglyphs, should be more vivid in my mind than Julia's face, her child shout, her fidgety hands.

She had long outgrown her little white polar bear coat. I remember she had a navy-blue jacket with bright buttons. But when I try to summon her features I see a wide-eyed storybook princess with golden tresses tumbling down to her feet.

Those were our best years. The illicit character of our relation only enhanced its flavor of sanctity. Secret I had to remain, not out of shame but prudence. Like some rare jewel that it is foolhardy to flaunt before the covetous eyes of the world, I preferred concealment.

I fancied Julia took pride in me. Was she not fortunate above others? Long winter afternoons I read to her fairy tales, legends, books of verse. She loved words; she loved them I fear at the expense of sentences. She would stop me in the middle of a passage to gape at a word like a child before the window of a pastry shop. We spent blissful, oblivious hours reading the dictionary. What a granary of visions! The word *archaic* conjured old, old men with thin white beards. Gigantic and gaunt they rose from gray bone heaps, their beards blowing like torches in the wind. She loved soft words most: *shadow* had a soft sound, soft as the wind and the flame of torches.

Thus we idled away many afternoons over a word glimpsed at

random. I loved her, I indulged her. All my hours were hers, Julia my only love, my sole charge. I did her homework for her. She was first in her class. While other girls were cutting out paper dolls Julia copied Chinese calligraphy and knew by heart the genealogy of Norse gods. Whether she shared my passion for missionary reports on savage customs, or merely tried to please me, I shall never know. She didn't complain. I was sure she thought herself privileged to be living with me. For so I taught her. Was I tyrannical? In my first fervor I shared everything with Julia, my little hobbies, my insect collection, my coins, my love of recondite lore. It was only a phase. Years later I repented and taught her to forget.

9

Why did Julia have to go to school when she had me for a tutor? Of the school years the only surviving memory is the dismal black-ringed face of the clock and the rusty clang of the bell. I am still angered when I think of the wasted years Julia spent at the school desk. Was I there with Julia? I prefer to believe that it was through Julia's stoic endurance that we managed to get through the school years.

And what of the hours I spent without Julia? Gray, empty hours. Yet in a way I welcomed time for myself. Free to think my own thoughts, wander solitary, a shadow passing over the shadows of bare branches; or drift away, diffused in the gray sky.

I used to wait for her after school in the old cemetery. Sometimes Julia was late; she went to the park with friends. I was angry. Or she came eating candy. It infuriated me. Eating in the cemetery is an offense to the dead. I made her throw it away. I had been waiting for her all day and when at last she appeared she displeased me. Something soiled and wilted about her. Dulled by the schoolday. Inkstains on her fingers. I rubbed them off with snow. I undid her braids, ripped off the starched collar, let her coat fly open and covered her with leaves. It was an improvement.

We roamed through the woods. I did not care if the mud splashed up her legs and the wind made riot in her hair. That was my Julia! A leaping fawn. A forest nymph. A sister of the sodden earth.

Homeward the thought of the comments Julia's dishevelment would provoke oppressed me. If only they would punish her, beat her, starve her. But they only made inane remarks. I had to invent harsh parents for Julia. A wart-faced witch mother and an ogre father with tusks like a wild boar. I took turns playing the cruel parents and the kindly fairies who came to her aid. After I wearied of these games I invented other stories. She lived with an old wizard. He made magic for her. She would remain his prisoner until she learned his secret.

In later years I constructed Julia's relation to her parents with greater subtlety. I even allowed for family pride and piety. They were dead. There was no more danger.

10

My next ten years with Julia were spent mostly watching over her manners: keeping her from sticking out her belly, holding her head to one side, chewing her nails, sitting with her legs apart, laughing at the wrong time. Not a very flattering occupation for a spirit of my gifts; yet a trifle can engage the will when it offers the stubborn resistance Julia did. Small wonder I became somewhat prim and dreary, a regular schoolmarm by the time Julia learned to cross her legs properly.

I was her slave, her drudge. What didn't I do for Julia? I went on tedious hikes to keep her trim. Ate carrots that Julia's eyes might shine. And a thankless job it was. Julia began to drift away from me. Days I waited for her in vain in the cemetery. Where was she? Sitting around with the girls in the corner pastry shop? Reading movie magazines in the locker room? It would be like her to spend the afternoon hanging around the ballfield where the older boys played soccer. Unless she was just ambling stupidly along the road, blowing spit bubbles or picking her nose—but there were things I frankly preferred not to know about Julia.

I admit I was somewhat of a prude but the world will grant me Julia was not easy to take care of. Would my charge never grow up? I had to be on guard every second or she'd make a fool of us in public. The time we had to appear before the school principal, for example, I am sure she would have stroked his whiskers if I hadn't pulled her back.

No, Julia, I had to keep reminding her, this man is not your Daddy, he is Mr. Kraut, the principal. You can't call him Popsie. You must say Mr. Kraut, because he is the principal. His teeth may be like your Daddy's, his glassy stare is like your Daddy's, but still he is the principal, Mr. Kraut. See, he has whiskers. Your Daddy doesn't have whiskers, you know that. So say, Mr. Kraut. (Lower your eyes and you'll be less likely to giggle.) You mustn't stroke his whiskers, he is the principal, the principal, Julia! You don't gape or wink at the principal. (I'll buy you ten candybars, just please don't laugh now.) You can't touch anything in his room. Not even the monkey paperweight on his desk. Nothing. You mustn't kiss him when he gives you your report card, just curtsy, say thank you, and go back in line with the other children.

A moment's inattention could prove disastrous. Once during church service a detail of a cornice caught my attention; I was trying to make out the Latin inscription when I noted looks of consternation frozen on us. Julia, I realized with horror, had sat down while everyone stood in silent prayer, and what was worse, had plunked herself in the lap of the statue of Moses to our right. Her teacher promptly pulled her back into line with a yank whose mildness astonished me. Given the power I think I would have struck her dead.

What struggles I had with her! We quarreled endlessly about Julia's eating. Julia had no scruples about food. Anything tasted good in her mouth. I had made an extreme effort to overcome my natural squeamishness about the body. It was not easy. Each time Julia bruised her knee I had to hold myself not to flee at the sight of pus and blood. There was a period when the flow of saliva brought me to despair. The odor of excrement still makes me faint. Human excrement, I should say. The droppings of beasts do not offend me. I even confess to a liking of horse dung, those hard, dry clumps so much like clods of earth, with their mild aroma of hay. There is something sickly about everything human. But through arduous discipline I learned to overcome my loathing and to accept Julia's body. If Julia sneezing or cutting her toenails still disheartened me, I would never make an issue of it.

But food was a more serious matter. What gave the Kloppses and their servants their phlegmatic character and bloated aspect if not the food they ate? Partaking of their potato soups, stuffed cabbage and dumplings, I was certain Julia would turn into a Klopps. Next to the Klopps kitchen I had to contend with the candy store. A chocolate bar did not fit my image of Julia. What diet would I prescribe for her? Wild birds' eggs? Snails and butterflies? Should Julia eat cheese?

What trials we went through trying to codify a system of food taboos! I was difficult to live with I suppose. But so was Julia. What hurt me most was the way she could go off and play after our worst crises as if nothing had happened.

11

But I can't even be sure whether Julia willfully scorned me when, in fact, she simply acted as if I wasn't there. Judging from her behavior at the time one would believe she thought herself the only person in the world. Indeed, she was, if I may quote our cook, old Mathilda, so hopelessly "wrapped up in herself" as to be divinely oblivious to any existence apart from her own; and to the extent that she took in other persons and things they became a part of herself. Her most defiant gestures like the most submissive had a quality so blind and supremely indifferent, I sometimes wondered whether she heard me at all. The servants, I observed, found themselves in the same predicament. As for the Kloppses, they discerned nothing unusual or alarming in Julia's solipsism. Dismissed as another Klopps trait? No, I rather suspect they never expected Julia to intrude on their little tête-à-tête about Baby Klopps, and had she responded to their remarks by word or deed, I think they would have died of shock.

But perhaps Julia was playing a game with me; I thought so at the time and trembled moreover that she might give me away. Julia often came out with statements to the world like, "God is inside my belly," when threatened with divine punishment. It always made me jump. Alluding to me, the little snippet! As it happened I wasn't in her belly along with all the muck of half-digested dumplings, but since that's where she placed the powers that might be, that's where I made her feel a kick that sent the blood rushing to her face.

And all her weird little antics, her counting games, turning around in circles till she was dizzy, or skipping down the stairs by ones and twos and threes and up again and down again endlessly—why did she do it if not to confound me? She plucked out the eyes of all her dolls and hid them in matchboxes. Why? old Mathilda asked her. Why did you do it, you bad little girl! So they'll love me more, said Julia in her singsong way. But they were prettier with their eyes, Mathilda maintained. Don't like them looking at me, mumbled Julia. Specially in the dark.

Was all this some kind of counter-magic devised against me, or another Klopps trait?

12

Never would Julia have become the gracious Julia, the beautiful Julia without me. How I labored to make her over into a lady, a dream, an apparition! Within the space of a few years I accomplished miracles of transformation. I even taught her courtesy toward her parents. Others remarked on her improvement. Most important, however, was to give our best performance when we were alone. God is looking at you now, Julia, I whispered in her ear. You are alone before God. I spoke to Julia of God. I told her God would come and pluck her like a rose.

To see myself as Julia's guardian angel has ever been my happiest fantasy. Unless it was Julia's and I jumped into the role. Julia believed in angels for so she was taught in Sunday school, and I was careful not to infect her with my cynicism. I offered my services. Was I shameless? But there was no other angel around whose place I usurped. Why blame myself then and say I postured when I acted in blind faith, I, this naked I, this paltry pronoun, this nothingness. If only I would have been sure of my calling. A mere nod from on high would have made me a better spirit. If it had only pleased God to seal my appointment, everything would have turned out differently. Julia would have become Julia, I would not have tried to live through Julia. No, I would have been content to be an angel with a nice nook in heaven to return to, my own halo, wings, harp and tunic waiting for me, after I have finished my task with Julia. And it may be so for all I know. God's ways are inscrutable. An angel on trial, I've told myself, and Julia was my temptation. I succumbed. I fell as all angels fall through lust, pride, curiosity, the presumption to imitate God's creation. If so, I am in good company.

But I was not her angel. I take it back. I want to believe that angels exist and one watches over her and sees her truly, not as I see her. I'm vile. If I remained with her it was for my reward. In the secret hope that I shall be admitted into God's world through Julia. And my years of service? Can I believe that I have not been altogether useless because I have filled a child's lonely hours? Good or bad I was her devoted companion. I amused her, played with her. The wrong games perhaps, I knew no others.

13

But I have not told the truth. I was unfaithful to Julia already at that tender age.

There were others I loved besides Julia, for whose sake I neglected her, at times came near to despise her. I can forgive myself my infatuation with a horse, a tree, the rain, although once I was ready to kill Julia for not being a tree. But my love for Caroline still fills me with shame.

For over a year I was sick with love. I would never allow Julia to suspect. Caroline was Julia's age. I confess I tried to model Julia after her. Imitate Caroline's laughter, her swift movements, the sudden toss of her head. To be like Caroline. Caroline, or the opposite of Caroline.

Caroline always dressed in white; no one could wear white like she. I see her up in a tree swinging her legs, crying Copy cat! Copy cat! while I blushed for Julia standing in her new white pleated skirt and white knit shirt, like Caroline's, so unlike Caroline.

Was it her eyes bewitched me? Her glance that flicked like a cobra's tongue. Or her body, lithe as a cat's. How she could climb and spring, then sidle up softly. Nobody could refuse her anything. Her hair fell over her arms and back in shimmering strips, almost silver. I could not take my eyes off Caroline. Her bare legs so slender and tawny and smooth as bone made me forget everything, Julia, myself. But most I admired her daring. I followed Caroline into reckless adventures; climbed barbed wire fences to steal a peach, ate wild mushrooms, plunged in the icy pond in December.

Caroline was cruel and perverse. She stole the teacher's purse and let others take the blame. She robbed nests, cut live frogs into pieces. Once she hung a litter of puppies on a tree by their tails and watched them die. Caroline spied on her parents; she blackmailed her father and his mistress; hid her mother's jewels. What a mouse Julia was beside her! This stupid, slow, honest Julia. I marveled that Caroline condescended to play with her. I adored Caroline. I became her slave. I followed her around and let her bully and insult me. I stole for her; gave her Julia's favorite doll and watched her tear off its arms and legs. I dreamed the impossible, leaving Julia for Caroline. To be united with Caroline was my image of heaven.

My worst agony was when Caroline lay sick for weeks, stricken by a mysterious tropical fever. Should she die, how could I bear to stay on with Julia? I wanted to die with Caroline. At the same time I found a morbid consolation in fantasies of Caroline emerging disfigured or crippled from her illness. Fortunately Caroline recovered. I was relieved when I saw that the six weeks of confinement had left her almost unchanged. She seemed if anything more plump and somewhat placid. At the end of that year her family moved to another town. And fortunate it was for us. With Caroline gone, it was only against her phantom I had to contend.

I cursed Caroline, and preached against her: woe to the man who has Caroline for a wife! Woe to the child who has her for a mother! Still she returns now and again, and the ring of her cruel laughter makes me swoon with longing and shame.

14

Childhood is self-contained. The years Julia and I lived in the attic, no other mode of life seemed conceivable for her or for me. However oddly mated we seemed at times, I never questioned that we were made for each other. And yet I distinctly recall fantasies in which I pictured Julia living a different life, a life with someone else, in which there was no place for me.

From our tower room I would sight the carved prow and orange sails of the ship bringing the black prince who would carry her away. Dark men at the oars, their mournful chant carried by the wind. Everything happened with ceremonial precision. Attendant women brought her a bridal gown of the finest gold web. She put out her clothes and the maidens washed and dressed her. They gave her a new name. She took nothing with her into the ship. Veiled they led her into the holy city. The chief's mother instructed her. In time she forgot the language she spoke as a child. Her day passed in a series of ceremonial observances, ablutions and offerings. She prepared meat for her husband and mixed a special drink. His face had a solemn beauty. His long fingers when he caressed her were gentle. She loved his blackness. She drew sacred figures in the sand.

I also had chaster dreams for Julia. God would call her. I saw her led down into the crypt in a winding sheet. Then she lay on the stone floor while the nuns prayed over her, waiting for the kiss of death.

Is it possible that the thought of Julia leaving me was with me from the beginning? Or did I see myself as the black prince, and loveliest of all God's dark angels? Very likely. Black is my color. Or were these Julia's fantasies to begin with, although I must have revised them considerably, for Julia's daydreams, as I recall, lacked any style or coherence. This possibility cannot be dismissed altogether in view of our intimacy at the time. A jealous husband, Julia could have no secrets before me. I did not think it prying then.

Daydreaming was one of Julia's vices. How I struggled to break her of this idle, shameful habit! To no effect, I fear. I remember how we bargained in the early years. Say I caught Julia, just as we were leaving the house, racing through town on the back of a motorcycle with Freddy, the maid's lover, I'd give her till the third streetlight to be done with it or no dessert for a week. She always asked for a little longer, just till the end of the block and so on. When I finally put down my foot she'd stop like a mule at the exchange post. I took over. I tried to entertain Julia with observations of nature and architecture, edify her with verses. In my final exasperation I would often resort to adding up the number on the license plates of parked cars. At ten thousand it would be Julia's turn.

Julia's daydreams as far as I can recall were quite inane. To be kidnaped by gypsies. Or be a boy so she could go fishing with the gardener's son and similar nonsense about joining boys' gangs or a circus, of which I strongly disapproved. Some of her fantasies were positively morbid, like her obsession with being eaten alive. Especially before going to sleep or just after awakening when I'm not on guard Julia would revel in the thought of worms nibbling passageways through her groin, wasps slaking their thirst at her veins and finally some ravenous wolf cracking her bones. A fish, she imagined herself speared, slit open, but imagine is not the word, Julia suffered the precise sensation of the barbed hook piercing her gullet, the cook's coarse fingers tearing out her guts, and with shudders of delight. A Klopps trait? But I cannot disclaim all responsibility for Julia's fantasies. I abused her confidence, an extortionist, a voracious leech, I gorged myself on her secrets and gave her most innocent sensations my sickly hue. Julia was strange. I'll not deny it. Yet not as I have construed her. And perhaps not strange at all but for being construed by such as I.

15

It was around this time that I resolved to make something out of this wayward, dreaming Julia. I saw her as a ballerina, a countess, a spy. But most of all I wanted Julia to be a child of God. Though at moments I was carried away by ambition, I understood my task was to preserve her in purity.

Secretly I consoled myself with the thought that it would not be for long. Like those whom the gods love, Julia would die young. Would it happen of itself, or was it for me to tip the scales? Looking back I must admit that I toyed with the thought of doing away with Julia ever since the first time I saw that round, freckled face in the mirror, when she burst into her mother's bedroom, took a sip from her most expensive eau de cologne and poured the rest over her head. At that time I was going to have her lie down on a grave mound in the old cemetery at night in the heavy snowfall. By morning the snow would cover her. But there was no snow that winter.

I tried several times to poison her. Apricot seeds, the cook once warned, eaten in a quantity over six were sure to be fatal. I had her eat a few dozen. I remember how we collected the stones over weeks, hid in the cellar and cracked them open with a brick against the cement floor. It did not even give her a bellyache. She was very tough. I interpreted it at the time as the verdict of the gods.

What deaths I dreamed for her! What hangings, stabbings, throwing over cliffs! Her death must be an expiation, her down-going as sheer, blind and sudden as the breathless plunge of a Peruvian child hurled down a stony chasm to placate the mountain spirit. What priest would sacrifice her, to what God? To wipe away what sins?

I had forever to restore her that I might sacrifice her anew. I had her laid out in white in a little coffin with four candles at each corner to make sure she stayed spotless. And for each time I hanged her, drowned her, pushed her over a cliff, I repented a thousandfold. I sat in ashes, I confessed, I said I shall die that Julia might live. I consented to Julia. Consented to die that Julia might live. Julia, my incarnation, my passion, my expiation.

I did not make long-range plans for Julia. Our first deadline was Julia's twelfth birthday. It was a fine day in late autumn, my favorite season. We wandered into the old cemetery and rested on a tumbled-down tombstone. I collected acorns, pods, bits of dead insects. Dry, brittle things. I did not question at the time the infallible instinct whereby anything with life in it was discarded, a bough still resilient with sap, a berry whose color warned me that decay was still at work. I reached out for things past corruption. Shells of which time had sucked out the rot, things that have done with dying. Light, dry and delicate like a thin snailhouse or an empty husk in a child's hand I wanted to become. A great peace came over me. It was growing dark. At home they must be anxious for her. The dusk deepened perceptibly. Julia stood with her hands clasped, shivering in her party frock. Peace made me magnanimous. I gave her another year's extension.

16

The child runs away in several directions. There goes the chubby girl with the puffed sleeves, the despised one, the Klopps girl; she curtsies to the guests and mumbles a rhyme with her fist in her mouth. There goes the witch child skipping down the stairs to bury her matchboxes filled with dolls' eyes under the porch. And another, a wraithlike creature dressed in leaves runs barefoot and disappears into the forest. It's years till Julia reappears a grown woman.

Where next? Julia's wedding? Shall I jump over the dark interim, straight to the altar? Julia nursing her first child, my lovely maternal Julia! And the years of floundering? Shall I not give her a better girlhood? I used to be much better at it in the old days. When Julia was still with me I could revise her life at a moment's notice. Dishonest of me? But I did not regard the past as a closed matter. Julia's youth could blossom again and again; it could suffer blights; a detail could be amplified, lines erased or reinforced. Her past lay spread out before me like a vast canvas that I was continually perfecting and restoring. The detail of Julia with her guardian angel enhanced the composition as it was at the time. And even if it was at a much later date, when Julia was already a mother, perhaps while she was bending over her child's cradle that this image of tenderness occurred to me, I would nevertheless put it in her childhood; that's where I wanted it; that's where it belonged.

The canvas of her life. Another metaphor. There could only be one canvas. Painted by several hands; I might concede that, nevertheless, a single canvas. The others were sketches and blunders. But which was the true one? Were they all true?

But could I worry at every moment about the composition as a whole? Whether a delightful detail that engaged me at the far-right corner was in keeping with the rest? No, because life was going on; we were changing, our style was changing. I could always fix it up later. Still I was uneasy. I could not truly believe in my little retouchings although they consoled me for the moment. I knew that God's eye saw all the layers in a simultaneous vision. Even I could see them. At times I succumbed to utter hopelessness, cursed God, the canvas, myself. And I would have ripped it to shreds, but how could I lay my hands on that intangible entity the canvas of her life! I would have to wrest it from God's own hands.

The canvas was inviolable. I could turn my back to it, immerse myself in Julia's here and now; until the moment wears out or explodes from its own density, and once more I am on the loose, I need a frame, a composition, I return to the canvas.

Part Two

1

I RETRACE the journey of the dark years, the lost years, the years Julia was changing into a woman. I mean the woman underneath the woman I foisted on her, the real Julia, or in this case, the not-quite-real Julia, but Julia nevertheless, for there were those long periods when I turned away from her and occupied myself with philosophy. Left Julia to her stupid, harmless vices, window shopping, bubble baths, waiting for her true love to appear, paging through endless stacks of fashion magazines.

2

Our relation changed with the onset of Julia's monthly flow. I knew of course that Julia was a girl. Moreover, through Gundolf Klopps's well-illustrated medical books I had ample occasion to gain familiarity with facts pertaining to the female reproductive cycle. I may further mention that some months prior to the attainment of puberty Julia had attended, if somewhat fitfully, a series of Health Chats which the school in collaboration with the local churches held annually for the benefit of pubescent girls, where scientific information on this matter was dispensed in a cheerful and confidence-inspiring manner. I knew and yet I did not know. The sight of blood brought it home to me.

I am still trying to understand how the child changed into the woman, a transformation so mysterious and violent that I am tempted to say that they are two different creatures. We parted ways. Our conversations became clandestine. We could no longer live together in broad daylight. Suddenly I see her in a room with pale organdie curtains of which I have no previous memory; the bedspread, the chaircovers, the apron of the vanity, all done in the same pale flower print. Julia went on to dancing class and silk stockings. I wanted to stay in the child's world; run down the green slope, away from the growing girl.

It happened overnight. Sunday evening she went to bed in her white flannel nightgown and Monday morning she was no longer a child.

I remember she tossed and moaned all through the night. Her sleep was woven with a weird tapestry of dreams where each picture was a different hue of pain. The sky was a swelling. The tree trunk a sore. The apples were blisters. The moon was a boil. Headless dolls hung on a branch, their ivory knees displaying lipstick wounds. What was their crime? Julia danced around the tree with the seven dwarfs. The tree they cried was The Tree of Life. She saw it written on a signpost in red. She turned and fled through the deserted town. The sewers were overflowing. She waded barefoot through the flooded streets looking for a house to go in, but a witch sat in every doorway, the same witch with the same crooked grin, rolling the same apple in her outstretched palm. Then there were many witches pulling worms from their apples and clacking their tongues. But they would not tell her why the dolls had to die.

And when she returned to the tree only the moon hung on the branch menacingly white. She screamed and fled. The moon turned and flipped in her belly. It was scaly like a fish. And when she ran outside it was midsummer night. The moon was falling from the sky, soft and mottled as a plum. She tried to catch it. She spread her skirt not to bruise it with her hand, but it burst against her thigh.

There were frostflowers on the windowpane. Were the frostflowers part of the dream? All I remember is the moment she stood before the window when it struck me that she was changing. Was it the moonlight from the snow falling on her, gave her skin that spectral hue? Everything had grown paler, her hair, her cheek, her eyes; and there was in her eyes the look of someone else.

I was afraid. It was her pallor, not the pallor of death or apparitions, but a whiteness known only to lovers, a fleshly white that appalled me, as I saw her hair fall on her bare shoulders, and the small hairs of her eyebrows against the white of her forehead, and the remoteness of her glance, lost to something vast and foreign to me.

Day was breaking. Julia stood by the window clutching her soiled nightgown. When the sun showed between the branches she crept back into bed and pulled the sheet over her face. So she remained, motionless like a corpse and scarcely breathing, while I ranted Hail Marys and snatches of nursery rhymes over her.

Why was I so helpless? Why didn't I try to hide Julia when I heard footsteps up the stairs? It was the German governess, Miss Prunzel, coming to fetch Julia for breakfast. I recall a struggle when Miss Prunzel having failed to elicit any response from Julia by the command of her voice, began pulling at the sheet. Julia lost grip. The sheet flew off. Julia screamed; she reached frantically for the quilt, the bedspread, anything to cover herself. Miss Prunzel snatched away the bottom sheet with a triumphant snort. Julia tried to crawl under the mattress but Miss Prunzel yanked it out from under her. Just then the maid appeared, followed by the cook and the gardener's wife and I thought the whole world, and stood around gaping. I thought it was the end. Julia was dying of shame and I with her. She tried to coil up into a ball. The cook whacked her on the buttocks and dragged her out of the room. The scene in the bathroom comes back to me. Julia still struggling while the cook cursed. She boxed the cook, the cook pinned back her arms; she was about to bite, but instead pressed her face against the cook's fat arm where she found a sudden comfort. She stopped crying and suffered the cook to wash her and bind her up.

She came late to school. I was too mortified by Julia's behavior to think of forging a note of excuse. I forgot how the rest of the morning passed. Suddenly I was sick. When Julia got out of school I didn't want to be with her. I sent her to the movies.

For a fortnight or longer I went about in a trance. I was sure Julia would die. I pictured her on her deathbed not as I had last seen her, with her face, her arms and legs, even her fingers strangely elongated, her hair longer too and more lank, while under her cotton shift two slightly tapered breasts had pushed forth and trembled when she moved; but in the child image fixed in my mind, wearing last year's party dress which she wore the year before too, with a wide ribbon around her waist. There she lay in white anklets and black patent leather shoes, doll-like, her small firm hands folded on her flat chest.

In later years Julia's lunar phases became a source of wonder and fascination. But at the time I was simply crushed. It was as if my death warrant had been signed. The child, however irksome and contrary at times, was still my sort. But a menstruant maiden?

I had a horror of Julia walking through the street, going to school in that condition. I wanted her put away in some secluded place, behind drawn blinds, the wall hung with charms, women at her side, whispering women's secrets in the dark. What was she doing in geometry class? What was I doing with her?

I suffered pangs of moral anguish, haunted by the ghosts of those unborn babes whose rudiments were hopefully elaborated in her womb, month after month, only to be blotted up in sterile pads and unceremoniously flushed down the toilet. Julia became a generatrix of children of blood, a voluptuous flower overflowing with seed, crying to be fecundated.

I performed secret rites. In the old cemetery I built a mound roughly in the shape of a woman. Here I would come once every month at the onset of Julia's throes to place a gravemark for the unborn child: two twigs tied together with Julia's hair in the shape of a cross. I had Julia bring offerings, flowers, bits of ribbon, sweets.

The earth women took on life. It was Julia with her belly stuck full of crosses and bunches of grass sprouting at her armpits.

Though the child has been laid in a coffin in funeral white, she is unquiet in her death; roams about, stands in doorways. Sometimes I see her sitting crosslegged on a tombstone, chewing a blade of grass. Her features change. Still in her party frock she appears in the form of a toad, a mouse, a dwarf child, her small, pinched face, prematurely old.

Even now her gaze rises through layers of rotting leaves and fills me with a sudden loathing.

3

Can I draw clear lines of demarcation like textbooks of history? The end of an era. The period of transition. A chapter in the dark ages. There is a gap; an obscure stretch of time. I have tried to fill it with odd fragments, sundry incidents from Julia's life. I'm not clear what belongs there. Was it a period of seven years? Five? Or even less? Sometimes most of Julia's life falls in that strange interim; parts of her childhood, all her youth, even periods of her marriage suddenly become detached from their context, and whirl around like loose pages. I lose myself in the gap. My present ramblings without Julia take me back there.

I have called them the dark years, the lost years, the years of my estrangement from Julia. For long periods I forgot about her existence as if she were some half-finished sketch I put away in the drawer. Other projects preoccupied me. I gave her up. Not entirely, perhaps. Every so often I toyed with the idea of Julia. Sometimes took refuge in playing Julia. Julia combing her hair before the window. Julia the chaste novice, raped the night before she takes the veil; Julia the temptress, kindling the lust of a young monk. But I ceased to believe in Julia.

Was there a Julia? I am surrounded by the idols at whose feet I sacrificed her, for whose pleasure I perverted her youth, sold her into marriage. More phantoms, yet how can I curse them, how not revere them, for they have been nourished by her blood. Can I requite her at their hands? I want her back. Every moment of Julia's dark years is precious to me now. It's the lost parts, the parts of Julia drifting or decaying somewhere at the depth of time I want back.

What was she wearing? But we went through so many phases. Ophelia. Saint Theresa. Jezebel. The Duchess of Muscovy. A humiliating incident comes back to me: her favorite teacher commented quite severely on her dress and makeup. It was a black satin sheath with red trimmings, somewhat décolleté in the back. Was that Julia, got up like a little vamp? And those ridiculous chandelier rhinestone earrings, did she buy them behind my back? I don't remember her having a friend after Caroline left town. What did she do after school? All day in the summer?

But Julia was absent so much of the time. She simply left. I could never be sure for how long for she went without notice and sometimes I wouldn't be aware of it till hours after, or the moment I caught her stealing back. She might be gone for an afternoon or a few days. It seemed quite natural at first; just what I might expect of Julia. For I assumed she was with God when away from me. Her departures were like journeys into other worlds. When she returned she seemed to have no recollection of where she had been, only the sense of bliss lingered on.

Sometimes I would catch her just as she was emerging from a handful of beads, or dissolving in the fragrance of fresh mown grass. I did not know what to make of Julia's capacity to become literally absorbed into things. Was it a state of blessedness or gross sensuality? Was she a mystic? I tried to interest her in the works of Dionysus the Areopagite. In vain. I fear I spoiled Julia by doing her homework for her. Now she vaunted her undisciplined mind. How insolent she had become! Pantheism was still too academic. Epicure put her to sleep. I gave up trying to find a philosophical frame for her vagaries. Was she an illuminist perhaps? Or simply mad? I feared that one day Julia might disappear altogether in the color blue.

When Julia left for more than three days I became fearful, suspicious, morose. Could I be sure she was with God? Could I be sure of anything? A week without Julia I nearly went out of my mind. I do not like to speak of Julia's absences. When I'm alone I want to hide. But I have to substitute for Julia; put on her face, produce her voice. Suddenly I stand exposed. Julia evaporated into a pious illusion. There never was anyone wearing Julia's smile, the mask of flesh. The nights are the worst. It's as if she locked every door to sleep when she left. I pull out the gaudy costumes from the chest. I open perfumes or read tragedies aloud to survive the long night.

Why am I chained and she free to roam about? It seems all wrong. I should be the one who leaves on mysterious errands. It's her house after all. I'm only a guest here. Why can't I go off like Julia into smoke, or nothingness? Why can't I even for a minute when I will it? I am free to wander about from room to room. My prison is spacious. I can go out in the street but I haven't really left. I envy Julia who is free to go and leave me with all the chores. Her prisoner, her slave, her drudge. And suppose I won't, won't keep up appearances? Let the house fall to shambles. And when they knock on the door not answer. Or call out in my raucous voice, She's out. She doesn't live here anymore. Go to the devil!

When she returns it's like awakening from a nightmare. My grievances vanish. The rehearsed reproaches I swore I would fling at her fill me with shame.

Take me with you, Julia, I plead with her, take me wherever you're going. I want to be gone with you, lost with you, absent with you.

Her journeys became more adventurous. Once I caught her in a bower undressing before the gardener's son. The act of undressing seemed to be happening over hours. The boy stood, his head in the branches, staring entranced. I remember naked bodies touching. She went there often. Sometimes I caught her in his hair, his eyes wild like a gazelle's, or caught just barely in a vanishing glimpse, the image washed out and blinding white like an overexposed film, his face pressing against her thigh, or perhaps her breast, I couldn't make it out. They never spoke. Their embrace had something languid, dreamlike, no different in quality from the way Julia might sink into a bead. I did not understand. I tried to dismiss it. Preposterous, he was a year younger than Julia; a few inches shorter, too. True, one of Julia's greatest pleasures as a child was to watch him urinate. But that was long ago. Was Julia deceiving me? For when she saw the boy in the garden she scarcely looked at him. They did not always greet each other. One day when he happened to be sprinkling the grass near our bench, I observed him at length. His skin had none of the misty allure I recalled from Julia's meetings. On the oily side. Well-formed features, Latin. But his expression was lacking in nobility. I dared Julia to ask him the time. He came closer, rubbed his nose, shrugged; he didn't have a watch. His diction was slovenly. Also I found his eyes dull. What in the world did she see in him?

I think I disenchanted Julia in the gardener's son. Their trysts became less frequent. There were others. But Julia had become more secretive. The clues grew increasingly scarce and baffling, an odor, a carving over the doorway, snatches of a tune. Sometimes they seemed to be planted to throw me off the track. There were parts I could not connect with any known persons or places. The midriff of a man, bare to the waist; a blurred hand, apparently engaged in unbuckling the belt; the silver buckle shaped like a horned buffalo caught my eye, the image explosive with terror. Was he getting ready to rape her? To whip her with the belt?

I spent weeks hunting for the owner of the horned buffalo buckle. Wherever we happened to be, in school or out on the street, I cast furtive glances at every passing male midriff. I developed an animus against buttoned jackets and coats, they seemed to be designed specially to thwart me. All my efforts were for naught. The one horned buffalo buckle belt I spotted in the course of my extensive search was out of consideration. Its owner was a five-year-old boy. A comely child I will admit. But Julia wasn't that perverse.

The image of the bare male midriff, the elongated navel, the buffalo buckle, continued to haunt me. I remembered vaguely, months ago when Julia was coming home from the beach, there were men working on the road, itinerant laborers. Bare to the waist, I believe, although I did not take notice of it at the time and certainly paid no attention to their belts. I recall I was reflecting somewhat gloomily at that moment on the decline of the Kloppses' estate, the devaluation of Julia's trust fund through the inflation and how this might affect our future. The sight of the workers evoked in my mind the possibility of Julia, or rather myself, reduced to hard labor. A thought which I found profoundly depressing. But of course the connection of the buckle with the road workers is sheer conjecture. And other images were even more baffling. What, for example, was Julia doing with old Professor Grubbe, the piano teacher? True, he was appealing, delicate as a sprite, the face of a woodpecker, but he was well past seventy, with grandchildren almost Julia's age. Yet I found her naked with him behind a bush. Old Grubbe wildly kissing her belly while Julia seemed to be teasing him. I don't remember the words, only her murmur, full of laughter, as if she were saying, Now, now, Heinrich!

4

Julia was going on fourteen. What would become of her? I was not concerned with a career, of course. I had more lofty interests in view. Her person, her image, her destiny.

I wanted Julia to be. To be as truly as a tree is. No difficulty here. Julia had no professional ambitions, the ruin of so many fine women. She had me, of course. Inventive, ruthlessly ambitious once I set my mind on it. She could have become a great actress with my training; a painter, a dancer, a concert pianist. I would have subjected her to the most rigorous discipline. A writer. Was there ever a more fertile mine of ideas than I? What stories we would have invented, tales of love and adultery! But why limit myself to the arts? She could have been an explorer, a lion tamer, the founder of a new religious sect.

Nothing was impossible with me behind her. But then it wouldn't be she. It would be cheating; the world, and what concerned me more, cheating myself of Julia. For all I knew it was my only chance to be in a woman.

I confess I did at times toy with some of these possibilities. The dance was a great temptation. I dreamed of Julia transfigured into pure motion. I saw her leap and whirl with mounting frenzy and like a flame that burns up the log on which it feeds in a moment of ecstasy leap her last and go out. And though Julia did not dance, my dreams of a dancing Julia put her body on fire, sometimes brought her near swooning. How dreams abuse the flesh! An active life would surely have been saner.

I still regret my decision. But at the time I thought I had no right. I would be too ruthless with her, I feared. And then there would be the others, the ballet master, the choreographer, the agent, the public. I would no longer be her sole master. I was afraid of losing her to those others.

Practical considerations finally forced me to reject any vocation for Julia which required sustained effort. Alas, my traveling companion was simply not equal to an arduous journey. Men have bewailed that a third of their life passes in sleep. I had to resign myself to the bitter fact that besides this lost third, the greater half of Julia's waking life was claimed by the turbulence of her monthly cycle. A week of premenstrual depression, an equal period of cramps, fatigue and general misery, to which must be added the day of her ovulation when she was usually too distracted and fidgety to apply herself to anything. In view of her constitutional weakness, then, I did not encourage Julia to pursue a profession.

Was I timid? Did I doubt her gifts? I suppose I was disappointed that Julia was a girl, or rather that she was not a boy, for what did I know what a girl was? As I recall, Julia's sex was a source of some perplexity to me around this time frequently bordering on alarm. For one thing, I like things out in the open. Where was the banner of her sex? Julia was a glove with the thumb turned in, a wrinkled purse. A mere repository, a trench, a sponge that absorbed everything; whatever she touched seemed to impregnate her. She could not even cast her own water from herself without wetting her bush. Her acts could only be construed as states suffered. Wouldn't I have to rewrite her entirely in the passive?

But enough of the melancholy topic of the cunt. The missing member was enough to disconsole me, even apart from the nightmares I projected into Julia's concavity. I wondered how I could ever dream of Julia tackling any serious task. With what? When I watched the young men with eyes aglow planning sea voyages or writing satirical verse, I could almost see them shake their cocky snouts and semen-like spray issue from their mouths. I imagined they dipped their member in the inkwell when they wrote, beat time with it, caused cities to fall on its point; that not the thumb, nor the upright posture, not even the added convolutions of the brain, but the male spout was at the origin of all human accomplishment.

I looked wistfully at every bitch that had a tail to wag and was envious of the elephant cow for her trunk. While I suspect my feelings about Julia's sex were strongly influenced by certain works of psychology I found in Gundolf Klopps's library, her shapelessness at the time tended to confirm them.

Julia was late to flower. Indeed, up to the time she married, I had grave doubts whether she was a woman. One might think that the missing appendage would allay my uncertainties; but this only proved that she was not a man. The monthly geyser of her blood, then? The tumescence of her breasts? But at the time these seemed more like fearful disorders and malignancies than emblems of sex. What was she? An anomaly? I didn't believe anything well shaped could issue from her.

Put her in a convent! It seemed the perfect solution. While Julia hardly inclined toward unworldliness she was naturally attracted to the more sensual aspects of the rite. The idea of living in the austere splendor of a medieval abbey more than appealed to me, of course. But would I let her locks be shorn? Could I bear to see her body discolor in its dark confinement uncaressed through the years? And what about her periods? There is something positively obscene about a menstruating woman in a convent. No, she must marry, be wife, mistress and mother.

But those were the war years. The best were on the battlefield; there was nothing to do but wait.

Oh, they were hard war years! I saw her pine away her youth in that ancient, decaying house, where now only old Mr. Klopps, paralyzed and reduced to idiocy by the stroke, sat in the living room, strapped in a wheelchair, attended by the cook and a doddering, arthritic butler, the last that remained of the servants. Death would call on them one by one, until she would be alone in the house, her best years behind her, a shade wandering among the shades of the dead. Eventually she would go mad.

Marry she must. But what were her chances of marriage? At the time the number of marriageable females was far in excess of the number of marriageable males. According to the census figures one out of every four women was doomed to spinsterhood. Estimating the number of marriageable women in our town at forty thousand, I calculated a total of ten thousand future spinsters at the modest count. Twelve thousand would be nearer to the actual figure since more men than women choose the celibate life. Twelve thousand spinsters in a single town, a legion! And Julia among them!

I tried to take a cheerful view on the prospect of spinsterhood. Wasn't I somewhat of an old spinster myself, or should I say bachelor, perhaps? The consolations, nay, advantages of the celibate life presented themselves readily to my mind. To think only of the still unread volumes of Gundolf Klopps's library in the attic! A lifetime of peace, leisure, solitude, freed from domesticities, devoted entirely to the cultivation of the mind. Yes, I would have been content to putter around my insect collection, I could easily amuse myself learning medieval Pahlavi, inventing new phonetic systems. I might even take up painting. But what about Julia? Could I bear to see her languish as the years go by and her body never yield its fruit? No, I would rather see her dead.

Perhaps under the circumstances I should have considered the life of a single mater familias raising children born out of wedlock. Now, if it were for myself, this is exactly the role I would choose: a formidable matriarch, a queen-bee. But I am somewhat eccentric. It wasn't Julia's way. She was made to belong to a man, to adorn him like a jewel.

Gloom hung over our lives in the war years. Julia moped about. I grew morose. Why didn't she have any aims in life? Hadn't she been a nasty child? Did she ever in all her life give anyone a single moment of joy? A vain, heartless girl. She didn't even have a tear for her mother the day she died. Her only thought was how she would look in a black hat with a veil. And when she almost fainted before her mother's corpse it was not out of grief but revulsion.

Could Julia ever make up for being such a bad daughter? But why try to make Julia virtuous? True to her nature, I swore. But how if she was destined for evil, her portion not grace but hell? For some months I indulged my obsession with the dark Julia. Or did Julia's own murky depths surge up in me? A livid flame flared up, hissing, Let her poison the old man, put fire to the house! Was Julia capable of a great crime? Was I ready to perish with her? The image of Julia buried under the charred ruins of the Klopps house at the age of fourteen still makes my heart stop.

There were other circumstances besides the shadow of the war to dampen my humor. The grounds surrounding the Klopps house were being built up. By Julia's twelfth birthday, the old mansion no longer stood by itself on the hill but was flanked by apartment houses and within a few years the unspoiled country stretching from our door to the sea was blighted by summer cottages and hotels. Gone were the forests, the scenes of our former legends, gone the old cemetery where I buried the child Julia and Julia's unborn children. The Klopps house itself was in danger. Following Mr. Klopps's death during the war, there appeared on the scene cousin Oswald and cousin Felix who, as I learned to my dismay, had in the absence of a will been made trustees of Julia's property. Cousin Oswald was of the opinion that the house, being so well situated, should be modernized and eventually rented out to summer guests. He intended moreover to draw on Julia's trust fund to finance the projected renovations. Cousin Felix, however, argued that in view of the high real-estate value of the plot at the present moment the house should be put up for sale and the money reinvested, preferably in munitions stocks. Julia at that tender age could hardly be expected to stand up to her cousins. Indeed, dependent on their good will she had to suffer their moist looks and more than fraternal embraces unprotesting. Since cousin Oswald and cousin Felix could not agree, the house was neither sold nor renovated but simply deteriorated in the course of the years. The cousins returned to the house periodically and sent contractors, now to assess the property, now to estimate the cost of renovations into a hotel. And although nothing came of it, throughout the years of Julia's adolescence I lived in constant apprehension of being evicted from our castle.

5

From Julia's fourteenth year to the time of her marriage I kept a notebook of a sort. Possibly to fill the lonely hours when Julia was away. Or as a way of keeping in touch with myself when Julia threatened to overwhelm me. It contained reflections on my reading, drafts for a new epistemology, personal meditations on existence. Some quite morbid. Gems of insight perhaps. Lost when the Klopps house burned down. I would not pack it with Julia's things when she went to be the wife of Peter Brody. The day before the wedding, I wrote, This shall be my last entry. She shall not take me with her where she's going. I shall remain between the pages, flat and dry as pressed a leaf.

The notebook which I had occasion to reread at the last of our annual visits to the Klopps house surprised me as much by its omissions as by what it contained. Nothing of my fears and hopes for Julia. No record of incidents which assumed such importance in her life. How could I pass over the loss of her virginity in silence? My entry for that week consists of commentaries on Schopenhauer. Was I so engrossed in my metaphysical studies that I simply returned to my books as if nothing had happened? A disagreeable interruption, perhaps, a lost evening of work?

Or did piety forbid me to touch upon her person? I am inclined to believe that if Julia is absent from these notes, and even in the single reference at the end, never mentioned by name, it was because she was so sacred to me. Though I felt free to speculate on the anatomy of angels, Julia remained my one taboo. I thought it sacrilege to look her over like some profane object, note her daily habits, probe her motives. As improper as to observe a fly buzzing around the host during communion. I must add that I am particularly susceptible to such irreverence, yet I would never grant a lapse the dignity and permanence of the written word.

The sense of awe I felt before Julia was without any sentiment of tenderness or esteem for her. Indeed, it bore no relation to any trait of her character or her appearance, unless it was the brute fact of her sex. I had become an intruder in her life.

It must have happened the years she began wearing silk stockings. I remember when she rolled them down in the evening I instinctively turned away. The hose and garter belt hanging over the arm of the chair the moment of awakening always gave me a shock of being in a strange person's room. I don't remember the hour, or the day, imperceptibly the room where I had lived so long turned into a shrine. My presence there, so scandalous, I refused to believe it. I was too stricken by shame to inquire into this outrage or attempt to justify it at the time.

Yet there I was, locked in the holy of holies where at any moment the high priest may enter to perform a solemn rite. I mustn't be found here! In my panic I scurried from corner to corner like a trapped mouse. What could I do? I hid between the folds of the altar cloth and waited for the ceremony to begin.

6

Julia turned fifteen. Fifteen and still unbetrothed! How long would she remain in this larval state? I was impatient to have her unveiled, confirmed in her sex. Where would deliverance come from? The boys at school? A rowdy pack of pimply faced pups! They scratched her name on the walls of public urinaries and made obscene sucking sounds and barked when she passed. All my hopes were vested in some unknown soldier fighting on a distant battlefield. For him I kept Julia chaste.

I will not say that we were sorely tempted. Yet I had reasons to fear that Julia might commit a folly with someone outside her class. While ordinarily somewhat shy, Julia was alarmingly at ease and familiar with any delivery boy, plumber or street-cleaner. Perhaps she thought it didn't count. But I suspected a family trait. The Kloppses, it is true, never discussed Grandmother Fuchs's promiscuities beyond remarking that she was prematurely oversexed; but I did recall rather spicy stories about a certain cousin Prudella who was brought to childbed thrice by different butlers, not to mention our Aunt Etta who though she died a spinster consoled herself with many a groom as well as his horse. Such deviations may be the privilege of a declining upper class. But I had better hopes for Julia. What was I there for, if not to save her from the Klopps fate. Thus I doubled my guard in the presence of domestics, road workers, foreign laborers, and I must add, frail old men and boys of a still tender age. This office gave me, if nothing else, a sense of purpose. However, the days dragged, and though our prospects remained dim, I could always boast of one accomplishment: I kept her a virgin. Living as we were in a loose age, where a girl might wonder whether her virginity was a prize to save for her husband or a minor obtrusion she would do well to have removed at the first opportunity, I took a firm stand. Unsoiled I would deliver her into her husband's hands.

That Julia would marry a virgin bride was dogma. I will not deny, however, a powerful inclination toward more than one heresy, prompted, I must hasten to add, by the very sanctity encircling her virginal state. I simply couldn't imagine Julia's deflowering performed by her husband. The breaking of that sealed vessel called for an act of violence, brutal and illicit, free of any sentiment which might mitigate its quality of a pure transgression. The idea of being raped seemed, moreover, to appeal to Julia. I recall a particularly hair-raising fantasy in which she was surprised on a dark road by a band of gypsies, who pushed her in a ditch, pinned down her arms and legs and forced her in turn. Their number varied from three to six. I never went so far. And of course I would never permit Julia to walk alone along deserted country roads at night.

Another favorite fantasy was that Julia sacrifice the flower of her youth to a nameless soldier. Not that Julia was the kind of girl to be dazzled by the flash of a golden button, the military belt, the holster. No, it was the impersonal hue of his uniform. He belonged to the world of barracks, transport trains. His body under the uniform partook of the impersonal. It was as if he stood naked before her already. She was seized by a sudden anguish for every white-faced soldier leaving at dawn. When she yielded to him she felt the fear of trenches, the desolation of the wounded and dying on battlefields. I was torn between the violence of rape and the tender gesture of offering. But I could not renounce my image of Julia as a virgin bride. Finally, I must confess to my own secret fascination for prostitutes. A sneaking glance at one of those sad vampires was enough to plunge me into agitation. I never seriously considered it as a way for Julia. But for me! I could not pass one in a backstreet without a tremor of kinship. I was never so envious of the town's beauties as of their rouged pallor, their tawdry adornments, their look of an abused doll.

On which altar would I offer Julia? There were so many gods I would have needed as many Julias, one to be a whore, one to marry in white, another, no, at least a dozen little Julias to be raped in turn. Mere fantasies to pass the long winter afternoons and lonely evenings.

That same year, her fifteenth year, Julia was deflowered.

It happened on the night of the Christmas dance at the mayor's house. The ballroom was thronging with soldiers, home for the holidays. Squeezed between steaming bodies I held my ground, watching for Julia's reflection along the mirror-lined walls. I went prepared for an ordeal. It was a matter of obligation. How could I know if it wasn't Julia's chance to meet her man?

After a while I lost track, dazed by the commotion of stamping feet, Julia yanked about, changing hands as the boys cut in. Red-necked boys with perspiring palms. The next thing I knew she was leaving the dance with a soldier. They crossed the road to his car. Should I have protested? But I was powerless. Oh, I have found out since, when Julia is alone with a man she ceases to be my creature. It's as if she were launched. Without warning the gangplank is raised. She sails and I cower in the hold, a wretched stowaway. I recall a sense of mesmerized panic, clear as doom, as we were racing through the night alone in a car with some strange soldier called Bruno. I never caught his last name.

If at least she had been raped. If he had dragged her in the bushes and forced her against her will. But it did not happen so. She smiled when he unfastened her brooch. What should I call it then? A mere stupidity? Shall this blunder be entered in the book of life? Or can it be reconciled with my image of Julia? It was his last night before returning to the army post. It was not Bruno, it was a soldier. It was not Julia but any girl in wartime. Julia wanted to be that anonymous girl.

The details are irrelevant. Why do they intrude upon me in all their original oppressiveness? The moment Bruno asked her for a dance still makes my ears burn. Julia was just about to take a third round with a dogged and taciturn sailor when two gentlemen in uniform simultaneously requested her pleasure. It was a matter of a split-second decision. She looked from one to the other, both officers of the same rank and past the first flush of youth; the one big, bland and beaming, the other small, fierce and swarthy, hesitated an instant as the little man's eyes seemed to snap at her, but finally accepted the offer of the more generously proportioned suitor. I had a rather favorable impression of Bruno, even though he was baldish and his volume was distributed in breadth rather than in height. No prince charming, to be sure, but agreeable, well mannered and a welcome relief from the raw youths Julia had been dancing with. When in the middle of the dance he suggested that they go somewhere else for a drink, I saw no objection to it. He would surely take her to one of the better places in town and Julia, I thought, must feel enormously flattered to arouse more than the passing interest of a man who may have been in his early thirties and an officer too. Not until he was already helping on her coat did I reflect that by her leaving thus with Bruno, apparently to escape the stringy little officer, Julia in fact expressed a preference for him in favor of the other, and possibly a desire to be in his company in a more intimate manner than she originally intended. Their flight, moreover, was quite unnecessary as the little officer with the snapping eyes was just then making his way to the cloakroom with his prize for the evening, a stately blond, leaning coyly on his arm. It is easy to say now that she should have backed out of it then. The moment Bruno helped her on with her coat there scarcely seemed cause.

He did not start the car immediately but sighed and kissed the tips of her fingers and looked at her at length. Oh, what did that look mean? And why was he smiling at her so stupidly and pursing his lips like a baby as he whispered her name? Why whisper all of a sudden? Before they were alone in the car five minutes it was clear that Bruno was afflicted with a most deadly passion for Julia. Before they had been driving another five minutes it was clear, furthermore, that Bruno was not taking her to one of the cafes, but to the tavern where he was staying just outside of town. Wasn't that the moment for Julia to protest? Demand that he take her to a cafe in town or straightway home? But how could Julia be cool and sensible when the man beside her was consumed in the flames of love, in a state of most pitiful agony, induced, moreover, by her own radiant person? For while I cannot vouch for Julia's feelings toward Bruno, I can say that the spectacle of Bruno's rapid deterioration swelled her vanity besides engaging her compassion. Could she be so insensitive as to inquire about time or place or purpose when the man beside her was in so stricken a state, breathing hoarsely, stretching out his face toward her, his mouth hanging open and staring like a fish—a disgusting sight, no doubt, yet could any woman be so callous as not to show pity on him? What does he ask for, after all? To clamp his lips on hers and stick his tongue in her mouth, squeeze her breasts and, yes, finally cuddle his swollen member in her fold. For all her innocence Julia knew where it would end. Yet how could she refuse to quench his thirst, especially since it was her irresistible charm that reduced him to this helpless state?

Bruno had stopped the car before they reached the tavern, apparently incapable of steering while the fit was upon him. I flinched while he inflicted his suffocating kisses, wondering if the stringy little officer was using his companion in a similar fashion and if it made the least difference in the world how the couples were matched that night. His hands groped under her skirt, up her thigh, touched her bush. To my great relief Julia squirmed away and, complaining of the cold, requested that they proceed to the inn. Of course, Bruno said, distractedly, and started the car. All the way to the tavern I was spinning in a frenzied circle, thinking, now we're in for it, he has touched her bush. Oh, he touched Julia's bush, now there's no turning back! As if this starting intimacy had to be made good somehow, and could not be made good unless she went through with it to the bitter end. Julia's fate was sealed by the time they entered the tavern. True, up to the eleventh hour my voice kept ranting, he hasn't pierced her yet, she could still be saved; now they are alone in his room, he has ordered the wine, but she is still a virgin; now she has undressed, he has seen her naked, but she is still intact, there still is time. But as soon as they lay down in bed my voice was silenced. I capitulated. My reactions, however, may not be to the point at all.

Was Julia looking to me to save her? But not at all. She had a bold air. She entered the tavern on Bruno's arm poised as a queen. Perhaps just a bit too exhilarated. Out with an officer. Fancied herself quite an adventuress. The man's eyes hung with adoration on every visible detail of her person, he catered to her little whims. He was in her power, or so she thought. They had a drink in the tavern. Bruno ordered a bottle of wine and some fruit to be brought to his room. Now she was bought, caught. Up the stairs Julia's courage began to falter. When she found herself alone in the room with Bruno, all of a sudden she could not speak for fear of bursting into tears. She bit her lip; strolled stiffly about the room, to the window, back to the table, absently examining the glass figurines on the mantelpiece. What happened? Her position changed suddenly from a conquering lady to a captive.

After some amorous attentions and a glass of wine, Bruno excused himself and disappeared into the bathroom. To prepare for the slaughter. Julia was at a loss. Did he expect her to undress? She slipped off her shoes then put them on again. Went to the mirror and tried to tidy her mussed crown; gave up, took out the pins, sat disconsolately on the edge of the bed playing with her hair. Bruno came out of the bathroom in a pair of drawers. His torso, though not Apollonian, was firm, if shaped somewhat like a seal's. He leaned over her, exuding a strong compound of talcum and eau de cologne. Julia was on the verge of tears. He inquired if she was in her monthlies. Then Julia informed him that she was a virgin. Bruno's face melted. He reassured her that in just a little while that obstacle would be surmounted. In the course of the ensuing struggle Bruno's expression altered: an air of professional competence replaced the lovesick looks. Perhaps he regretted the evening more than she. He would have preferred an experienced woman. But I want to be just. I was touched by the way he appraised her body before he actually fell upon her.

My confusion from the moment of the assault was too great to be attentive to the details. I don't like to think of hands fumbling in the dark around those sacred precincts. In an instant of pure terror Julia's body assumed the aspect of a fortress under siege, panic behind the walls. The enemy crashed the gate. Bruno's palm clamped on her mouth to stifle a scream. Julia felt pillage and fire, her halls demolished, the curtains ablaze.

I became totally dislocated. Was I in Julia? Was I in Bruno? I was sick for days after from the physical trauma alone; not to mention the shame.

Julia's first moment of womanhood was a defeat. My purpose moves toward the consummation of the image, but Julia opens into a depth where I lose foothold. Her body lost its clear outline; she seemed to spread indefinitely.

They sat naked on a long-haired rug before the fire. No, that was another time, with someone else she sat naked before the fire, someone who accosted her on the street and she went just to be naked with someone.

They finished the grapes. The conversation became sentimental. He said he'd find her when he returned. I think he meant it for the moment. I think Julia believed him for the moment. She thought of him every so often in the years that followed, maybe every third month, or so; and even after she married, once or twice a year she remembered Bruno.

It was almost dawn. Bruno worried her parents would be angry about her coming home so late. His younger sister, he remarked, would get a lashing if she came home after dark. I felt crushed. I did not want Bruno to think she was a loose girl. Tell him about the house, the garden, the servants, I urged Julia; that your grandfather haunted lions in Africa. But she just sat silent like a little sphinx.

They had to rouse the innkeeper to unlock the door. Bruno couldn't start the car. He called for a taxi. I was relieved he was leaving the next day. He said he'd call her in the morning when she got into the taxi. But he didn't. He probably couldn't remember her last name.

As we turned in the road leading to the Klopps house, it dawned on me that Julia may have gotten herself with child by a man whose last name and address she did not know, and with whom, moreover, I would not care for her to establish a permanent relation. I imagined Julia's life as an unmarried mother. Bruno would fall at the front. She would have the child in her father's house in defiance of the world. Her life would be dedicated to raising him. For a fortnight it looked as if Julia's fate had been sealed.

Julia did not have a child. Bruno did not die in battle. When I saw him three years later on the beach he walked past Julia with an older woman. I don't think their eyes met. I was appalled by his thick, hairy calves.

Shall I be held to account? But do I know what moved Julia? Am I Julia's keeper? Is she like some voluptuous beast I periodically unleash to watch it bound and roll? Sometimes I see myself as an old pervert who has young men rape his daughter while he peeps through the keyhole. But this is only part of the truth. More often, I feel, the reverse is the case. I fancy she is my puppet when in fact Julia leads me by the nose.

7

Julia shamefully deflowered at fifteen! A bruised peach. Her beauty fell from her. Do I still wring my hands and groan, Why did you do it, O why did you do it, Julia? Did Julia care? She fell into bed without washing her face, slept till noon; and when she awoke the makeup clinging to her skin gave her pleasure and she gazed at length in the mirror. For days she cherished her body's pain. God was in his heaven and all was right with the world as long as her navel was in the middle of her belly. And no regret? But I don't understand these things. Perhaps regret was so much part of the experience that she relished it with her soreness. Why weep for Julia, she wanted to be pierced, rammed, filled, she wanted it. Because of the way she is made I suppose, with a crack, a slit, between her legs, poor thing; a hollow in her flesh she wanted filled with flesh, a man's or a child's. She would have filled it with other things, I suppose, if I hadn't been watching her.

Julia my virgin was lost, wanton, thrown away. I despaired of her life ever attaining to coherence. What was there left? I turned to metaphysics, the only pure thing left in life. But this time my own voice mocked me. What! Search out the elements of being in a skirt! For a moment I was tempted to burn Julia's dresses, cut off her braids. But why seek congruity when I was made a monster? I would pursue my ends in this frilly masquerade. Keep vigil with Aristotle in a corset; fast with rouged cheeks. Still, the shadow of her earrings falling on the page brought me to distraction. Her scented sleeve brushing past my desk made jest of my labor. Whether to appease her or as a gesture of spite, I goaded Julia into promiscuity. What was to be gained through chastity, now that she was no longer a virgin? But it was I who was left with the bitter taste. Our relation reached a breaking point. How could I concentrate on my cosmological treatise with the phone continually ringing for Julia!

No, we couldn't live together. It was Julia or I. Julia had her chance. But what of me? I, behind the masks of Julia? Would I remain in obscurity, covered under this rag of a girl forever? Why did the world take no notice of me? Was I not the nobler part? But it was always Julia! Julia's dress, the tilt of her nose, her dimple, her little toe, the slightest detail of her attire seemed to concern the world more than my most delicate insight. Away with her! Now it was my turn.

I still lived off her, like a hermit feeding on grubs and roots. A mere body she became to me, a potential carcass, that lingered on, churning its brackish juices; whose sole right to exist was through my strict, fastidious, incarnal presence, to serve as a host, a mere larder, to the princely parasite I fancied myself.

What was Julia doing all this time? When I summon up the hours given to my solitary flights, only my distorted image of Julia bears witness. Julia struck me ridiculous, ugly, unreal. How arbitrary her face, how nonsensical her limbs! To think that I, a spirit, should have any connection with her, actually live in these sewers! Each time I dozed off, I was wracked by nightmares of swimming through marshy waters, thick with bloated pollywogs and gray shreds of corpseflesh tangled in rotten weeds. But even the outside disheartened me. The covering of soft, moist skin, with patches of hair only pointing out its nudity. Why had this uncouth abode been allotted to me? The relic of some antediluvian age. Why not a sphere, a cube, any regular solid, smooth and hard? I longed to dwell in a perfect crystal, a snowflake, a drop of dew. A beetle was beautiful compared to Julia. In vain I tried to cure her body of its succulence, shrink it into a mummy, at least a facade more in keeping with my temper and habits. The beast was magnified through my abuses.

I even forgot that she was a woman. Her flesh assumed an obscenity which rendered her sex a matter of indifference.

Of my flights only the twisted armature of the preposterous flying gear; the plumage gone. I was not equal to the challenge. My notes of that period bear witness to fruitless self-preoccupation ending in incoherence.

Or do I do myself injustice, and I was on the path celebrated by mystics as the dark night of the soul, or on the road to extinction described by eastern sages; but for love of Julia swerved short of the goal? But no. My tracks wound inward like a burrowing worm's. The point around which I circled was not deliverance but uttermost bondage. Not God, but I. With each turn I was more hopelessly walled in. The sense of my existence, far from diminishing, grew more acute, and at last became excruciating. I was seized by the terror of my indestructibility. Nothing that I was, nothing could annihilate me. Even if Julia's heart stopped, I would go on, spread over the rug, eat my way into the woodwork. I saw myself crawl like a blight over the fields, poisoning the wells.

I must have abandoned my project for a new cosmology, for in the notebook begun in the spring of Julia's fifteenth year I found no reference to it, nor, indeed, any mention of the topics which formerly engaged my most passionate interest. Nothing on grammar or invertebrate anatomy. How did all the joy go out of my studies! My solitary pursuits, once a happy escape, a delicious vice, were one by one enlisted in a grim regiment of punitive exercises against the creature. Suddenly I found myself on trial. To putter around the attic, or chew my way through Gundolf Klopps's library, which, besides, was quite outdated, could not longer contend me. I needed a purpose. But what was demanded of me? Would I write an opus? Who engaged me? Perform acts of devotion? To whom? Void the mind? I found myself slipping into a semi-imbecilic state staring for hours at a spot on the rug. Make something of myself, then. But how could I bear to be anything less than a perfectly unconditioned and necessary existence? The rankling suspicion that in truth nothing was demanded of me further undermined all my efforts. No one called upon me. I was giving orders to myself. The task of finding some figure for my predicament finally obsessed me to the exclusion of aught else.

There is little in these notes which could claim originality, unless I include the first five or six pages, which, however, can scarcely be called reflections, since, language apparently having failed me, I rely solely on punctuation marks to convey my meaning. On the first page, I recall, I had placed only a question mark, the sign of my bewilderment. It seemed most apt at the time: a point hovering over the abyss pursued by an indefinite curve. The following page showed a series of small question marks in a row, which seemed at the time to signify some progress in the development of my thought. The third page could be taken for a sample of Morse code but is in fact an assemblage of exclamation marks running now sideways now up and down. I have forgotten their meaning, except that I perceived some hidden connection between this sign and the first-person pronoun: turn me upside down and I am an exclamation mark. It made sense at the time, and being so totally at a loss as I was, to see myself as an inverted exclamation mark seemed a step forward. In the next few pages I explore the colon and the period. The colon first, it struck me so noble, balanced and constant in its nature; it revived my faith in the possibility of speech. I proceeded to fence in those monsters, the question mark and the exclamation point, between colons. But I had still to settle with the point; the point in which all my hopes were finally vested, that most treacherous of all signs. For besides the single point, the true period, there were those double, triple dots, signifying the absence of beginning or end, the very image of my terror! For another few pages I pursued my inane game, arranging the signs in various sequences. Not until the seventh page, written months later, did I regain my articulacy and embark on an attack on all previous psychologies. The last week of November, Julia's sixteenth birthday. Oh, my heart bleeds! It's sad enough that a girl is sixteen only once, but Julia was never sixteen. Sixteen and seventeen are a blank in her life, a bleak void where sits a fat spider drooling his sickly web.

I, not Julia, I declared in a fit of spleen, From now on I would be I, not she. But what was I? I didn't even have a name. Not that I was envious to be called Julia Klopps, but by my own name. And my place in the order of being? Had my sort of existence been noted in the works of men? Had it been investigated? My extensive readings in theology, mythology and popular spirit lore, all led to negative results. Though I would have been pleased to claim family ties with many a fabled beast, hobgoblin or sprite, to do so would have been another imposture.

Did I exist? Was I a thinking substance? Descartes's *Discourses*, though they occupied me some six weeks, did not persuade me on this matter. Unlike Descartes I did not presume to doubt everything. Far from it. I never doubted that the sun shone, if not on me, on the wheatfields. Nor was the existence of my desk or my chair a problem. The world I have always found to be all too solidly there. It was only my own existence I doubted. To say then, that here is something beyond doubt, namely, that I doubt, does not advance me a step further, if anything it enjoins upon me a step back: an endless series of certainties regarding the existence of a doubt. As to the leap from *I think* to *I am*, it takes such an effort and in the end I discover I've been hopping on the same spot, without, perhaps, touching ground. Assuming that I think, I doubt, what follows from it? That I am a thinking substance? And so I am at peace in a little jar with a Latin label. But I am not. All that follows from I think, I doubt, is more thinking, more doubting. Thinking substance, indeed! I could easier believe I was a backache.

I resumed to my quest turning to religious works. But the writings of the theologians, the testimonies of mystics and saints only increased my despair. For I know I am not what they speak of, not this mystery, this handiwork of God, a living soul. No, the more I read of these pious works, the more the awful conviction grew upon me that I was some sort of malignancy, a flaw in God's creation. Indeed, during these months of darkness my one solace was to meditate certain passages in scripture which speak of the casting out of spirits. I saw myself in the place of that foul demon the moment it emerged from its unhappy host and stood dazed and cringing before the Christ. The mortification of that filthy spirit as it crawled out of its hiding, his stricken amazement as he withered up under the gaze of the savior, were the only blessedness I could imagine at the time.

I had found out what I am: the ugliest thing in the world. Yet was I truly humble even then? Or did I take pride in being a sore? And while I groveled in the spittle of my self-contempt, think my groans and genuflections more precious in the eyes of heaven than any natural act of Julia? I entertained mad schemes to bring about my destruction. Let her take the veil. True, I would be bringing her to the cloister gates. The motives, the project would be mine. Yet the rites performed on her would annihilate me. But could I be sure? Having survived Julia's baptism and her confirmation, I feared the rite of initiation would be equally powerless to exorcise me. And to imagine I would follow her inside the cloister, whisper obscenities in her ear!

What a fraud I am. But I will confess all. I come to the strangest juncture of our lives, when I decided to give myself up. No one had discovered me. I could have left it at that, taken my stolen treasure and devoured it in secret. But I was seized by the craving for recognition. Why couldn't I break out on Julia in the form of a rash? I resolved to take matters in my own hands. I would give myself away, even if it should ruin Julia.

But how? And to whom? A written declaration? Saying what? Throwing a fit would be more effective. But I wanted to avoid theatricalities. Make myself known as I truly am, a gray, nondescript spirit, cold and sober to a fault, without the trimmings of fiery eyes and clotted hinderparts. I started to draw up a statement.

But who would I tell it to? The girls at school? Professor Grubbe? The cook? Old Mathilda was the last person to whom I'd confide my secret. She knew too much. I'd never give her that satisfaction. But perhaps the Latin teacher, he had a somber look. Or better a stranger, the balloon man in the park or some old charwoman. No, the world would think us mad. And the one thing I vowed must never happen was that Julia join the ranks of the illustrious members of the Klopps family who wound up in the madhouse, among whom I am sorry to have to name that model scholar and antiquarian, Gundolf Klopps, who it is said ended his days in an asylum skipping rope and tying ribbons in his hair, having at the age of seventy, after twenty-five years of solitary meditation, emerged from his study firmly convinced that he was a nine-year-old girl. No, my own intellectual pride, as well as a residue of vanity as far as Julia was concerned, enforced my determination that we must steer clear of the madhouse. Besides, I couldn't bear to live in an institutional setting; I had put my foot down the time Julia's cousins wanted to send her to a boarding school.

My exposure would have dignity. To no other than a servant of God would I entrust my case. How would I arrange the interview? Request it by note? How would I sign it? Julia Klopps? God forbid. A pseudonym, then? But I had sworn I was done with impostures. Present myself in person? Whose person, Julia's? How would that look? Would I have to throw a fit, after all? I waited for the opportune moment.

One morning just as we were leaving church, the priest drew her aside for a word in private. I trembled. Had he seen me? There I sat right on her forehead, covering her face. I prepared for my great moment. But the good priest had asked her in the sacristy only to pass on some compliments he had heard from her piano teacher, to which he added his own, and finally to invite her to a small gathering of young people to be held at his house the following Sunday evening. I sulked in silence. How could I speak up under the circumstances?

More than once when Julia passed the convent, the nuns invited her in. But each time I went resolved to give myself up, a curious change came over me. I cannot account for it to this day. No sooner had we entered, I was numbed, it seemed, by the sheer physical impact of the setting. A picture on the wall, the pattern of the rug, hues, shapes and the cadence of voices etherized me by their imposing presence. Eyes that looked past me and rested on Julia; dwelt kindly on her face. A voice that spoke to Julia. I withered up in shame. But no, it was painless. In fact I felt a sudden relief. Light and giddy, I found myself dancing with the motes in the sunlight, while the nuns showed Julia around in the cloister, happy to be of so little weight, almost nothing.

But as soon as we were out I'd revive and take my vengeance on Julia. There I'd be waiting for her outside the gate, ready to spring on her neck. Poor girl, she didn't know what was happening to her. What was that thing struggling in her? I'm sure she felt me twist and squirm, now in her belly, now at the roots of her breath, in her throat, between her eyes. She tried to flee from me. She'd run till the branches blurred and the moon swung like a lantern on a string, till there was nothing but the wind in her head. But when she lay panting on the ground I'd be there again riding on her breath like a child on a seesaw, now on top, now on the bottom and wouldn't get off. Her visits to the convent became more frequent. I should have been pleased, but I wasn't. I was sick with envy. Julia got all the affection, all the praise for my labors. Wherever we went, it was always Julia. Not even the priest took notice of me. I was seized by an insane longing to be caressed. Long after I had resigned myself to live forever in the background of Julia's life, the craving lingered on. Indeed, the older I get, the more childish. I dream of one day stumbling on a little hut in the middle of a forest where lives an old witch, the one witch who will recognize me. She will look past Julia's brow, look through her eyes and see me only and call me by my name. I will crawl out while she claps her hands and cackles over me. She will call me her darling and scold me and spank me and scrub me clean. And Julia? But there'll be no more Julia. A fond fancy. Bit maudlin, too. And to think I was once so proud.

Return to Julia? I had nowhere else to go. But Julia was a disorder. It must have been then that I began my search for her, haunting corners we've passed for her exploded moments. Till weary of my search I came to rest on Julia's graven image, her forehead, the swell of her breasts; took refuge under her scarves and skirts.

Having failed so ignobly to free myself from bondage to Julia, honor required that I make some formal gesture of capitulation to signal my acceptance of defeat. I considered burning my books, my notes, my insect collection; destroy all trace of myself. I could not think of a greater sacrifice. But I feared that if I set fire to the attic, Julia would be blamed for it. So instead I locked the attic door with a solemn oath never to set foot in my former haunt again, rowed out at night, and committed the key to the bottom of the sea.

Yet what of my notebook entries the week before Julia's engagement? The day before her marriage? Was the key returned to me after a fortnight in the belly of a fish? Would that it had been so, for then I could have called it fate. But no, the door was forced open one day when cousin Oswald's agents made inspection of the house, a circumstance which did not touch upon my oath. No, I had no excuse for entering. That I had forgotten some things of Julia in the attic, her jade earrings and the Japanese kimono she was so attached to? Phah! I have no character.

My notes during the month preceding Julia's engagement, three brief entries in all, including the last, hint, if somewhat obscurely, to the closing of a chapter. In the first, I am prepared to dismiss the entire question of myself as unreal, one of those pseudoproblems to which we are led through the peculiarities of language. Yet on the next page I resume my inquest in the form of a commentary on a passage of Saint Augustine on the darkness of the creature; one would suspect me of piety. This, I recall, was followed by a page covered with curious curvilinear scrawls. Possibly an attempt to carry out an earlier vow to renounce discourse.

Perhaps I should also mention as a factor which may have played some small part in bringing me to my senses, that in Julia's eighteenth year her dowry was established at a rather handsome figure by cousins Felix and Oswald.

Part Three

I

THE TIME for frivolities was over. I was ready to follow her like wandering Bedouins their sacred camel; pitch my tent wherever the holy beast chose to stop.

But what was the matter with Julia? How strange and sullen she had grown. Now she bolted now she balked, now she went around in circles, when we had a destination and so little time to make it. She didn't want to be anything? But Julia, I pleaded, I need a house and clothing. I cannot be without a face. Day after day she went out into the fields kicking the clod in the same faded jodhpurs and broken sandals. It was only by appealing to God's law that I could prevail on her to wash her face and put on a skirt. God was a magic word with Julia; it soothed and reconciled her. She would even comb her hair for God. I feared she was becoming religious. Was it so preposterous, living in contact with me?

Julia would not be rid of me until she met my equal, to possess her, body and soul. Someone would have to take my place, challenge to combat and slay the old dragon keeping her in captivity. And I would have to make all the arrangements! Find the hero who shall slay me, provide him with the magic weapons, dress her for the occasion, have her lie in a locked room, my sleeping beauty, see to it that the key gets to the hero in time, rush back to the gates in my dragon gear snorting and spitting flames from my seven heads. I was dejected at the prospect of having to plot the entire thing. Julia was wearing me out. I could barely make the effort of washing her hair every five days. And now to have to contrive my banishment and her rescue!

But I wouldn't let Julia down. On the job from morning till midnight, I pulled her out of bed, arranged her dates, dressed her, combed her, made her face to go out with the young men. I depended entirely on her appearance. All of a sudden I found myself cast in a bizarre role of a worldly mother baiting young men in behalf of her nunnish daughter.

Her lethargy was bad enough. But when she got it into her head to do something, I really flinched. She developed a sudden passion for weaving; nothing could tear her away from the loom. She'd weary of it as soon and take up clay pottery. Let the young men wait while she was messing around. Next she wanted to breed dogs. Then she was seized by an irresistible urge to travel. I was in a state of panic for weeks wondering whether I'd find myself on a steamer to New Zealand or to the Canary Islands. She spent her days going from one travel agency to the next and had every clerk in town working for her, making out elaborate itineraries, calculating time schedules and fares on the Shanghai Express and Cook's bus to Bombay. Between travel offices she loitered around the pet shop. She almost bought a pair of full-grown Saint Bernards, but in the last moment thought the better of it just in case she should want to take the Shanghai Express. My worst scare was the morning she set out to town to join the Women's Naval Auxiliary Service. Julia! I cried, Where are you taking me? Where are you going! No, it was to be the convent after all. Was she on her way to the Mother Superior? To the train station? To the beach to drown herself? How did she ever make it to the public gardens, past the flower woman at the gate, past the ice cream stand and the balloon man, to the fountain where a young man was waiting for her?

Was Julia indifferent to men? Not at all! What else was on her mind while she moped about the house in a dirty old kimono but how her true love would one day suddenly appear.

Julia's dream man! But I won't get into that. Suffice to say he never appeared as a decent young man in a white shirt and tie, the kind she was likely to meet at a garden party. I had my doubts whether Julia would ever turn into a decent woman. But where ever did I get my image of a wholesome, womanly, woman. An innate idea to be sure, for I never confronted one in the flesh.

While I had only the vaguest notion of the sort of man Julia ought to marry, some professions were clearly excluded; the peasantry and laboring class, even such appealing and poetic types as fishermen and locomotive conductors. Neither a hangman nor an undertaker were for us, however hallowed their office. No, Julia was a lady and we had to be realistic. Shopkeepers, small merchants, civil servants, functionaries, agents, lackeys, regardless of their rank, were naturally out of the question. This left the so-called nobility and the professional classes. The former was unfortunately in its last stage of decline. As for the latter, I had only a few strictures. I would not want Julia married to anyone in daily contact with crime, disease or poverty.

A scholar? It would depend on his field of interest and stature. The same held for scientists and inventors. The wife of a clergyman? Never. A judge? Heaven preserve us!

Thus we patronized the town's artistic circles besides faithfully attending every dance and garden party to increase Julia's chances of a good match.

I will confess that for all my efforts, I couldn't believe that Julia would ever get married. Wasn't her fate linked to mine? Was I ready to sell her in cold blood to the highest bidder? Julia was incapable of making a commitment for life. For all I knew she did not take to the idea of marriage at all and would have preferred a series of indefinite courtships. Or why didn't she say, Yes? I waited, listened, waited; I counted to a hundred but Julia just stared into space smiling vaguely as if the moment were sufficient unto itself.

I had to take the step for her. I signed the papers. In time she'd turn around and see it my way. She'd have to. Hers would be the duties and the honors, hers the children. I only helped her across the threshold into a world I would never enter. My last service to her. The day would come she'd be grateful to me. No, she'd never know.

2

I still say we couldn't have made a better choice. Who was there after all besides the very boring young men, who, I should add, never received sufficient encouragement from our side to make a proposal. A Roumanian count, if he was a count, the affair was too brief to allow me to verify his title. But he appeared genuine enough with a monocle, gold teeth and a saber scar across his cheek. He proposed to Julia in the middle of the third dance, ranting of his fatal passion for her, his horses and estates in Transylvania which he laid at her feet amidst the most ferocious displays of love. I think he was serious for the following day he sent a basket of roses to his future countess with a note that he hoped for consent that same evening. He was rather outlandish; but we gave it a fortnight's consideration. The wife of an elderly nobleman living on a country estate, with servants and horses, she could do worse, after all. I had visions of Julia coming down a white marble staircase in a heavy velvet gown, hung with precious family heirlooms, to receive her guests, all ancient nobility. I saw her driving through the grounds in a stately carriage on her way to church, waving graciously to the peasants. But to lie at his side every night, be squeezed and pinched by this desiccated frog? It would be an unhappy marriage, of course. But could anything be more wretched than her present state? She was bound to suffer with any man, let her at least suffer in style with satin cushions on which to lay her aching head. She could devote herself to her children, after all. Find consolation in religion. One day, a young man, the son of the neighboring baron, who had been away studying law or medicine would drop in to pay his respects. As the young baron took shape before my imagination it became increasingly clear that she would not be safely married to the count.

Ulrich Schultz? A most unlikely partner for Julia; yet he intrigued me. Hearty, hairy, corpulent, he could, after all, have been her prince charming in the disguise of a bear. For I never saw Julia laugh so hard as when Uli lifted her by the heels and swung her around.

Uli was a painter. A bad painter, but he was immensely pleased with his huge blotchy canvases which reproduced from every conceivable angle the lusty disarray of the one-room flat where he slept, cooked, ate, painted, washed, made love and grew garden vegetables in wooden crates. Uli liked to make love at all hours but preferably in broad daylight smelling of garlic and turpentine with the pot simmering on the stove, the children shrieking in the courtyard and the delivery man banging at the back door. It was the furthest from what I had imagined for Julia. May this be a sign that it was destined?

I made a supreme effort to accept Uli. A warm, expansive nature, I said. I fancied his face had character. A Roman face of the late imperial period. But I was embarrassed when I saw them walking together. Sloppy Uli with his loud tie and perspiration-stained shirt. Wouldn't Julia begin to spread around the waist living with him? And even granting that eating stew from the pot in bed with Uli had a certain charm, how would it look in ten years? With six children? No, Julia Schultz didn't sound right.

Conrad Richter would have been our man. A man with a hawk's beak, a tiger's glare and a daredevil grin. A wild, willful, hard-loving, hard-drinking, torrent of a man. Long before he took an interest in Julia I observed him avidly from a distance. Richter was one of the town's more notorious characters. Thrice married, now widowed and living with an actress, he had been a journalist, gambler, stunt pilot and theater producer in turn and was currently writing operas. While Julia lay giggling with Uli I envisaged passionate love scenes and quarrels with Richter. The fact that he was past forty and scarred by life only enhanced his charm.

But could we trust Richter? A man who had gambled away a small fortune! Naturally I was suspicious when he proposed to Julia after two weeks' acquaintance, during which, I may add, a kiss on her forehead was as far as he'd allow himself to go, it being his fond conviction that Julia was a virgin, a point on which I did not think it prudent to enlighten him at the time. The man was after her dowry, I feared. While this was not a great sum, they could live comfortably on it for a few years, time enough to finish his opera. Indeed, Richter had intimated to Julia his dream of buying a small farm an hour or so from town where he would retire with her, a reformed man. A likely story. He'd buy that little farm, all right, but he'd never be there. After the first week Julia would be alone on that farm feeding the chickens and cleaning the sheep pen, while Richter lay rolling in the arms of some boozy old actress in town. Oh, I saw it all!

Perhaps I judged the situation too much like a sensible old aunt. Thrice married, I thought wedlock cannot be too sacred to him. Julia deserved better. Still, there weren't many men around with his seductive charm. Possibly a genius! But what if he was simply a *raté*?

The insipidness of their relation finally decided me against Richter. Was Julia so overwhelmed by Richter that she dwindled into a little rosebud in his presence, or had she no choice, because it was Youth and Purity, his saving angel, he sought in her? She charmed him with dawny, dewy looks, dimpled, pouted, crinkled her nose. I could have slapped her face. Perhaps she met him too late in life. In any case, my dreams of a tormented passion were not fulfilled; he must have saved that side of himself for the aging actress. Richter undoubtedly cut a better figure than Ulrich Schultz; if only he could have seen in Julia a different sort of woman, a tomboy, a tart, an enigma, his double, anything but the always fresh and fragrant little flower he wanted to possess in her. How tiresome it was; to think that we were almost caught in that trap! Perhaps it was simply to escape Richter that we rushed off with Peter Brody. Julia was the worst coward about terminating a relation. She just let the suitors accumulate until we had to scatter them with one blow, sending out the wedding announcements.

Peter Brody was different. Peter had something fine. He was tall and delicately built, with the clumsy charm of an overgrown boy. Peter was a little shy, a little withdrawn. He wore glasses. Of course he was not the man I imagined for Julia. Peter's features were too rounded and there was something about his posture that reminded one of a newborn colt standing on its legs the first time. Peter had a small head. People said a small head is noble. He had a fine head, a noble head, people said. It took me long to resign myself to Peter's small, round head. I disliked Peter at first. Peter was very intellectual; somewhat gray. A bit too much like me. But after a while he won me over.

Peter was not yet thirty but already held a responsible position at an important shipbuilding firm. An exceptionally brilliant young man, indeed. He completed his postgraduate work at eighteen. At twenty-five he was considered one of the country's most promising naval engineers. Peter was, moreover, the last male representative of one of the oldest families in town which meant that a considerable property now held by aging female relatives would eventually fall to him and his heirs. The most eligible young man in town, people said. But as a matter of fact, although Peter had been seen at social functions with almost every marriageable daughter of the town's small aristocracy, he displayed a marked indifference toward women until he met Julia. I ought perhaps to mention at this point that Julia was on her knees scrubbing the front doorsteps the fateful afternoon Peter Brody happened to wander up the lane to the Klopps house to inquire whether it was the Bristol Inn. She had been impossible all week, until finally I put her to work: clean out the cupboards, wash the floors, boil her underwear. Needless to say we were not expecting visitors when the young man appeared at the foot of the steps dressed in afternoon formal holding a bouquet of choice hothouse roses and looking somewhat forlorn. Julia straightened herself, brushed her hair out of her eyes with her forearm the better to behold the young man, and began to direct him to his sought destination. But Peter Brody was in no haste to proceed to the Bristol Inn with his bouquet, now that he beheld Julia. Flushed, dusty, and perspiring, her blouse torn at the armpits, more likely a servant than the daughter of the house, Julia roused his passion.

Indeed, Peter was a little disappointed when he found out that she was not a servant. He often remarked even after they were married that she should have been a servant girl to make it perfect. Well, I say it was pretty nearly perfect as it was. After all, the Klopps house was practically a ruin, the family name had been on the decline ever since the last century, and Julia's dowry was a drop in the bucket of the Brody estates. The manner of their meeting, I should add, gave their relation from the start the stamp of the inevitable.

Everyone in town was eager for Peter to marry, but none so much as his guardian mothers, Aunt Eulalia and Aunt Eudora. The aunts, or rather great-aunts, for they were sisters of Peter's long-deceased grandfather on his also long-deceased father's side, were getting on in years and understandably impatient to entrust their charge to the solicitude of a wife, who besides would provide the family with an heir to carry its name. Great was their joy when Peter brought Julia to the house and announced their engagement. No questions were asked. Julia was hailed as Peter's salvation.

Peter was a delicate man. A wonder he survived outside an incubator for thirty years. Although it should be said his aunts took every precaution to approximate that model; they regulated the temperature of his room and bath water, controlled his diet, determined every article of clothing he should wear and held several councils a day on the state of Peter's health. The task absorbed the two of them; Peter for all his timidity was not always tractable. For one thing he was addicted to work and would never have left his desk for food, rest or air if not for their conjoined effect. Peter, moreover, drank secretly since a very young age; a factor which naturally increased the aunt's conviction that he needed a wife. Peter drank steadily and without ever getting roaring drunk. He sat at his desk bent over a blueprint and drank quietly, as his father and grandfather had done before him. It was obvious that Peter needed a wife or he was doomed to destruction and the Brody name with him. Julia was truly godsent. Aunt Eulalia and Aunt Eudora embraced her, heaped praises on her, showered her with gifts, surrounded her with all the anxious solicitude they formerly lavished on Peter: Julia must have everything, she must be happy, healthy, strong, the better to take care of Peter. I must say, Peter's health did improve considerably in the marriage and this despite Julia's less stringent observance of the hospital rules set down by the aunts and the additional drain on Peter's health of a rather irregular and probably excessive sexual life.

Peter was not exactly an easy man; but then he was very highly bred. He had his special brand of tobacco, shaving cream, lighter fluid, paper and ink. In short, a man of discrimination and refined habits. He loved his glasses; he had ten pairs, I believe; one for ordinary use, another for reading, a third for precision drawing, a fourth for ordinary use in the sun, a fifth for reading in the sun, with an extra pair of reserve glasses for each. Always neat and immaculately clean, Peter never went barefoot for fear of fungus. He wore socks even on the beach and rubber swimming shoes when he ventured in the water. But Peter had no objection to Julia going barefoot. He loved to see Julia go barefoot. But then he loved her in every condition, busy or indolent, disheveled or dressed for the opera; perfumed or with the odor of the bed about her.

His aunts having made his health their mission, it is understandable, moreover, that Peter should oscillate between hypochondriac caution and the most wanton recklessness where his physical wellbeing was at stake. Experience proved nothing. For Peter his work output was his sole gauge of health. When his engineering genius stalled he would in desperation alternate between an herb tea diet and assaulting his sensitive system with such amounts of coffee and sausage as would make a strong man quiver. I couldn't say whether Peter was more difficult to live with on a diet of herb tea or when he methodically poisoned his system. I suppose that with anyone as neurasthenic as Peter was it doesn't make much of a difference. It was clear, however, that married to a man like Peter Julia had no choice but to become the most gentle, gracious, considerate, faithful and solicitous wife imaginable. If not for Peter I doubt whether Julia would have become the good Julia.

Finally, there was something touching about Peter. Behind his preoccupied manner, his casual, matter-of-fact tone one suspected there was a very tender man. Peter had a secret sore around which the whole man was bound like a bandage. A sad childhood he must have had even with all the efforts of his good aunts to make life pleasant for him; his father dead of drink before he knew him; his mother, an opera singer, must have been a very possessive woman. Gossip from the servant quarters had it that she publicly vowed to kill herself the day her son married. Alas, we missed the performance for her kidney burst when Peter was twelve.

Peter was happy when he held Julia in his arms. A little hesitant, almost incredulous, at moments amused. He couldn't believe it. His expression turned from anguish to bliss, from bliss to anguish. Would Julia ever find a man who loved her as much as Peter? Who brought out so much good in her? Her life, I felt, was not in vain as long as she made one person in this world truly happy.

Part Four

I

SHE MARRIED. She became Julia the woman, took on the qualities of night, vegetation, of the sea. I shall never know now for I wasn't there. The moment the bridesmaids slipped the wedding gown over her head I was caught up in a sudden trembling. In a shudder of joy I perished. My joy was premature as it turned out. Yet for a period of about a year I seemed to have disappeared entirely from her life. Julia's one year of sheer happiness without me. Where was I? Asleep? Suspended in that twilight region where I lingered before I came to Julia? So small and drowsy, my presence in the marriage chamber was as little offensive as that of Julia's newborn child. I slept and while Julia nursed her little one I dreamed that I was that infant suckling at her breast.

I came to, one way or another. Not quite my old self. In fact I did not think of it as me. When Julia entered her season, I too became transfigured. Pure, remote, angelic, I basked in the morning sunlight that fell upon Julia's hand serving coffee, or brushing her daughter's hair, suspended in gestures of tenderness that hung about the family like a fragrant aura. The holy family! Do I strike the old pose? The queen's chronicler; her majesty's portrait maker. I swelled in my office, at last an honorable post. Unburdened of my advisory function, my task was to administer her cult. With what loving devotion I went about to revise her life. A portrait of Julia her husband could hang in the hall. A life of Julia fit for her children to read.

Day in and day out, when she lay wrecked by birth-pangs or smiled at her infant nursing at her breast, while she set the table or smoothed her husband's brow, I hovered like a host of cherubim around her head, singing with one voice. Praise be to God! Amen. In the performance of her humblest household chores, Julia partook in some sacred drama, far beyond my paltry comprehension. Yet I basked in its aura. With time, of course, my first neophyte zeal yielded to a more perfunctory observance at my offices. My amens did not flow unceasingly but only at prescribed hours. Toward the end, I found my concentration flag even during service. Perhaps I was getting too old to mount the steep slope of Julia's ecstatic journeys. But I made myself useful in other ways: planned the menu and prepared shopping lists for the following day while man and wife made love. Every so often I'd contribute my amen. But in the beginning my hymn of praise accompanied her every move. Julia did not sew on a button or put a bowl in its place but my angelic choir sang, Amen. So be it.

2

What I remember of the weeks before Julia's engagement is like a dream pieced together upon awakening. Julia seemed to be whirling through town in a trance; men in theatrical costumes kept emerging from behind doorposts and streetlamps, one after another they took her by the waist and twirled her around. She'd spin twice or thrice then break away, dancing her way out of the town into the fields. At some point I must have entered the picture. While Julia was turning in her enchanted orbits I was engaged in a quest. My physical image of myself is a very thin gentleman in black with a cane; a cleric or an undertaker. At the same time I appeared hard, shiny and segmented; possibly a beetle. I recall checking periodically whether I still had my white handkerchief and suede gloves; but I hastened along, very preoccupied; tapping, tapping, now with a cane, then with my antennae. All this before the dream took a dramatic turn. I was content tapping. It was the thing to do. Julia seemed vast, all pervasive. I had difficulty disengaging her from the landscape. I kept asking questions, unaware that they annoyed her, until suddenly I perceived that she was running from me. Even then, I continued to pursue her. Doggedly, with a sense of righteousness, saying, It's my duty. I stopped every so often to steal a glance at the watch dangling on a chain around my neck. With increasing frequency as the action progressed. I felt a tinge of guilt about consulting the time. But I had no choice. A great celebration was taking place and I was in charge of the arrangements. I was hot in my black suit, giving orders and explanations, but in a festive spirit. We were getting there! It was going to be a village fair, a wedding. But what was the funeral hearse doing there? My role combined diverse functions: priest, undertaker, uncle, at moments a theatrical producer, or an industrialist, Julia the commodity I was selling, or Julia was the event itself, the festival I was arranging.

The dream went on; perhaps another dream, for I was no longer in the picture. The hearse must have been for me. I remember following her down the streets into the public garden, past the flower woman and the balloon man up to the fountain where Peter Brody was waiting for her. But the miracle by the fountain belongs to Julia; I had no part in it, except for random impressions, the toy ship sailing, a pigeon's feather, gold candywrapper and a child's ribbon at the bottom of the basin. Julia stood by the fountain; the wind blew her hair in her eyes. But Peter Brody didn't see her face. He was sitting on the rim of the fountain, her skirt touching his cheek, looking up her waist, the swell of her breasts. His hand stroked her skirt, to smooth a fold, to brush off a bit of pollen, or simply to feel the fabric which was part of her. He stroked her skirt, his hand sought hers, their fingers clasped; his arms bent around her waist and he pressed his face against her thigh. A miracle was happening; it was not for them to know it; they were part of it. I have called it the miracle by the fountain. There they remain for all eternity before the fountain. No, they walked away, arm in arm. He bought her a bunch of bluebells and pinned it in her hair, they went out through the iron gate and down the street. I forgot how the day ended.

3

For seven years I celebrated Julia's marriage. Even after the tide turned, Julia ebbed, and the burden of sustaining the sacred order of things fell on me, I did not cease my song; even after Julia may have already left. I say seven years, I find comfort in the number seven, although it may have been less or more. Even now, long after it has ended, the worn formula still springs to my lips, I make the gesture of benediction over the unswept hearth.

Seven years. Can I account for a single day? Or was every day so much like another? How was she so used up that she had scarcely time to go to the hairdresser? True, there was the house, Peter, the children. But she had Aunt Eulalia and Aunt Eudora to help with the house and the children. For they came faithfully to help the little mother. They would arrive in her seventh month just in case the baby should be born prematurely as was the rule for every Brody male child, to be there to celebrate the boy; and stayed till the infant was practically weaned. They came summer and winter, although Aunt Eulalia was loath to come north which was so bad for her rheumatism, and Aunt Eudora died each time she entered the house that was so full of sad memories. With two women in the house what was there for Julia to do? Oddly enough as I recall when the aunts were helping in the house Julia was busier than ever. Aunt Eulalia would be telling her to put ointment on the baby, disinfect the strainer, but before everything else, disinfect the chamber pot while good Aunt Eudora would be screeching at her all the time to stop rushing about and take a rest or her milk would stop. If Peter and the children and the house did not wear Julia down, surely the aunts did.

I do not say it was all felicity. Not infrequently while I sang hosannas, Julia groaned. Oh God, Oh, God! But we were beyond happiness and misery. Beatific horror, wretched bliss, whatever it was, however bewildering, dreary, pitiful, inane—it was life!

Do I need to account for my state of delirium? That each time Julia rinsed a diaper or suffered her husband's quirks, I exclaimed, This is reality! This is Julia! My image of Julia? What made every commonplace act seem a miracle? I can only explain it through the mysterious chemistry of Julia's system. For in the period I speak of, Julia was, when not otherwise used, either pregnant or nursing.

She smothered me in her voluptuous mass. The Julia who made her appearance at dinner or at the opera, coiffed and perfumed in a silk gown and pearls, was like a tantalizing mirage, a mere shimmer on the surface of opaque depths, made up of sensation indistinctly infernal and exquisite and suffused with the odor of souring milk, blood, urine and excrements.

While I do not have a clear image of Julia in her blessed state I must have been present during her pregnancies in the form of the curious lucidity of the mind under ether. I recall being in a tortured involvement with Julia's foetus. For nine months we wrestled locked in a strangling embrace. Did Julia feel the intrusion of that alien life in the thick of her flesh as acutely as I did? Its heedless, triumphant growth, feeding on her marrow? I was prey to nightmares: the black foetus; Siamese twins, hermaphrodites, monster-births of every description haunted me. My amazement each time Julia was delivered of a little girl, pink and comely, with not a joint missing or a limb too many.

With each delivery I thought the child was giving birth to the mother. Emily. Laura. Jenny. Each was a flowering of Julia. She would fill the house with children. Julia herself was unfolding in each child, in the shape of its head, its eyes, its moods, blossoming in multiple forms and destinies. I could not wait for them to grow up, marry, have children. I lived with the legend she became for her grandchildren.

It's curious, come to think of it, that while I could imagine Julia at a great age, a magnificent grand dame at eighty or even a hundred, her abundant snow-white hair in a bun, beautifully erect in a pearly gray dress—the idea of an aging Julia was simply inconceivable. Julia at forty-eight, thirty-nine or even at thirty-two, never! Perhaps I hoped that that cold chronology would be annulled in another time, the mighty rhythms of childbearing. I don't recall noting Julia's twenty-fourth birthday or her twenty-eighth. It was by her children

I used to count the years. The year she gave birth to Emily, I said; the year Laura was weaned.

All these years I had labored in the void trying to make Julia into Julia, when her true destiny was to be wife to a certain Peter Brody and mother to a series of unknown creatures. She belonged to them, lived though them. How simple it was! God forbid that I should ever commit the impiety of probing their relation. Did she really love Peter? Did she want to raise children? Did she consider the step she was taking in bringing living souls into the world? Or was it to arouse Peter that she loved, and to luxuriate in her own fecundity? Peter was never so mad about her as when she was pregnant. Her belly! Her swollen belly! There she'd be sprawled out and naked on the bed when Peter came home from work. She'd watch him enter in his neat suit, wipe his glasses and grow pale and begin to tremble when he saw her lying there, her hair spread about the pillow, her naked belly heaving in the air. After washing his hands he'd go straight at her belly button. Julia ceased to have eyes, a mouth, a face. Oh, Julia! Peter groaned. Oh, Julia! Oh! while she grinned in the dark playing with his ears.

But my voice failed when Julia's breasts were flowing. I bowed before her power, I reveled in it. Who was I after all, beside Julia? I owed everything to her. The Brody house, the wood-paneled dining room, breakfasts on the veranda. I was grateful that I was allowed to enter Julia's bedroom, sniff her perfumes, watch her put on her jewelry. How did I come by all these riches, the little girls with their dolls and teddy bears, the fine linens, cheese soufflés for lunch? Did I gain them through my own merits? No, it was through Julia. Of course I cherished and exalted her.

4

I admit that at times I found the house oppressive, and increasingly so with the years. All so neat and decorous, the waxed floors and starched curtains, not a speck of dust, not a scratch, a wrinkle or a stain to be seen, every object always in its place. There wasn't a single room where I really felt at home. Often as I watched Julia set the table, I reflected with a certain horror that every day for the next twenty or thirty years she would be going through exactly the same motions, distributing the knives and forks, the wine glasses to the right and the crystal salad bowls to the left. I would be seized by an irresistible urge to change the order, mix up the silver, mess up the linen closet, tear down the walls and throw everything together in a great barn. Or at least declare a week of rest from the incessant housecleaning; my old temper rearing its head. Obviously this wasn't my style. But I wanted it for Julia. Julia was to be mistress of the pantry and the linen closets. There was an old shed in the garden which suited my needs perfectly: a dirt floor, some broken wicker chairs, stacks of old magazines. Here I would retreat every so often. I kept a bottle of gin, and some playing cards to pass the time. I had long renounced a life of my own, but I needed occasional privacy.

Alone in my shed my thoughts remained with Julia. Every so often I took stock of the situation. Had Julia any cause for complaint? She couldn't have a husband more loving or blind to her faults. Peter did not gamble or chase after women; he never beat her or used obscene language. He was neither dull, nor bald, nor podgy. All in all, a most considerate, well-bred, hard-working and presentable husband.

Not that Peter was always sweet and amiable, which might have made him somewhat of a bore. Mornings in particular he was habitually irritable and morose; but then, Julia was a bit disorganized herself. Breakfast time neither husband nor wife were at their best; they knocked against each other and the furniture, overturned glasses, passed the salt when sugar was requested and were prone to mumble to themselves. Peter couldn't see straight, or make any sense for that matter, until he evacuated his bowels, as if their contents obstructed his frontal lobes as well. Peter's preoccupation with ridding his tubes of yesterday's waste, so as to start clean the day's work, was worse than Julia's after delivery. Every day was somewhat of a trial since Peter's system was quite unpredictable and while on certain days the most violent purgatives could not make his intestines budge, on others a teaspoon of lemon juice sent him in a three-day cramp. What should

Julia's stand be on this issue? Peter constipated was insufferable. But Peter in a cramp was not very agreeable either. Peter had his weaknesses, I'll be the first to admit. He couldn't stand a quarrel or, indeed, the least display of emotion. The sight of a tear was likely to drive him out of the house, and any sign of sadness or strain on Julia's part was sure to precipitate a liver crisis. And when Peter couldn't find his automatic silver pencil, which, I must add, he habitually misplaced, his whole universe and, as a consequence, ours, was thrown out of kilter. Was this reason for Julia to think herself unhappy? Married for better or worse. Another husband, I said, would have other faults.

As for Peter's eccentricities, they were on the whole endearing. So solid, so decent, so correct in every respect, yet Peter had a touch of perversity. He was not aroused by a woman unless she was either highly pregnant or a tart. Ideally she would be both. Needless to say he wanted the woman he married to be a chaste wife and irreproachable mother. Nevertheless, in the nuptial bed he would insist on Julia wearing the most lurid garters, black lace stockings and extravagant hats with ostrich feathers. Every so often, especially when he was sorely overworked, he made what seemed to me somewhat extravagant demands; but this was rare. Usually he was content to fart in her hand. I suspended judgment over these operations, though they hardly appealed to me. Aren't all men fundamentally perverse? Uli, for example, couldn't make love properly unless there was near certainty of being caught in the act. And if it was the dead of night all the lights had to be on and the blinds up, in the hope that a late passerby or an insomniac neighbor catch a glimpse.

A naughty streak I found particularly touching in Peter was his greed for Julia's milk. Luckily his work took him out of the house for the day so that he could only indulge his gourmandise at nocturnal hours or there might not have been a drop left for the baby. Even so, the morning feedings had to be supplemented with the bottle, and of course Julia had to take the blame from the aunts who would attribute the scarcity of her milk to Julia's carelessness in her diet, to her keeping late hours, or not thinking the proper thoughts.

Julia was obviously the perfect wife for Peter. And could a woman have a more perfect husband than one for whom she embodied perfection? It is true that they hardly spoke to each other beyond ceremonial requirements of the day. But then, Peter had his work. Every moment he spent away from his desk filled him with visible anxiety. And while he may have had a genuine passion for blueprints I believe he was driven not so much by mundane interests to advance his career or aggrandize the Brunschig Shipping Firm as by a religious zeal to accumulate working hours on his credit with no one else but his mysterious god. With Peter the universal fear of wasting one's precious ration of time on earth may have been more acute than with most men; and who are we to judge, after all, whether the posture of kneeling is more pleasing to God than that of Peter Brody bent over his desk? It is quite understandable therefore if Peter considered the sexual act as much as he dare give of himself to anything outside his work. Not that Peter was a recluse. Besides his numerous social functions he would spend a Sunday on an outing with the family and take his wife to concerts and the opera as frequently as any other husband. If Peter did not appear very lively on these occasions but indeed assumed the wooden aspect and vacant stare of an Easter Island idol, he was scarcely to be blamed. He had after all withdrawn these hours from his desk and what he did not spend might still be credited to him.

The debt he incurred in the hours of nocturnal passion must have been a source of great anguish and terror to Peter; sufficient anguish and terror in fact to nourish a secret hope that he had in part already been stoned for them. Would Julia ever find a man so hopelessly bound to her as Peter?

Of course I had my moments of doubt. Was Peter a rare blend of opposites or was he a contradiction, a mere confusion, an ambiguity so that one wished that he would be either one way or another, either soft or hard, hot or cold, sweet or bitter. Faced with Peter's complexity how could Julia possibly know whether Peter's sweetness was at the root of her discontent or whether it was not rather Peter's bitterness; or whether it was the fact that he was a blend of both or whether her discontent had anything to do with Peter at all. The latter seemed to me the most likely possibility. For Julia was irked now by Peter's attentiveness, now by Peter's negligence; now by his earnestness, now by his jokes; now by his long woolen underwear, now by his leaving without his galoshes. Oh what was the matter! Julia still had at least ten years to go till her menopause. Was she simply giving out like a used battery? Running out of smiles and caresses, words of comfort for her family? I shuddered to think that we still had some thirty or forty years ahead of us.

The day I had to take over the role of Mrs. Brody, I confess I sometimes gagged on the lines. Why couldn't Peter take a second serving of fish or put on a tie without Julia's permission? Every morning when Peter left for work Julia had to stand by the door and wave to him until he reached the end of the lane, and then go upstairs and stand by the window that Peter might have a last glimpse of her before starting the car. It was clear that their relationship was sustained by these little ceremonies. To omit a word or look of reassurance was to undermine the entire edifice. I liked to see Julia performing these rites; she did it with such grace. Was it not touching that a grown man, as able and independent in his professional life as Peter, should place himself entirely in her hands? Is it possible that Julia did not really want to be a woman, was not a real woman? Or was Peter's adoration simply not enough and she needed a whole congregation at her feet? But was there such a thing as woman? I began to doubt it; an effigy hung with little boy fancies, that's all it amounted to in the end. Of course I never allowed these misgivings to interfere with our daily observances.

These were her best years. I was in bonds. Julia lived at last, her own life at last. I did not look too closely what sort of life. It was enough to wake up in the morning and to know that her life was mapped out for her to the grave. What matter whether the way was rough or smooth, we were on the right road. I was content to remain in her shadow. And although now she eluded me more than ever, the house of which she was mistress, every piece of furniture, Peter, the children, continuously reassured me of her presence. Indeed, she could have left without my knowing, I believed in her so firmly. As long as she was Mrs. Brody nothing could shake my conviction in her existence. Julia could slip away, simply vanish sitting on a park bench one sunny afternoon and it might be years before I noticed it.

5

I shuffle through the old portraits, go over the past accounts, the past attempts to understand what became of Julia.

Julia's married years fall in three distinct periods: the Early, Middle and Late Julia. Jenny's birth marks the transition to the Middle Julia. But where shall I set the beginning of the Late Julia? For I perceive symptoms of the Late Julia already in the Middle Julia; yes, as early as the Early Middle Julia, say when Jenny was around two. They subside and then assert themselves with increasing virulence after the affair with Paul Holle. Can I make that affair the decisive factor in Julia's decline? Or was it the last stage of a process of deterioration that began with Jenny's birth or possibly earlier, with Laura's, or Emily's. Unless Julia never entered into the marriage: I went into it alone with Julia's trousseau, her dowry, and it was I alone with Peter and the children from the beginning. No, that's going too far. I'll put it all on the affair with Paul Holle; from that point her life entered another depth plunged into a disorder from which there was no recovery. And the affair itself, where shall I place it? It doesn't really fit anywhere in the outline of Julia's three phases as a married woman. It belongs if anywhere in her adolescence. Or to another destiny altogether. As to the Late Julia, I would dispute whether it was Julia at all. I really don't see any connection except the name. No, the scheme doesn't work. I give it up. The wrong approach altogether.

6

The first years of Julia's marriage correspond to what I subsequently designated our age of faith. I wasn't in the picture. From the moment

Julia became mistress of the Brody house I firmly believed that I had ceased to exist. Whom was I trying to deceive? Myself? God? But I believed in magic and miracles. I was playing Julia, to be sure. But with what devotion! My former impostures became acts of piety. I could only make these token offerings. What I performed in play, God accepted in earnest of my faith ardently affirmed a real world where a real Julia lived a real life, a world to which I naturally had no access.

Of course, so delicate a relation is fraught with perils. I was prey to momentary delusions of identity. In a fit of drunken elation I would fancy myself the lady of the house. It was almost inevitable. An actor carried away by his role, at moments I really lived Julia; this was my connubial bed, these my ivory combs and flasks of scented water, the white forehead, the breasts offered to a caress, the parting lips, mine. Mere lapses. Actually, our relation reached its maximum distance at this period. Never was Julia so opaque to me. I took the decisive steps. In a sense, I bowed out. I restricted my province to the imaginary; the rest was God's good world. Julia walked in those gardens. Or perhaps it was a wilderness. It was not for me to judge. That was between Julia and God.

So I would have gone on shrinking and becoming progressively more abject each time Julia swelled, brought forth and suckled another babe. But as it happened Julia emerged from the delivery of her third daughter in so lacerated a state that a waiting time of several years was urged upon her before she embark upon the making of another, and as it was hoped, a male child. Her sense of physical decline, her disappointment at not having produced the much-awaited male heir in three tries and finally the bitter realization that she would never in this life have produced six sons before she turned thirty are sufficient to account for the change that came over Julia around this time.

She came to my shed on a rainy November night, the eve of her twenty-ninth birthday. She did not have to speak. I understood everything. It was to be expected after all. In my opinion she had had too much of a honeymoon of it and only a foretaste of the seriousness of marriage. Bitterness and sorrow, a secret discontent seemed to me part of a married woman's lot, and with my help she would bear it with dignity. What other alternative had she after all? Leave Peter? I would never allow Julia so much as to entertain the possibility of breaking up her marriage. Divorce is ugly. I say so. Besides, anything was preferable to having Julia on my hands again. There was clearly only one course to follow if we were to steer clear of shipwreck: she must gain a new beauty through resignation, suffering and forbearance; she must rise to the gravity of her station. Now was the true test of Julia's womanhood.

I shudder to think what would have become of Julia if I hadn't come to her aid. Once the initial surge of excitement passed, it was I who sustained the marriage. I was continually at her side to remind her of her blessings. Look at your dressing table, I whispered, the mirror framed with gilded cherubim, the jars of ointments and flask of scented water, your jewels, your drawers full of fine silks. Caress your furs, the marriage bed with the lace cover, the velvet drapes. Now we'll go to the dining room, to look at the china and the silver. Don't weep, look with pride; the soupbowl is one of its kind and the candelabras were made by the best silversmiths of Italy. Hear Aunt Eulalia playing the harpsichord in the drawing room? A gracious soul. But now to your husband's study. There he sits at his desk bent over a blueprint, the good man in his fine camel's hair housecoat. Doesn't the smell of leather and fragrance of his tobacco fill you with gladness? Go up to him, kiss him on the back of his neck. His perspiration should be sweeter to you than wine. Ask him if he desires a cup of herb tea. Aunt Eudora has taken care of it? So much the better. Ask him when he will come to bed. Don't worry; he will be up working another three hours; we'll have time for our gin and solitaire. Now up the stairs, to the nursery, see the little angels tucked in. Emily's toe sticks out, pull the blanket over it. Look at Laura hugging her teddy bear, there never was a sweeter sight. Oh, that smell! You better change little Jenny. Don't tell me you're tired and the maid will see to it in the morning. It's your child. You want a sweet-smelling baby. For shame, Julia, your tears are soaking the baby's shirt. Shame on you for weeping over the child because it is a girl child, and you a woman! Don't just leave that diaper festering in the corner, rinse it and put it in the pail. What will the maid think! Now lift her gently and put her back in the crib. Before I knew it, I was diapering Julia's baby and doing her chores. I didn't mind. No, I considered it a privilege.

When she could not sleep at night she'd come to my shed to drink gin and play solitaire. Or she would sit paging though old magazines and pictures. I boosted her spirits recounting to her the accomplishments of the day. Moreover, I would conclude as I observed her hands clasp and unclasp the arm rest, there is nothing wrong with a woman in your position and with your responsibilities drinking gin and playing solitaire late in the evening.

Nor had I the least objection to a light affair now and then. On the contrary, I encouraged Julia to go out. It will keep you young, my dear, I said. You will be a lovelier wife, a better mother. I heartily approve of small flirtations. They embellish a woman, like her linens, her jewels, her children. Of course she must have admirers. By all means go riding with Captain Hosch, it's bound to advance Peter's career; have lunch with the director of the conservatory; dine with the chief of the archives, doesn't he awaken fond memories of Professor Grubbe? Each is a mirror in which you can behold yourself from a different angle. See, you are a whole gallery of portraits, portraits you can live in. Here you are gentle and demure, almost saintly; naughty on another; a child full of mischief on the next. Each has captured something of your nobility, your charm, your sadness, your strange repose. See, you abide; they catch your ephemeral reflections.

Consider it as part of your functions, I said. There was no question of Julia's faithfulness to Peter at this time. After an evening holding hands with the chief of the naval archives, Peter wasn't so bad after all. Of course she enjoyed it. She enjoyed being a woman, dressing up, having her hand kissed, didn't she? I don't really know. Perhaps the only thing Julia really enjoyed after a while was drinking gin in the shed. Weary of her admirers she sought my company more and more. She'd sneak away from the nursery just to sit in the broken rocking chair rocking to and fro, taking a sip of gin off and on, paging through old magazines. She'd rather spend the evening in the shed than dine out. After midnight she'd still be out in the shed with me.

Is that how it ended, Julia drinking gin in the shed, while I dealt the cards; till one day I looked up and I was alone with the empty bottles, the old magazines? I prefer to believe that Julia abdicated on the night of her first visit to my shed. She laid down her ring and her keys before me. Slipped out of her wrap, sank down on my cot and never rose again. When it grew light I threw on her wrap and rushed back to the house to dress and feed the children, send Peter off to work. I like to think that Julia never returned to the house.

And the subsequent events of her life, are they to be ascribed to me? I, having an affair with young Holle? Giving birth to his bastard? Did I sleep with Deolger? Hosch? I'd like to spare you, Julia, if it were up to me I'd close the books before you reached thirty and take the blame for the rest; but that's going too far. Who went on living in that house, then, setting the table, emptying the ashtrays, sneaking out at night? Was I truly incarnated in Julia, wedded to her to the bitter end, Julia the slut, Julia the corpse I'm hiding in the shed? Or did I recoil from that plunge, afraid in the last second of perishing with Julia, boiled into Julia's banality, dirt of her dirt. I pushed her over the cliff and remained standing on the rock, her survivor. Shall I not celebrate myself? But where is Julia? Where shall I find her? In the past? The future? Here and now?

7

My last picture of Julia is in the public gardens late in August some weeks after she was delivered of Jenny. The pallor of her cheeks, the languor of her body, a glowing sorrow, fuse in the aroma of mother-hood. Watching over her jewels, Emily in saffron, Laura in blue, Jenny in white. No, it must be later. Jenny's hair is in braids. She has put a fistful of grass in her mother's lap and run off to play. I want to remember Julia in the moment of her ripeness; her last splendor, just before her fall.

The past year has flowed away with scarcely a ripple, like one long Sunday afternoon. Without so much as the faint shudder elicited by breakfast dishes on the veranda seen through a flood of sunlight and the flicker of turning leaves.

Life goes on. I won't say it's Julia's life, or mine, or ours.

She bides her time, like fishermen who have set up their traps, lowered their nets, and now there is nothing to do but wait.

I still say she. Do I mean Julia? I don't know. It's I. The shadow I cast. I in the third person. Am I still trying to save her face? Julia then. I'll say it's she.

She has not been indolent, but her occupations in the house only serve to bide the time and wait; not for something extraordinary to happen, but for the moment to pass, the hour, the day, the week, the months and the years, and in that passage undergo a kind of distillation. When she dresses the children to go out, or when she sits on the park bench with a book she does not read, watching the leaves turn, gazing past the children in the sandbox, she wonders if one day, ten years hence or twenty, an instant of this afternoon will come back to her, a sudden image plucked from the monotony of mornings and afternoons, perhaps the blue of Emily's skirt brilliant against the sand bring tears to her eyes, or the lacy shadow of foliage cast on the gravel catch her breath.

True, memory was my reward. But first it must pass through Julia's soul. I imagined her soul was shaped like a kiln, that by some mysterious alchemy extracted the precious ore from the dress.

While Julia folds the little petticoats or mixes the lemonade I skulk around her skirts like a bored, petulant child.

Sometimes I'm cranky. I whine and nag. Not loud. I hate myself. I wish she'd put me to sleep. From my little stool in the corner I watch Julia turn about the kitchen as if she were a servant or relative. I am struck by trivial details, a run in her stocking, the inflection of her voice when she calls the children. Emily, Laura, Jenny. I don't know what I'm doing here. Julia, I have nothing to do with you. I would break with Julia, but this is no longer she. Aunt Julie I'll call her. The meals are oppressive. I don't like the children. Do they see me?

Thank God for the daily toils! The milk that has to be brought in and poured into glasses. The children asking to be fed, buttoned, their shoelaces tied. Julia puts so much devotion in tying little shoelaces. She always goes down on her knees as if by assuming the posture of prayer she was fulfilling childhood dreams of cloister life. Jenny fidgets, twists around to watch Laura squirt milk at Emily through the straw. Julia does not allow the movement of her foot to interfere with her task. All her strength is concentrated in her fingers. She ties a fine bow. Oh to serve! She feels herself used up in the day's thousand minute ceremonies; the vessel from which pours the daily life of the household.

She has passed into the picture; a moving tableau. Is that how it ended? Julia was poured out on the altar of the household gods. Just before the end, her image flares up for the last time, deceptively bright in a passion of a fortnight.

8

A portrait of Julia the adulteress? Julia and Paul Holle are not subjects for a portrait. Only a flash camera or the devil's eye would so rudely discover their entwined limbs. I shall leave them to that dark world of bodies construed not by sight but caresses, their very eyes become all flesh, palpitating, appetitive deep-sea creatures.

A portrait of Julia alone, then, the fallen women, her head bowed in shame, her dress loose, hair disheveled? But I see Julia sitting beside her husband in the opera in a satin gown and pearls. Is this Julia the adulteress?

I pass to the family portrait of a year later. The lady in blue, holding an infant son in her lap, who is she? Not Julia, for I'd rather see her dead than so false. Yet there she is in an oval frame, Peter at her side, three little daughters around her and an infant son in her lap. An infant son. Oh, joy! What matter who fathered him when he brings joy into all their lives. Joy to his little sisters; joy to Aunts Eulalia and Eudora. But most of all joy to Peter. The happy father. He could be his father after all. Perhaps he is. Unless Julia was already with child from her lover when she went to bed with her husband. But we don't know. Julia accomplished this feat with blindfold haste so as to obscure and perplex and confound both past and future forever. Now we'll never know, Julia. Never, never, never. So let's enjoy our little family circle.

We have come out of this rather well, I would say, we have come out of this anyway; we haven't lost our head running off with a young nobody, we haven't lost face in the eyes of the world, and we have got a little son, isn't that what we always wanted? Shall we cry over Paul Holle? There will be another. And another. And another. Now we are busy writing invitations for the party. We have a big household in our hands. As for our honor, who cares? Who, I ask you, cares? Emily has her tenth birthday tomorrow, and Julia must show a nice face. We have blundered, but essentially what we've got here is a happy ending.

And that affair long ago with a student from the capital, well, not so long ago, even if the last months took longer in passing than the ten years of her marriage. Yes, that young architect Paul Holle. Whatever became of him? Why, we haven't heard. Returned to the capital, I assume. Nobody in our circle knew him. He was here only for a visit. Anyway, of what interest can it be to us how Mr. Holle is faring?

Does Julia miss him? Does she grieve for him while the priest sprinkles holy water on her son? His baptism was delayed till his sixth month, like all Brody male children he was delicate at birth. Does she take pride in her little son? Or, still under the spell of Holle, look for some sign of her child being his? Does Julia care? Is she at all there?

Yes, that is where she went; down with Paul Holle. Lost, her image. I have tried to fit her fall into the picture. But it doesn't work fitting her together from the pieces I have. I tried it and it doesn't bring her back. It looks like she has left for good. And now she will not grant me even a fleeting glimmer of her former glory unless I speak of Paul Holle. I won't do it. Not on Emily's tenth birthday. I have some honor left.

I keep saying it's not the first time after all that she went off suddenly leaving everything in disorder; not the first time she did a stupidity that had to be condoned, painted over, transmuted into something fine. And I did it for her, I cleaned up the house, I invented the perfect lie and lured her back. Why can't I do it again?

This is her house, this is her husband, these are her children: I study the family portrait taken a month or so after Petie's birth. The picture shows them in the living room; Julia looks surprisingly well for what she's been through. Still a young woman. What makes her so sure I will go on doing her chores? It's been months, it's been over a year or longer that she's left me and still I can't accept it, can't believe that this time Julia's gone for good. Blotched it up for good.

Alone now, back in the shed, the day's chores done, the children sleeping, the light still burning in Peter's study; alone with a bottle of gin, a pack of cards, or what's left of a pack, she's torn up the best and flung the rest around, I will give in. Sooner or later I always yield. I shall recall Julia with Paul Holle. Try once more to revive her with the name of her lover, to lure her back. And to take my mind off other questions; perhaps there is another hell besides ours.

We will pace or we will walk back and forth between the house and the shed as we used to do when she was carrying little Petie. I will follow her strolling in the garden or out on the street, as far as she wants to go, like the nine months when she was so restless waiting out her term, the child filling up her womb so slowly, pushing out her belly, he took so long to grow. But it was not for him she paced so restlessly, not for his little toes to unfold in order, not for the first kick of his heel she waited impatiently, or just to be delivered of her burden, but for her lover; yes, pined and waited for her lover to appear who may or may not have planted his seed.

I tried to console her then. And again after Petie was born I talked to her all night; I told her yes, name the child Peter; it will help. Shall we go over it as we used to, back in the old rocking chair? I remember she was crying; she was broken, she would never be the same, she moaned. She was too weak to walk, she could hardly stand, to sit was excruciating. It was the same after each delivery, I reminded her; she said the same thing after Emily's birth and Laura's and Jenny's; she would get over it like then and be her old self again. Then I recalled to her Paul Holle, his eyes, his hands, his words, his every move, to cheer her; she was so gloomy, I feared what she would do next. Her good friend, her old friend, her only friend, anyway, told her the story she wanted to hear. At her feet, back in the old role, her majesty's jester, or a wandering minstrel singing for his board. Oh, I felt wretched, abused, sold out, miscast, or worse, the old whore or pimp; I didn't know anymore which, Julia had so confounded me.

9

Have I made too much of it, Julia's one great passion, when it is just another banal story? A student from the capital with holes in his socks. By the claim in his eyes alone, he conquered her. Love of Julia, such as she was, or some fancy chick of his own? A young man's dream to rob another of his lady, taste the forbidden fruit, and to bring that lady low? A young man playing the part of the lover in the old melodrama; he loved her who came to him from another's house in lace-edged underwear and rings, hands that smoothed little girls' hair, Julia Brody, another's sheltered wife. And who was she? A woman past thirty waiting to be saved, ready at the glimmer of a hope to fall from the dignity of marriage and motherhood. How did we stumble into that trap? Julia had begun to drift, fade, blur. Did I push her into Holle's arms, create Holle for her, to pull her together, save her for me? But it seemed most proper and chaste at first. How did that slight, charming, innocent acquaintance grow into what it did?

10

It began in the public gardens. A day like every other. The children playing. Emily riding her scooter up and down the path, Laura digging in the sandbox, little Jenny waddling back and forth thrusting tufts of grass in her mother's lap and snatching them back again with little screeches of triumph. She has clambered on the bench, her red little face close, grimacing: chubby face, sly eyes gleaming behind folds of fat, wide, drooling mouth; a Klopps face? No, it's just me. I see fiends in children's faces. Julia sits gazing softly into nowhere, mouth curved in a delicate smile; she puts it on first thing after breakfast and wears it till bedtime. Easier than having to summon it for the twenty-five hundred occasions of the day. She sits gazing softly; now and then she lifts her eyes above the trees, perhaps trying to make out the hands of the clock on the church tower. How many more hours till noon? Till dinner? Till the evening drink? Her gaze falls, diffuses in the foliage. Too much effort to read the time. It's still morning. This day, also, will pass like every other, I consoled her.

So that morning was passing when I noted a change in Julia's behavior. She rose with a sudden lightness, waved gaily at Emily riding past her, then going to the sandbox squatted down beside Laura to appraise her mudcakes. Returning to the bench she lifted little Jenny in her lap more lovingly than I had ever seen her before. Someone was watching her. I was too embarrassed to locate the eyes for whose benefit Julia performed her little acts of motherliness which became increasingly outrageous. She encouraged the child to dishevel her hair, open her blouse. Fortunately the striptease did not proceed further, for Laura wet her pants and Julia like a good mother had to pack up cheerfully and start home. Her dignity, when she resumed it, barely concealed a new vibrant air.

Leaving the park, with a sneaking sidelong glance at the occupants of the neighboring benches, I carried out with me a glimpse of an expressionless young man in a dark suit and sunglasses. The flash impression recalled Julia's girlhood crush, the gardener's son: the old Latin cut, sensual, empty face. Shame on you, Julia, I said, at your age you should be interested in men with character.

For all of Julia's daydreaming through lunch, I believed it ended there. But I was wrong. The next day their paths crossed again, and for the remainder of the week the young man became ubiquitous. Wherever Julia's errands happened to take her, to any of the town's shops, the public gardens, the hairdresser, a dinner engagement, he was there, standing at a street corner, sitting at the table of a sidewalk cafe, looking at her through the window of a bookstore, coming toward her along a lane in the public gardens, or simply following her down the street. It was uncanny. Julia, I should mention, strangely aflutter since the incident in the park, sailed through town more freely than usual, her little jewels entrusted to Aunt Eulalia. Needless to say, she had the proper instinct to lower her eyes or look past him while maintaining her new exuberant air. My impression of Paul Holle from a dozen stolen glances was still the first: his face had nothing striking, a bit too blank, or just ordinary perhaps. A student, judging by his youth, his apparel, which though decent had something bare, and of course the fact he could idle the hours of the working day chasing Julia.

I had to be prepared for the possibility that he might approach her any moment. Was he worth our while? Should she involve herself even to the extent of a glass of wine? As a rule I forbade her to speak to strangers.

I remember the afternoon he entered the bookstore where we were browsing before Julia's appointment at the hairdresser. I watched him stride to the bookshelf past the counter where we stood and pull out a volume—a book on local monuments, I observed. He opened it, very intent on the page, or studying his opportunity, I couldn't tell, since the dark glasses concealed his eyes. Oh, how often since I have cursed fate he didn't approach her then! The answer was clear. No, she was busy; she was attending a soiree that evening, she had to be at the hairdresser and was already late, she had no time not even for a drink. If he had taken a step that moment, it would have ended then and there. I remember reminding Julia it was time; her gaze had drifted from the counter to Paul Holle's hands and lingered there. He shut the book abruptly and looked up. Julia hastily purchased a volume of poems by a young poet whose soiree she was attending that night and left the store.

I'm not certain if our paths crossed again on our way out of the mayor's house. For a second I thought I caught a glimpse of him emerging from a urinal just as we turned in the arcades; but I suspect it was an hallucination; by this time I was so rattled by his sudden appearances that I fancied every young man in a dark suit with sunglasses was he. The soiree had put me in a vile mood besides. Young Gadamer steaming with adoration before Julia; why did she have to suffer his deep looks, his perspiring tremulous hands helping on her coat; another wilted adolescent and a bad poet on top of it. What a relief, I thought, to be out in the evening breeze.

I confess I was up to my ears with my lady that night. Was it her high heels? Her fancy hat? Her lush perfume? Oh, it was everything, her stockings, her garters, her panties, her brassiere, her slip, her gown, her wrap, and the seven combs and forty-nine hairpins holding up her hair—the chef d'oeuvre of the town's best coiffeur. Did she have everything? Her handbag, her scarf, her hat, her wrap, both earrings—Julia was so mindless, she'd walk out of a restaurant clutching the napkin instead of her gloves. This time it was Gadamer's latest lyric poem and one glove. Its mate? Lost, of course. Left it, dropped it, who knows. I always calculated a pair of gloves in the overall expenses of an outing together with the hairdresser. Thank God, Peter was a well-to-do man.

I usually put Julia in a taxi as befits her status. But that night we decided to take the trolley home. Riding the trolley is one of my oldest pleasures. Years ago, in the Klopps house, I'd ride with Julia back and forth between the two end stations, just to hear the wheels rattle and the crossing wires hiss and flash blue-white lightning. We had to hurry to catch the last trolley; among the people waiting on the platform I perceived the young man with the sunglasses. Our young man, yes. He bade the conductor to wait for us, and we got on.

The young man sat down opposite us; he was holding Julia's glove. His look was hidden but his lips curled in a faint smile; a taunting smile, or just mischievous, he let the glove rest on his thigh. We were approaching our stop. What were we going to do? Get up and snatch it from him? Julia made no move. Whenever she was at a loss she assumed an air of transcendent serenity. The young man began playing with her glove: I was still trying to make out the nature of his smile. Sweet? Somber? Mocking? His smile was inscrutable. Or was it simply the way his mouth was shaped: long, full lips, slightly drooping at the corner? We passed our stop.

Smiling his inscrutable smile, Paul Holle played with Julia's glove. He played with it delicately, turning it in his hand, pulling the fingers apart, picking it up now by the back, now by the edge or tip of the thumb, to see how it would fall. After the last passenger got off at the firehouse, his improvisation became bolder; he slipped his hand halfway into the glove and made it move; an odd restless creature, it kept changing its shape, curled up in a cocoon, spread like a starfish, it grew horns, tried being a crab, turned into a bird testing its wings; it gave up and became a glove.

Julia laughed as in the days of Ulrich Schultz. Even I had to admit it was charming. So he was a bit of a clown.

He introduced himself when they got off at the end station: a student, as I supposed, finishing his degree in architecture at the capital. A project treating the layout of medieval cities had brought him to our town for a few weeks—he was vague as to the extent of his stay. He was twenty-three.

It was a long walk from the terminal to the Brody house. Paul Holle accompanied her home as was quite natural, indeed obligatory at that late hour.

He spoke on the length of the broad tree-lined street, of his travels and manifold interests, of the antiquity of the cobbles under their feet, the history of the mansions they passed, of the first settlers of the town, while she listened and over their heads spread the pale night sky, and the rambling leafy crowns of the elms nodded like sleepy old men.

Oh, they were beautiful walking side by side that first summer evening. I approved his conversation and her silence. Both so poised. But somewhere midway I remember I suddenly flinched: it was when Paul Holle launched into an account of the daily walks and habits of a certain Julia Brody. Witty, to be sure, but wasn't he impertinent, and her silence dangerous? Or was a bit of teasing to be expected from a young man courting a married woman? I didn't know then. And he flattered Julia, her beautiful children, the blouse she wore on Saturday afternoon. Julia smiled graciously; what was there to say? Suddenly she broke her silence to ask why he had been following her. They had arrived at the Brody house and stood before the gate, both silent and perhaps at a loss.

"You interest me," he said simply, and suggested that they drive out to the country after lunch the following day. There was an abbey he wanted to sketch. She might enjoy the drive, and they could have a drink in an inn afterward. And Julia said yes. Of course Julia said yes.

A drive in the country, indeed, why not? Keep it light. Keep it beautiful, I told her, and gave her careful instructions on fine points of behavior. I felt Julia's pull to be what she calls "simple"; I told her plainly, you may be simple, but the world is not; Mr. Holle may just want to play a game with you, so play a good hand. Anyway, I would be in the prompter's box.

I accompanied Julia like a watchdog on her first outing with Paul Holle. But his manner dissipated all suspicion. After a fortnight of sightseeing, I thought, at last a truly platonic friendship between a man and a woman! I never before believed it was possible.

It pleased me that he showed interest in Julia's taste and sounded her out on her preferences in artistic genres and styles. Indeed, his patience with her replies, which were at times strange, was touching;

at least he did not respond to them with a blank look, or rephrase her words as others so often did; he just smiled and asked further.

Several times a week Julia would accompany Paul Holle while he was gathering material for his project. It was good to be out of the house and such a welcome change for us to drive around the country, visit galleries, museums, and unknown corners of our ancient town—I tended to let pass much that displeased me about our driver. I made allowances for his moods and poses, his air of charming remoteness which irritated after a while. He is young, I kept saying to myself; and with Julia mostly silent, mostly wearing her expression of transcendent serenity, Julia, emanating her perfumes, flaunting her skirts and scarves, and somewhat moody herself, I thought Paul Holle managed quite well.

It is bitter to recall that while we were courting our ruin, I was lifted to a state of new hopefulness about Julia. Her future, which I had sealed in the marriage, began to open. She had lived too confined a life; I felt she should be more actively involved in the cultural life of the city. Of course, it was not enough to play the muse. Perhaps she could take up weaving and clay modeling again; I had fantasies of opening a gallery; why let all the Brody wealth rot in the bank? Paul Holle's allusions to Julia's latent gifts, I may add, increased his credit with me.

As these meetings continued I began to notice a change of mood in Julia. Why so pale and silent driving in the fresh country air? I found her growing listless and more absent than was necessary or prudent in our situation. Was she tired? I wondered. Not entirely recovered from Jenny's birth, perhaps these trips were too great a strain. Or was it Paul Holle's company? His conversation, in particular? For she seemed barely to listen to him. While he would be explaining to her the original ground plan of a church, I would catch her staring at his hand, gaping at it as if it were some strange and gorgeous beast. Worse than bored, her behavior at times betrayed irritation. I recall an incident in a small country inn. They were just finishing lunch; Holle was describing an old castle that made a particular impression on him during his student travels, when Julia suddenly broke in.

"So," she said, "have you made plans for next time? Will it be prints? Roman ruins? Another visit to the catacombs?"

She said it so bluntly, not with delicate sarcasm but like a sulky child, I was shocked.

I recall a vertiginous moment of silence, till Paul Holle said, "If you're bored, just say so. There need not be a next time." And his somber face vanishing behind the large folio of the menu: "Are you sure you wouldn't care for dessert?"

"Some more wine," she said crossly.

Did Julia feel scorned? Nonsense, I thought. She received enough compliments. Holle was all attentiveness and interest. There were moreover Holle's elliptic remarks to assure her of his regard for her. She had reached the age, I felt, to enjoy a platonic relation.

As to the consummation of this courtship, I did not see it as a problem. Holle was returning to the capital sometime in the fall. Julia was a married woman and there were limits. But the conversation during these outings was beginning to take a disturbing trend, or perhaps undertone, I should say, as Paul Holle had the habit of smuggling personal remarks—often provocative, sometimes positively shocking—in his running commentary on the archaeology of our region. This parenthetical device, even if jarring, neutralized the immediate effect of his remarks. But, when alone at night, they would return to me and raise the darkest suspicions about Mr. Holle's motives and character, dissipated by his modest and pleasant presence on the following day.

What distressed me more than erratic statements about his feelings were his pronouncements about her marriage. He inquired quite extensively into her life with Peter Brody and their three children. And no matter how glowingly she described her married state, spoke of her respect and affection for her husband, her absolute fidelity to him, her devotion to her children, Paul Holle's comment was simply, "I don't believe you're really married." And back to architectural gossip before I had time to gasp. A young suitor's insolence, I thought, and unworthy of a reply.

Why was he so preoccupied with her husband? Her marriage? Her future? What business was it of his? Who did he fancy himself? Her confidant? Her conscience? Her judge? And as for Julia, did she speak too earnestly? Was she evasive? Not evasive enough? Why did she bother to answer him at all!

Happily, the Brody house awaited us on our return from these airy excursions; there it stood firm and sound, three stories of solidly built stone girded with ivy, a fine lawn, and three little girls running to leap around Julia's neck.

We had reached the point where nothing spoke for continuing these meetings with Paul Holle. Fortunately, a natural way of ending the relation was in view. Peter was leaving for the capital for a fortnight or longer, and suggested that Julia accompany him—a little vacation from her household duties would surely do her good. It would do Julia good to be with her husband, I thought, and we would survive seeing Mr. Holle another week. But after my next outing with this gloomy and quarrelsome couple I changed my mind. If his company made her so ill-tempered, she need not see him again. I certainly could do without Mr. Holle.

I told her to call off the next day's tour of the old city walls. Simply call it off. But Julia went. Out of sheer apathy, I thought. The old problem, I thought: no will of her own. So acquiescent and long-suffering, my Julia. It was a mistake not to have put her in a nunnery. In God's will she would have found her peace. If only I could have believed in God! So I sighed over Julia two days before our planned departure to the capital. It's true Holle did not have a telephone; it was uncertain whether a note would reach him in time; and to leave a young man waiting in the park, no, Julia was a tenderhearted woman, she could not do that. She had to meet him.

She could not upset Mr. Holle while he was on the job, drawing his diagrams, forming his acute judgments, so considerate, my Julia—well, I couldn't blame her living with a man like Peter for over ten years. But afterward when they sat down to have a drink, why didn't she tell him then that she couldn't meet him again, she had no time, she had to pack, she was leaving with her husband for a month, maybe longer, make it clear to him it was the end? Why did she sit silent while they drank their wine, why did she let time pass, let him talk on, wait till the glasses were empty, till Paul Holle told her the plans for the next day? Or why didn't she tell him then that she couldn't, it was impossible; why, why did she say yes, yes, she would meet him after lunch at the public gardens.

Returning home that afternoon, I dimly grasped some great trouble. Julia was going to be sick, I felt the attack coming on. But what was it? Something she ate? An inflammation of one of her tubes? Heaven help us! The intricate twists and turns of Julia's reproductive organs were my despair. Was she pregnant again? God forbid!

Toward evening I began to discern the nature of her affliction.

By midnight I recognized beyond a doubt the symptoms of the malady I had read so much about during Julia's girlhood. Not that this subject interested me specially; it did not. But it was unavoidable by its sheer ubiquity in the realm of letters. Call it passion, or infatuation, or call it love, the symptoms are known to everyone. I never seriously believed in its existence, when Julia was a girl. Perhaps I thought passion belonged to a bygone age, like the bubonic plague. In any case, I considered Julia immune to it. Passion, as described by the poets, seemed such an artificial thing I suspected they invented it. And Julia was basically simple. The problem with Julia was to bind her to one man, the same man tomorrow as today. As a girl she simply like to be naked with a man, any man. She always found something to enjoy in him, she could go wild about a part of a man's body, she could be quite silly, but I have never seen her want a man, want to possess him entirely. But now she was sick with love for Paul Holle.

Julia was stricken; I had no choice. I tried to be a good nurse: to bed, I told her. The fever must take its course, to bed with him. You will wallow in it and be cured of it.

Did I maneuver to get those two into bed? No, there was a limit to my services. I would not do it for her, I told her plainly: I got you married but this you will have to manage yourself. I was concerned, nevertheless, that it happen gracefully. It would not do for Julia to throw herself at him. And seeing her muddled state, I gave her some advice. If your man, that block of wood, won't budge, I muttered, you'll have to put down the first card. No, not show him all your cards or you lose the game before you've begun. Just one card, Julia. Which one? Why do you ask me? I screamed. How should I know? But I knew I had to see her through. I suggested a strong opening.

No, come to think of it, I wasn't so nice. A crabby old nurse, wearing a tight smirk, I went with her the next day. Perhaps I still hoped I could spoil it for her. For her own good, after all. Anyway, Julia did it her own way.

The weather was in my favor. A foul day, low overcast sky. Julia seemed calm, or just spent from the night before. Halfway to the baptistery of St. John the Divine it started to rain. The windshield wipers clacked back and forth. There they sat side by side in the small humid car, silent and morose till Julia—on what impulse I shall never know—told him that she was leaving with her husband for the capital. Perhaps he had some suggestions as to interesting sights?

I was astounded. She had come to her senses and wasn't going to go through with it after all.

Paul Holle began to lay at her disposal his wealth of information on the archaeological treasures of the capital; he had plenty of suggestions, but why did she need his advice, didn't she trust her husband would show her around properly? His voice crackled, then hissed with suppressed rage.

"Why are you so nasty?" Julia interrupted.

In reply he stamped on the accelerator and the car shot forward with a sudden jolt. This was too much, I thought; Julia mad and our driver going out of his mind. Please! I wanted to squeak, please ask him to slow down. But Julia just sat back, smiling.

"I can't see a thing," I remembered her saying cheerfully. "Can you?"

We were racing in the squall. I stopped watching the speedometer. So this is how it would end, I thought, Julia Brody, her head smashed against a tree, thrown in a roadside ditch driving with a young man. I was composing the newspaper headlines when I heard Paul Holle's gruff voice.

"Am I driving too fast?"

"No, it's nice," Julia said.

So they raced on.

"Why are you staring at me?" he asked after a while.

"I'm just looking," she said, and her gaze remained fastened on his jaw.

"Are you in love with me?" he asked.

I gasped at his conceit but Julia was differently affected. She laid her palm on his wrist and wrapped her fingers lightly around it.

Holle brought the car to a halt. He turned to her slowly, took her face in his hands and looked into it intently till her lips moved toward his still, sealed mouth and they kissed.

They drove back in silence, more slowly now, his hand on her thigh. The clock on the church tower showed past four as they drove into town. Julia had two hours till dinner. I thought of the little girls at home as they got out of the car, the rain still boating down heavily. Would they have to go through all this?

And now must I go back to Paul Holle's room, up the five flights behind Julia and her lover? Mounting the stairs his breath on her temple they seemed to float upward past the Roman numerals chalked on each landing like the hours of some fantastic dream clock. Entering a bare musky room with the stove and sink in the corner, the bed to the left of the door, I wondered, were we back with Ulrich Schultz? The shades were drawn that afternoon. I didn't look around. Still in their dripping coats they embraced, their hands plunged mutely to the bare flesh.

She was about to step over a small pile of clothes on her way to bed and I beseeched her, Julia, do you know what you are doing?

I was literally in a state of shock till we walked into the dining room where Peter Brody was already at soup. All during dinner I struggled to regain my bearings.

It was not like with Peter, hovering over man and wife, thinking all is well, according to God's will, man and wife are making love. It would have been even nicer without my hovering over them; but that's nobody's fault, certainly not mine. I much prefer to be absent. That's what was a bit embarrassing with Peter, being there wide awake, having to find things to do.

It was not like it happened with those soldiers sometimes, knocked out cold, absent, the way I like it. It's Julia's business, I feel. But it was not like that. I was present but it was not I, or I was dreaming, tossed back and forth, strange images rising, all false, breaking like waves—oh, it's hopeless to try to describe the horrors I saw, ridiculous monsters, giant animal plants, a huge flat leaf folding over, devouring itself—no, I don't want to remember. Suddenly I recalled that just as she was leaving Paul had given her the key to his room.

"Come to me when you are free," he had said. More of his insolence! Or what did he mean? My mind was clear by the time coffee was served. This was not what I had in mind for Julia when I had her go to bed with him. Fortunately she was leaving with Peter the next day and would never see him again.

But Julia did not go with Peter. She told him she'd rather stay home; simply like that with her suitcase packed already. She didn't have to make up a tale or pretend she was sick; she had a way so sublimely vague, if I hadn't been with her at Paul Holle's I would have thought, like Peter, she was so firmly planted in her home she simply couldn't move.

Peter didn't mind. Peter understood. He agreed the trip might be too much of a strain. There would be those professional dinners; and he had conferences most of the day.

I was not so cheerfully reconciled to Julia's change of plans. Did she know what she was doing? Of course not. But it was clear to me what she wanted. Rush into her lover's arms or hell's fires—ruin herself, destroy her marriage—that's what she was driving to, whether she knew it or not. I knew I could not stop her from going to Holle, but I was determined to set a limit to her folly.

I had been ready to give Julia one afternoon to her lover, I would concede a night, seven nights, or till her husband returned, let them have their fill and wear out their bodies' lust.

The night after Peter's departure I slunk after Julia from the nursery along the hall down the stairs. She was going to her lover, where else? I saw her reach for her coat, the coat with his key in her pocket. Put on her best dress at least, I thought, be majestic, imperious, if she must demean herself. I told her but she took no notice. Go to him in your nightgown then, I taunted her. Go crawling on all fours dragging your hair on the ground and kiss his feet. She smiled vaguely; I think she would have liked that. But I made her re-dress; wear her gold embroidered opera wrap, at least. Overdressed? Not at all, I assured her. Suddenly her earrings seemed too heavy and ornate, her simple summer dress too expensive, she fancied she could run around barelegged in a cotton shift and her hair a mess just because she was having a fling with a young man. It hurt me to see her self-deceived.

Dressed like a queen we set out to Mr. Holle. The clock on the church tower showed half past nine. Would we find him in? I wondered. Alone? How could Julia take such risks! Crossing the bridge a ghastly thought flashed through my mind, what assurance had I that he didn't hand out keys to a half dozen other women in town, this mysterious Mr. Holle. Suppose they all took it in their heads at the same time to visit him this night—or perhaps he arranged for them to come on the same evening, the diabolical Mr. Holle. I pictured the scene of some half dozen of the town's aging beauties, hair tinted various colors, expensively dressed, all waiting solemnly in a dark top-floor room for the seducer. The scene became so real I fancied I had invented Paul Holle. He was a fiction, there never was such a man. Julia Brody was taking a bit of air strolling across the bridge. In a little while she'd turn back and we'd have our gin and game of cards as usual.

Laboring up the five flights of stairs the mirage of the six aging Julias faded progressively. It was dark under his door. Knock, just to be on the safe side, I advised Julia. He was not at home.

I was angry and ashamed for Julia. Could I persuade her to leave? You are nothing I told her. I made you Julia Brody. You have made yourself a nobody. It was my impotence that made me so spiteful. She sat waiting calmly.

Holle came in late. He was surprised to find Julia in his room

"Have you decided then?" he asked.

Silent, smiling, she curled into his arms.

She was hungry, she said; and while Holle looked in the cupboard, threw off her fineries, cape, bracelets, dress and all and wrapped his bedspread around herself. I don't remember what was said over that first midnight feast of sausage, wine, and not so fresh bread, only Julia's obsession with certain objects in his room. The oddly shaped stones on the sill, a piece of driftwood in the corner—were they his? And affixed to the wall over his desk, the photograph of a woman swimming in the nude, who was she? Just a picture he cut out of a magazine, Holle said; and questioned further if he had many mistresses before her, replied with a small shrug, which could only mean, whether few or many, they had meant little.

It was almost dawn when they rose from the table. Julia slipped off the bedspread, she even folded it up neatly and put it at the foot of the bed. She looked inquiringly at Holle who still stood by the window, his face dark in the light breaking behind him.

"Take off your ring," he said. "I want you completely naked."

Happily, Julia Brody's ring wouldn't come off; not with soaking the finger in soapy water and much twisting and turning, they couldn't get it over the joint. Little things like that are decisive for me. No, it's not all that simple, Mr. Holle; you're not quite what you fancy yourself. I felt the gods were on my side.

Paul Holle dismissed his moment of defeat with his customary poise.

"We'll get it off, don't worry," he said as they lay down. "Perhaps it will come off by itself," he mused on, "or we'll just have to chop off your finger," he whispered in her ear.

Little did I dream during those happy quiet hours while I did Julia's sewing what agonies were still in store for me. Each time his hand clasped hers I squirmed under the wedding ring. While Julia murmured foolish things to her lover, I thought of Peter far from home negotiating with naval contractors in the capital. I flinched before the trusting gaze of the little girls each time she stroked their silky cheeks with the same hands that had so recently caressed her lover's thighs. Out most of the day, all night, sometimes she wouldn't even come home to kiss her children good night.

Why did she have it so easy? We didn't even have to make up lies. The children and the aunts didn't need them; why, indeed, take the trouble to keep track of Julia's coming and going? Now she was here. Then she was gone. And lo and behold she was here again. Explanations would only have bewildered them. As for the servants, they wouldn't have believed them. Naturally, they had to be bribed. I am not boasting when I say I held that household together; I was the only one who cared. For the wrong things or in the wrong way, I'll be the first to admit; still, I did my best; I went on caring after nobody else did. But perhaps they were right, all the Kloppses and Fuchses, the idiot aunts, Peter and Julia on their way to the shelf with all those jars of pickled fish. Right not to care, they did better in their way than I doing my best.

Cooped up with two lovers for a fortnight, it's a wonder I survived. I still don't understand why they never went out to drive around the country like they used to, or stroll through the town. Even if they lingered in bed till late morning, they still had all afternoon and the long evenings. They could have done so many wonderful things: dance, walk by the sea, ride in the forest, make love in the ruins under the moon.

It just didn't happen.

If Julia suggested they go to the beach, Paul Holle raised his head, fixed on her a portentous look, and said: "Have you made your decision?"

If he stopped pacing up and down to propose they go see a play,

Julia sighed and said: "What really interests you about me?" and continued staring disconsolately in her lap.

Let her suggest they walk in the woods, and he would reply: "You can't go back to your husband. Not after this."

But suppose it was he who asked her if she felt like eating out, Julia said: "What do you really want me to be?"

Or should she attempt to turn his mood by urging they go to the bridge to see the fireworks, Holle turned on her suddenly and said: "Why do you come here, Julia, what do you want with me?"

Or should he want to be nice and offer to take her on a drive, she would give him her wide-eyed gaze and say: "Why do you say I'm unreal? Why?"

Julia might insist that they profit from the sun, but Holle would reply, his lips barely moving: "Julia, you must decide." And Julia walking away sadly: "Perhaps I don't interest you, really."

Did all lovers act this way, I wondered, or was this pair peculiar? Was there something wrong with Julia, as Paul Holle alleged—apart from the fact that she was in bed with him? Did she have a different face every day? Was she cruel? Evasive? Strange? Unreal? Wasn't she not all that a woman in love should be? A tender and loving mistress; passion by its nature is excessive. For however she might rave what she would like to do to him, she was never savage; maybe once or twice she bit him, but she didn't mean it I'm sure. After a while I understood, she could be fancy or simple, she could dress any way she pleased, and she would be right; if only she were not another man's wife. Yes, Holle made it quite plain: she was married to Peter Brody, that was what was wrong with her.

Was there something wrong with Paul Holle perhaps? One never knew where one stood with him. Let Julia ask what he was thinking and he'd say: "Nothing." Let her insist on knowing what was inside his head, bringing all her charms to bear on it, and he'd come up with wild retorts like: "Another head just like it." Was he insane, or just madly jealous of her rightful husband?

What did they really want, or their folly demand? To go on like this forever? Julia, I feared, was willing. She wanted Paul Holle, all of him always, to hold him, to feed him, wash him, turn him inside out, cut him up, eat him alive, bear his children, sail the high seas, live ten lives with him, be everything for him, anything he wanted her to be. As for Holle, though he was firm that she get up, stand on her own two feet, and make up her mind, the way he flung her on the bed and thrashed about inside her hardly helped to make her more sober, unless it was on the strength of his paddle he expected her to decide.

I prayed for the fever to pass; but Julia was sweeping me along. Was I guardian of Peter's honor? The caretaker of the Brody estate? My place was beside Julia. What if it was true love after all?

I was bold. I went up close to those lovers. I looked and I was terrified for it was not Julia Brody having an affair with a young man, but another, or not yet another, or not yet another, for she was all fluid, molten, ready to take on some other shape. Suddenly I had to ask myself could she ever go back to Peter?

Leave Peter? Impossible. It was not simply a question of leaving one man for another. Julia's commitment was not to a person but an institution, an order, a church whose visible embodiment was husband, wife, children, the house with its several stories and rooms, the linens and the silver.

But let us suppose Julia ran off with Paul Holle. Indeed, what was there left for her to do? Had she not already violated the sanctity of home by opening her thighs to Holle? The texture was rent. Let her take the consequences. Would Paul Holle be a husband to her? How? Can a woman have two husbands? According to the law she cannot have two at a time, yet she may with impunity have any number in succession. But secular law simply reflects the laxity of the temporal order. Take on the name of twenty husbands in time, yet which of the twenty would she bear in eternity? With whom would she stand at the final tribunal, with her husband? Her lover? Both? Or would she stand alone? Monday in one man's bed, Tuesday in another's, as many loves as there are nights. But with whom shall she lie in the grave when time runs out and the hours, rushed to their summation, are gathered and sealed forever in one eternal hour? Buried with the lot of them in a common grave? Peter on the right side, Paul on the left, with Bruno (the blood of her maidenhood on his head!) and some half dozen unknown soldiers stacked up at the foot of the grave? Oh, monstrous! But I am guilty with Julia. I paced long hours trying to find a way out.

Was there a decision to be made, when she lay naked between another man's sheets? But their days were numbered. Peter was returning in two days. Had Julia made her decision? She sat by the window with opiate eyes. Like some sea plant incapable of volition, yet responsive to every ripple; a fish brushing against its fine hairs would cause its cup to dilate and shut. He came up behind her and laid his hand on her throat. Her mouth went after it, lay open on his hand. Was that a decision? Had she crossed the threshold so that it no longer mattered whether Peter came home tomorrow, today, or yesterday? There was still Sunday, Monday and Tuesday; then there was only Tuesday; still three hours, two, still one hour left. Time, treacherous time. Time to turn around and turn around again. A game of chance it was. When the clock struck one, the trapdoor shut.

Their last evening together was their happiest. But I'm thinking of the evening before the last. Wednesday. Peter's letter arrived that day. Julia didn't open it. Returning to Paul Holle's room she put it absently on the shelf with the bag of groceries she had brought along.

They took long over the meal, even though it was only a bowl of salad. Silent and naked they sat through the dusk. It was late when they rose from the table, too late to go to the theater or even the concert in the park. He showed her some pictures of his family. How intently she studied his mother's face. Did she love him already as a child?

Then they played cards, sitting on the floor with a bottle of wine, and they could have been an old couple in Outer Mongolia or new-lyweds in predynastic Egypt. I saw the lovers playing oblivious in their dream. I heard Julia laugh. I wondered has she awakened in her lost childhood? Suddenly I remembered the house under the elms, Peter Brody, and the children. You're dead, Julia, I said. Looking down on the worn carpet tacked on the sloping floor, I saw her face at the bottom of the river.

Did I stand between Julia and her new life, and only now, posthumously, make a token offering of Julia to her lover? Watching it all from the loges, I covered my eyes in horror and indignation. But how could I be sure? Even Paul Holle wasn't sure. He didn't understand why she cried after reading Peter's letter. She didn't open it till Thursday noon, sitting at the table after breakfast, when Holle asked her if she wasn't going to open and read her husband's letter.

Peter's letter was short and simple, confirming his arrival Friday around noon. He missed her very much. He found the capital tiring; she was wise to stay home.

Holle asked her what her husband had written. But Julia couldn't speak. She gave him the letter to read, lay down, and cried. For shame? For what she had done to her husband and children? For grief? Did she cry at the thought of leaving her lover? For shame and grief both? I don't know. Paul Holle kept asking her why she was crying, but Julia couldn't speak.

They quarreled in the night. Holle threw her out of bed, she could go right now, he didn't want her as a whore he said, and started putting her things together. She refused to go. He flung her on the bed. Then they embraced again.

They slept badly. At daybreak she got up from that tousled bed, made coffee, and started to dress. Of course she had to be there when Peter arrived, why didn't Holle understand? He tried to prevent her from going back to the house even to tell Peter and see the children. "If you leave now, you'll never come back," he said.

Sitting at breakfast, they tried a few more times, he to persuade her, she to make him understand, till she lapsed into silence. Then, as if somewhere else, not in that room but in some remote hall of destiny it had been decreed she must leave, Paul Holle's face darkened, his words became increasingly taunting, cruel, contemptuous. "So your little holiday is over," he said.

It's over now. Just another banal story. Why must I keep going back to that room with the faded wallpaper, to the table by the window overlooking a court where they sat at their last breakfast; keep hearing his words over and over again speaking in the same uninflected tone, while Julia sat silent, only asking now and again what time it was.

She stayed another ten minutes and another, rapt in the play of sunlight on the breakfast dishes.

"You will forgive me," he said. "Or worse, keep me as a precious souvenir. I should kill you now," he said wearily, and rose to get her coat.

I wish he had killed her then. Because Peter wasn't the sort of man to lift an axe and split her head in twain, even if he knew. Perhaps I do Peter injustice. Shall we find out? Shall we tell him now when he comes back from walking little Petie to see how he takes it? No, he would have had to discover them in bed to gain the necessary momentum for such an act. Should I have seen to it, perhaps, that he does? Oh, Julia, you little slut, leave me in peace. You didn't think this love worth dying for, so why should he? Besides, he had his career to think of.

He went down with her and accompanied her as far as the bridge. Julia walked faster and faster. He stopped her when they reached the bridge. "You have the key to my room," he said. She groped her pocket, put the key in his hand without looking into his face, and turned. "I have planted my seed in you," he said, as she started to cross.

The children were up when she arrived home. No one asked where she had been or wanted to hear her explanations. Jenny had a tummy ache; Emily was being punished because she spilled ink over Peter's desk; Aunt Eulalia complained that the milk wasn't delivered in time. She would stay, of course. How could she ever imagine leaving them? And the names of endearment she had spoken to her lover, how long would they echo in his room on the other side of town?

She dressed the children in their prettiest frocks; they waited all morning. At noon a telegram came that he wouldn't be home till late that night, not to wait up for him. What difference could that telegram make? Yet, a few hours later, after she had fed the children and laid them to sleep for their afternoon nap, Julia left the house and started out in the direction of Paul Holle's room. Walked out of the house in an old coat and scarf he bought her. Crossed from one end of town to the other, up the stairs, to his door. There was no answer. The concierge said he had left half an hour ago. She sat down at the corner cafe and ordered a lemonade. She walked around the block, asked again, but he had not come back. She had a brandy. How long would she wait? She remembered the moment she gave him back his key. A large black key; she loved to feel it at the bottom of her pocket. She pressed her hands to her eyes. She rose at dusk. Walked around aimlessly in the district. Then headed toward the bridge.

She stood on the bridge looking out over the city; the streetlamps were soft against the paling sky. I don't know how long she remained on the bridge. It was a moonless night. Only the cathedral clock stared in the dark; its hands pointed sharply, but I couldn't read the time. The traffic had almost ceased. A tramp accosted her but she did not turn. It was growing cold. After a while she started slowly back home.

There was no light in the house. The children were asleep. She was still standing in her coat in the dark nursery when she heard Peter's car coming up the gravel path. She went to her room, undressed and crept under the covers. Peter felt his way toward the bed. She snatched his hand and drew him down to her. Peter was surprised. "I haven't known you like this for a long time, Julia," he said. "I should leave for the capital more often."

What was I to do? Expose her shame? Publish her infamy to the world? Let her be branded and put in stocks. Or go quietly. Yes, I should have left her then. Given notice and handed in my resignation. Let her find herself another conscience.

I did not do it, of course. I couldn't simply leave her in the lurch. Perhaps I was hoping she would die in childbirth. Always that last hope. And then there was little Petie to take care of, the announcements to be sent out, the letters of congratulations to be answered, the long convalescence. I had to bolster her spirits. Night after night I walked with her and explained how everything happened for the best.

You have had what you have had, my lady; you have waited for it long enough, I told her, ten years faithful to your husband. Let no man dare call you a slut.

As for Paul Holle, maybe he was the right man for you, Julia. But of course he was right! It's always the right man at the wrong time; it's hard on the flesh, I know. But it cannot be otherwise. It must be so. He couldn't be older. You couldn't be younger. You couldn't have met ten years ago. And if you had, you would have looked past him.

You have grieved enough, it's time you understand: there is no Paul Holle at thirty-five. Paul Holle comes from eighteen to twenty-four; at twenty-five he is already someone else. Ruined by the wrong woman? Perhaps. Let's leave it at the number twenty-four. And as for some magic to make you a young girl, it wouldn't do the trick. Paul Holle at twenty-three is interested in Julia Brody, mother of three children; it's the perfume of her past, rich and subtly blended that lures him, not a raw and rosy Julia Klopps.

But let us suppose you could have met ten years ago, yes, let us go back ten years, my lady, for you still don't believe me. I hear you sigh and draw in your breath. We shall put Paul Holle on a bench in the public gardens ten years ago: there he sits, a young man with an expressionless face, dark suit, smoking a cigarette.

Julia Klopps—not exactly raw and rosy-cheeked, somewhat strange, troubled, tired, but at twenty a sleepless night gives a girl a glow. Up all night wandering from room to room in that big old house, at sunrise you went walking along the beach. I, your guardian, quite worried at the time, was puzzling over what was best for you and what you truly wanted. You couldn't tell me. So I went with you to the sea; perhaps you needed a swim, it would put you in tone; perhaps you would drown yourself.

I was resigned to anything you truly wanted. You walked till the sea wet the edge of your skirt and turned back. We waited for the world to wake up. After nine you would go and speak to the Mother Superior at the convent. You were going to be a nun. That would settle it. You didn't really care, I had the impression; you'd make the best with Uli or Richter or Peter Brody or any man, you'd find something to please you. But would you stay with him? I had every reason to fear that you'd wander off with the next man. We couldn't have that. I couldn't at least. You'd be safe in a nunnery, doing God's will, rites to keep you busy all day and the gates locked at night.

It looked like the perfect solution as we walked along the road that morning on our way to the Mother Superior; you, my simple one, my wonderful, foolish Julia, fingering your beads, when for all you know you may be counting the hairs on the devil's tail, while I puzzled over the number of angels that can dance on the head of a pin. I saw you a young nun praying with entranced eyes, as we approached the cloister. It was not all my fantasy, dear lady—those statues of the Virgin Mary holding her infant son or his bruised corpse made you stop and gape and more. I do not wish to embarrass you now, but it worried me at the time. What a strange thing is woman, I said to myself—we were looking for the right man for you, remember? Or at least my Julia is strange; she looks past a man, she can't see him unless he is in a cradle or on the cross. Well, in the cloister you could have had both.

But you walked away from the gates after lingering a little while. You stuck a few blades of grass in the grille and walked away with a gay spring in your walk. And I had to reproach myself; what a fiendish idea to lock you up in a cell!

I didn't know what you wanted. I didn't know where you were taking me when you took the turn leading into town. I followed you as you roamed aimlessly through the streets stopping to stare at window displays; I remember you stood before the travel bureau for the longest time, looking at the map of the world and photographs of distant lands; perhaps you'd still be standing there if I hadn't pulled you away.

You had a date at noon with Peter Brody whom you had known two weeks and found quite nice, and it was already well past eleven.

I wasn't sure whether you'd make it; we still had to buy a comb and a pair of white gloves. You were a few minutes late entering the public gardens; Peter Brody stood waiting by the fountain as you came through the gate. I had to remind you, walk, don't run, you're a young lady now, the world will forgive you being ten minutes late if you're wearing white gloves.

The young man looked worried as you approached; he frowned, then he smiled and frowned again; you turned away from him, leaning over the rim of the fountain caught the sprinkle in your palm; that may have put him at ease. Then, while you stood absorbed in the play of water, he sat down on the rim and began telling you how wonderful you are, his voice so troubled; I kept asking myself, is this how a man speaks when he is about to propose to a woman, or when he wishes her to understand that she is simply too much for him?

Peter Brody wasn't clear. I wasn't sure. Perhaps Peter Brody wasn't sure either, yet he kept repeating how wonderful you were, that no other woman ever made him feel the way you did—the old line, I know. You turned a little toward him, your gaze somewhere else, in the leaves, the shifting colors of children moving about, a pigeon feather floating in the pool. I though he should appeal to you, apart from all that spoke for him in worldly terms: he was shy, he was frail, he adored and needed you. He was saying he loved you, he would do his best to make you happy, he didn't really know how you felt about him.

He paused, his head leaned toward your thigh, your hand moving to touch his hair, your fingers tracing the coarse, curly strands to the root. His voice drier, more firm, he spoke then of what he had to offer you. Your hand lay quietly on his head, which reared up with a little toss when he spoke of contracts. He had a confession to make to you, he said with a small laugh, and stroked your skirt. There was something he loved more than he could ever love a woman: ships. A ship, he said, and drew in his breath, for a moment speechless with rapture. He continued talking somewhat brokenly, laughing, a little foolish, the same thing over again, how he loved you, loved ships, had to tell you, didn't know how you felt.

Your hands clasped his head, perhaps more firmly than before, the fingers wove through his hair. He pressed his face against your thigh and you encircled his head with your arms; perhaps your gaze was still on the water.

He raised himself, his hands around your waist, and asked you if you would be his wife. You never said yes, you didn't even look into his face, but from the way your arms encircled his head I interpreted you to mean yes. Peter Brody did too. Your hands clasping, as you walked out together, sealed the contract. Did I misinterpret? I did my best to read you. Peter understood you to mean yes. In the restaurant, just a few steps from the park, he spoke of wedding arrangements. The house was ready. You could marry in ten days. Perhaps I simply took his view of it. I said, amen, so be it.

As for Mr. Holle sitting on the bench, an expressionless young man in a dark suit—how shall I put it, my lady, not to offend you? First of all, he wasn't watching you; secondly, he does not strike you—I speak of first impressions only; you will grant he does not look like the kind who'd swing you by the heels like our jolly Ulrich Schultz, nor the wildly romantic type, I mean our friend Richter. No, he is quiet, bare, expressionless, and to a girl of twenty, not so mysterious. Don't mistake me, my lady, I'm not suggesting your lover was common, just an ordinary young man; oh, no, he was rare. Understand this once and for all, and you will stop grieving; the Paul Holle you loved is a plant that blossoms for a Julia Brody on a certain day of her life and for a certain time only.

So I tried to explain to go on. Make Julia go on; save her image. She must have slipped away; while I was talking, I didn't notice; I went on talking to myself.

And now it is too late. I have lost her. Lost Julia's beauty in the water. She walked out of the picture and left me with all the mess. Sometimes she returns for a moment. She sits on a bench in the public gardens as if Paul Holle were looking at her.

I see Julia set out across the city on Tuesday afternoon. She wears a soiled raincoat, advances with long strides, her head high, looking straight ahead. Who would suspect the treasure she carries with her? As if she had taken her heart, her fate, all her glory and shame, taken her soul from its safekeeping out into the street, clutching it in her hand, a living plant she had uprooted, or a new fledged bird she had scooped out of its nest. Years after, as I pick up the toys from the nursery floor, I still follow her down the boulevard panting, Who are you? Walking along the pavement block after block, driven by what obscure promise, following the phantasmal chalkline that leads to a certain door.

Part Five

SUDDENLY it's over before it has ended, like a dream interrupted by the alarm.

She rises feeling her way along the wall. She moves with as little sensation of moving as an idol mounted on a cart while the shrubs file past in dense procession. Her past has been transposed into another tense, its episodes spaced like stone figures in an Italian garden, staring past each other indifferently.

No it is not Julia.

Julia standing on the bridge when the streetlights turned on—was that my last glimpse of her? I don't know. The doors I open are picture doors.

Has Julia become a little girl once again? She skips into the room dangling her doll before me. Julia, I will explain, listen to me, child. But this is Jenny looking at me with such round eyes—have I said something to frighten her? Run along now child. How shall I tell her, tell Jenny, looking at me with Julia's eyes?

She lured me on with her pleasure in a berry, a wandering gaze, a smile. Hasn't it all been a mirage, the child tramping through the woods, the girl in silk stockings, the bride? I follow her through the thronged ballroom weaving in and out between the dancers to a room in a tavern and back into the night; I follow her into other rooms, other beds, other men murmuring her name in her ear in the dark. I look for Julia in the daylight. Somewhere in the tall humming grass a child crouches heedless of voices calling, Julia. I wander through the old Klopps house, up the winding stairs to the attic back to my first dreams of Julia.

I look for her sitting on a bench in the public gardens on a summer day. I don't know which summer.

I don't know where Julia ends or begins. I don't know where she is. Lost. Out of time. Not in God's timelessness but sunk to the depths of time. The debris of her days still sifting downward.

Or is Julia in the house, combing Jenny's hair in the room flooded with sunlight, only I may not enter? This is Julia's vengeance on me, to bury me alive in her past. I tried to put a hedge around her and I fenced myself in. She escaped me.

So she is gone. Well, good riddance, and forget about her. Go back to the house where there is a job to be done, the cupboards cleaned, the children fed. I like ironing their little ribbons, sewing doll's dresses. Sweet Jenny, it's a joy to brush her hair; the only true joy in life. Stand still, my darling, while I tie the ribbon around your head. I must stop talking to myself. Time to go back to the house. Say any agency sent me, a volunteer worker. I'll turn into an angel, yet. Bring in the milk. Put on the kettle. Dress the children.

But what about Peter? What sort of a wife will I make? I can imagine a worse bedfellow. Women are such bitches after all. No, I can't bring myself to it. I lost the old flair. Well, be his mother. Tell him you're beyond that sort of nonsense. He'll understand. He can always find himself a mistress. But I don't want that, Julia's husband taking a mistress. That's not how I wanted it for Julia. Go on, be his cunt. Why not? What have I to lose now that Julia is gone. Why yes? To be angelic. Yes, be his old cunt. Does that make sense? I'll go back to the house for Julia's sake. It's dark. I don't find the way. Julia, won't you come and lead me back? I must stop talking to myself. Time to go back to the house. I must stop talking. I must. Go back? I?

I. We. She. No, I give up. It's a poor metaphor. A wonder it carried us this far, lurching, circling about from some initial point to where we are at present. I haven't explored all Julia's territory, only a narrow path through the wilderness. I hacked it out. No, that's not so. They were there, the stuffed animals in the attic, Caroline, Bruno. I'll never forget Bruno lying naked, his tense body arched, like a rubber man. There was the house under the elms where Peter Brody brought her to be his wife. Paul Holle's room; I didn't invent it, or Julia brushing her daughter's hair. It's a lie about myself. There was no I. I didn't say I then, think I. There was only Julia. I sheathed in she. No I or she, only Julia. The day I said I, Julia was dead already, gone already. One day I woke up and remembered. Remembered all wrong.

THE PATIENT

I HAVE no past. I was born an ageless, sexless, invalid, months or years ago, possibly in this bed. Or, if in another bed, another room, it was in no significant detail different from where I am now. Whatever I know about myself begins here, with things I've been told by the psychiatrists, Fuchs, Glatz, Engel, and others.

I lie on my back, powerless to move. Not that I will but cannot move. I cannot will to move. Sometimes I wonder whether I am not paralyzed, or possibly encased in a plaster cast up to my chin.

No one here seems to think that before proceeding any further, we should first establish my physical equipment, my age, sex, and former status in the world, if any.

Glatz, it is true, brought up at one stage an impressive body of material about a certain Judd, or Judy, Kopitz, J.K., for short. J.K. was supposed to be me. The fact that I didn't see any connection only proved Glatz's case. My resistance to J.K. stood between me and the first step to recovery. I never spoke to Glatz about any Judd or Judy Kopitz. It's something he pulled out of the files. Assuming that the J.K. data weren't simply a case of clerical error, I could only suppose that it's something I confided at one time to Fuchs, who forwarded it to Glatz when I was transferred to him.

Since my recovery was made dependent on it, I made some effort to get involved in the problems of J.K. I wondered what the Kopitz child looked like. Listening to the data, the first image that sprung to my mind was of a slight girl with a pinched face and jaundiced complexion, but it could equally well have been pink, with large sweaty feet, and a faint moustache, one of those fat boys whose testicles haven't descended.

Actually, since the data presented dealt exclusively with J.K.'s fantasies, it was impossible for me to come to a judgment about his or her sex. Indeed, it was never clear to me whether he or she was one person, suffering from the delusion that he or she was two persons; or whether J.K. was not in fact two persons, suffering from the delusion that they were one.

Glatz's manner of referring to J.K., now as the "latent male component," now as the "latent feminine complex," added to my confusion.

After a while, the case study to which Glatz so slavishly referred began to sound vaguely familiar, perhaps from hearing it so often. Still, I couldn't honestly see myself as the Kopitz child, male or female. This, Glatz kept telling me, was highly symptomatic.

I had quite a different theory. Assuming that the J.K. data related to me, was it not possible that the years of treatment under Fuchs delivered me from J.K.'s strange obsessions, so that, as a result of the therapy, I cease to identify with the J.K. complex? Was Glatz trying to rectify the work of Fuchs? Did Fuchs go too far? There is the further possibility that the case was already quite ancient by the time it came to Fuchs.

Curiously, the sessions with Glatz seem to terminate with my discharge. Perhaps out of sheer exasperation I finally assumed identity with J.K. All that I actually remember of this is my utter incredulity the moment Glatz patted me on the head and wished me good luck. The previous day he had declared me cured.

"You do see, now, don't you?" he said, in his nasal drawl, some dozen times. "Your dream clearly indicates that you see."

I also recall him saying, "Just remember to breathe from the center, and you'll be all right."

Shortly before my discharge, or possibly during the interval between my discharge and my readmission, I had the following dream. We were in the lobby of a hospital. Glatz and Fuchs were shaking hands energetically, as if they had just concluded a most satisfactory business deal. I stood on an elevated platform, a larger than life-size mannikin, with a rather handsome, empty face. They screwed off my arms, legs, and head, making ready to fit me in a box in which I was going to be moved. Although I was not told anything, I surmised that I was being relocated to a place for incurables.

The male mannikin has not appeared in my dreams since. I suspect that they never got around to removing me from the box and reassembling my parts.

It's difficult for me to believe that I actually walked out on the street with my discharge slip as man, woman, or child. Yet if I did, of which no trace of memory remains, I did not manage as well as Glatz supposed I would; otherwise, I wouldn't be where I am, or in the state I am. No, obviously, I failed. Perhaps, deliberately, out of spite. Just to prove Glatz wrong. The impertinence of pronouncing me cured! The humiliation of being cured by someone like Glatz. This, at least, was the opinion of Miss Engel who succeeded him.

Of the duration of my stay in the world, assuming this was a considerable stretch, I have not retained a single incident, face, or impression. I suspect I never got as far as the other side of the street. Yet, for all I know, I have lived a whole life, loved, suffered, and lost. In short, earned my peace, in which case their efforts here to make me somehow fit for the world are frivolous.

Of all the therapists to whom I had been assigned at various stages of my malady, Miss Engel stands out most clearly. In the beginning it was only through her voice that I could form any impression of her. That was because I could not open my eyes.

"I'm blind," I used to complain.

But she told me I would see all right if only I would open my eyes. I couldn't, however, no matter how hard I strained. It was useless for anyone to pull back my lids by force, because my eyeballs were turned the other way.

Miss Engel's voice was neutral. "It's my job," she used to insist, "to be neutral." She spoke in a quiet monotone, enunciating each word with equal care.

Her voice struck me as very youthful at first. She had a strong lisp.

I kept wondering why I had been assigned to a lady doctor and such a young one. It was obvious that she could not be very experienced. Probably because I was a hopeless case, so that her mistakes would be of no consequence; one of those old maimed frogs they give to high school children to cut up. Unless it was hoped that the contagiousness of her youth would produce the desired therapeutic effect. A woman, since I am a man, or perhaps because I am a woman. It would make sense either way.

In any case, her ingenue quality made me feel rather like a cranky old man. I began to entertain lecherous thoughts, and wondered if her undies were pink, white, lavender, or lemon. Had I been certain that I was in fact an old man, I would not have hesitated to ask her either. But suppose I am a little girl or a woman her age, my remark would have been in the worst taste. How could I respect the propriety of the situation, or to use their term, relate to Miss Engel, unless my own status was defined?

It was of no use asking Miss Engel. She never answered my questions. This, she claimed, lay outside of her province. My questions were treated as symptoms, which she interpreted together with my behavioral disfunctions. Often a dream would confirm my state of ignorance as to who or what I was.

"You see," Miss Engel would observe triumphantly, "your dream tells us that you don't know who you are. We must wait till the self consolidates, till you find the answer in yourself."

She meant the self I can't get at by hook or crook, to which only she has access by picking at the threads of my dreams.

One day when they wheeled me in the therapy room, I was resolved I would not be put off any longer.

"I demand to know," I said sternly, "how old am I?"

"Don't you know," she said, "the unconscious is ageless and timeless?"

"But I am a person!" I tried to insist.

But Dr. Engel only sighed sadly. "You're not ready. When the time comes, you will know."

Once I regained my sight I could judge for myself that Miss Engel was, or used to be, a woman. She must have been in her eighties. Her lisp, I then perceived, was due to loosely fitting dentures. Everything about her was old and dry. She always wore mauve, the color of her wallpaper. Her pale eyes never changed their focus behind thick-lensed, rimless spectacles.

The windowsill to the right of her displayed a row of potted plants in which Dr. Engel took great delight. She would get up sometimes in the middle of the session to water them, or give them vitamins through a medicine dropper, and was fond of showing them to me. I will never forget the time a rare plant from Mexico which she had tended for years flowered at last. She stood holding it in her hand as I was wheeled in the therapy room.

"Look!" she said, holding before my face the exotic blossom, ver-million with orange splotches, an intricately valved vaginal plant.

I never knew quite what to say. I wondered what the plants had to do with me. I was afraid of flowers.

"Is it carnivorous?" I asked at last.

"Oh, no," she replied, quite offended. "I don't grow carnivorous plants."

While I did not believe that Dr. Engel truly cared for me—if she had, she couldn't sit there like a dummy hour after hour and watch me writhe—she did make me feel that I was an interesting case; perhaps not as interesting as I thought I was, but nevertheless worth her while. She did not, for example, yawn or doze off as frequently as Glatz; nor did I seem to have the depressing effect on her that I had on Fuchs. She further gained my confidence by depreciating my former analysts.

"No, Glatz didn't understand, did he?" she would concede, with a little smile of complicity.

As to Fuchs, she would just sigh, "Ah, Fuchs, he has grave difficul-ties himself, you know."

Finally, I welcomed these talking sessions because they helped to distract me from what was going on in my head. Miss Engel, I should say, had no patience with my insectomorphic fantasies; confessions on my part that I was a roach or a gelded toad left her entirely cold, and whenever I ventured to suggest that I was immobilized by a plaster cast, she simply burst into giggles.

My need to define our relationship formed the topic of most of these sessions. We must have spent months, maybe years, on this. Dr. Engel let me rave on.

"Mine is a peculiar profession," she would every so often concede.

I examined the whole range of human relations, without finding a satisfactory analogy. Lovers we were not, nor friends, for there was no element of reciprocity between us. Were we like parent and child? But I never understood that. The relation between a mechanic and a malfunctioning machine seemed to me at one point best to describe the situation. Miss Engel, however, objected to the image; she didn't think it was good for me to think of myself as a rusty old phonograph, or a busted-up bicycle.

After a while it seemed most natural to think of Dr. Engel as some kind of Mother Confessor. Her celibate state (or so I assumed), the fact of her abdicating all personal existence (in my presence, at least), and, finally, her incredible faith in my possessing what she called a self, all served to confirm this impression. I wondered at length, did she belong to a church? Who ordained her? Was she answerable to higher authorities? The fact that she personified an office, and yet had no institutional backing, made me uneasy.

Dr. Engel, I must say, did not encourage the ecclesiastic analogy. Her favorite image of herself was rather that of a midwife or a gardener, and, in time, she forced me to think in terms of these figures. After some years with Dr. Engel, I began to feel like a foetus in the third month. Dr. Engel, whose diagnosis was always more optimistic than mine, declared me an overdue baby. In the last stages of the treatment, she dropped the biological metaphor in favor of the botanical one. I became a root, a radish. Any day I would sprout a little green stem into the light.

At first I offered resistance to Dr. Engel's staunch conviction that I possessed a kernel of self. The idea was too preposterous, or, as Miss Engel put it, it threatened my psychic economy. She must have worn me out, however, because there arrived a moment when I was on the verge of taking her seriously. I remember tears came to my eyes, and I felt the corner of my mouth quiver.

"Do you really see it?" I quavered. "Are you sure?"

"As sure as I'm sitting here," she replied, pounding her two thighs with her two fists in confirmation.

"What is it?" I asked, quite breathless. "Man, woman, or child?"

Dr. Engel merely smiled at my crudity.

By the end of the seventh year, Dr. Engel succeeded in planting in me the notion of birth. Rebirth, she called it. But for me who had no recollection of any existence to speak of, it was to be my first birth. It plunged me in a state of agitation and distress I had never before experienced.

"It's not right," I kept protesting. "Being born shouldn't be so hard; I shouldn't be feeling the pain. I should be asleep when it's happening. I shouldn't be present at all. It cannot happen while I'm present."

Dr. Engel said it was not the birth but the dying that put me in such agony. If I would only give up struggling against it and yield, the birth would follow painlessly of itself.

I listened to her. How could I resist? What could be more beautiful than dying the true death? I was told not to try, but my throes became intolerable. How I envied her plants! I wished Miss Engel would put me in a pot, and cover me with earth, fine, black porous soil, and water me. Then I would flower; then she would delight and take pride in me. But she only pointed to her plants, holding them up before me to admire.

"Look at this handsome Sipia," I remember her exclaiming with joy. "A month ago it didn't have a single leaf. I found it in an ash can. Someone threw it out. And just look at it now!"

Miss Engel kept assuring me that I was making progress. But this I felt was only a therapeutic expedient to help me over my *idée fixe* that everything was at a standstill. She was unfailingly hopeful, but I knew she did not delight in me. I wasn't making progress like her flowers.

The longing to blossom took root in me. I, who had formerly thought so little of myself, nor cared whether I was well or ill, lucid or murky, was wretched with longing to flower for Miss Engel. I alternately clamored for food and refused it. I scratched at my sores, befouled myself, and abused the attendants. During my sessions I either assumed a sullen silence or broke out in delirious accusations.

I was in the midst of these agonies when Miss Engel passed away one summer afternoon. She died sitting upright in her chair in the middle of a session. Mine, or possibly someone before me. I cannot recall whether she greeted me when I was wheeled in. I was silent as usual for the first ten minutes or so, and then began to mumble incoherently. After a while, I began to feel that the session was inordinately long. I spoke about my sense of the length of the hour. I asked her the time. No answer. Growing panicky, I asked her if I would have to lie there forever. Terror was gaining on me. I had the sensation of falling down a dark, narrow shaft. I tried to accept her silence.

She is testing you, I told myself. She just wants to see if you can terminate the session by your own forces.

But I was unable to summon any forces. I began to wonder if perhaps I ought to yield to this fall into darkness. But I was as unable to yield as to resist.

"Answer me!" I screamed.

After a while, I was powerless even to scream.

It had become pitch black. I must have lain motionless for I know not how long. Suddenly someone put on the light.

"Get up!" a voice said. I blinked, but still could not move. Miss Engel sat straight as a bolt in her chair, her lips compressed, staring like an owl, her chair flanked by two orderlies.

"She's dead," they announced. They lifted the fauteuil, and Miss Engel's feet rose in the mauve pumps. As they skirted around the small table at the head of the couch where I lay, one of the orderlies knocked over the Mexican plant. The earthenware pot shattered, and the soil spilled over the rug, exposing the naked pink roots of the plant. I thought I saw the roots writhe and slither after me. I swooned.

Within a few days, I was assigned to a certain Dr. Wichita. The first time I was wheeled in, and saw her head emerge from behind the tall back of a leather armchair, I was not sure whether it was a man or a woman. But after my first good look at her in daylight, I decided in favor of her being a woman. The imposing hawk's nose could have been a man's; her eyebrows also were thick, and she had a man's haircut, the back of her neck carefully shaved. But her heavy lips were painted a bright crimson; she wore big button earrings, and a colored bead choker around her short neck. Her hair was dyed a delicate shade of orange, rather uncommon for a man.

It's much better now. I think they have given me up for a hopeless case. Every so often, as I lie here churning my spittle, I wonder, is this the death Miss Engel meant, or is this the rebirth?

Dr. Wichita, with whom I discuss my sessions with Miss Engel, only remarks, "Who the hell cares what she meant? She's dead."

"And me?" I ask tearfully. "Will I grow into a wholesome, red-blooded..."

"Don't you think it's a bit too late for that?" Dr. Wichita interrupts, as my voice fails.

Miss Engel used to say it was never too late. She often spoke to me about a patient she treated who was seventy-three years old, and blossomed like a child. He took up sculpture, started a new magazine, he even remarried and had a son.

I am ashamed to tell this to Dr. Wichita. I know she'll say, "Bunk!" So I just cry quietly. Dr. Wichita, who is good-hearted at bottom, lets her mouth drop, which is her way of expressing sympathy.

"You must resent having talked out your heart for eight years to that bitch," she snorts. "And where are you now?"

"I don't know," I say. "Here. Talking to you."

"And what the hell do you expect from me?"

"Nothing."

But I'm lying. I want Dr. Wichita to adopt me. I would become a little girl with yellow hair down my back, so sweet and dainty she couldn't resist me.

Each time I went to a session, I expected it would end by her taking me home. She would show me to her husband, a small, balding, jaundiced man I imagined him, who had always wanted a little girl so much, and they'd been childless all the twenty years of their marriage.

Dr. Wichita would want to spend all her money buying me pretty things. She'd give up her part-time job at the clinic to devote herself to raising me. She'd groom me to become a film star.

"I can write you a certificate of discharge," Dr. Wichita barks, interrupting my fantasy.

"No," I quaver, although I know she doesn't mean it.

Dr. Wichita is indulgent. She lets me play with dolls. Occupational therapy, she calls it. It has helped me a great deal. I think I'm beginning to move about a bit, crawling on my belly.

I chatter a great deal to Dr. Wichita about the dolls. One of them has come to life. Maybe it's me. She is nine years old and spindly. I wind her in wide billowing skirts because she is such a frail, bruised little thing.

"Girls, I understand, are castrated boys"—Dr. Wichita nods authoritatively in reply—"and there's a wound, that little bleeding mouth between her legs."

For although she's only nine, she bleeds already. Her name is Ellen, and she is bald. But I glue an orange wig on her pate, and call her by flouncy names, Annabella, Beatrice, Francesca.

"Beatrice has no breasts," I shyly confess to Dr. Wichita; "maybe just the slightest swell around her little nipples. But no pubic hair," I insist, "no beard around the pale lips of her wound."

"Why no beard?" Dr. Wichita challenges me suddenly, laying down the newspaper she has been absorbed in and stroking her stubby chin.

And since no answer was forthcoming on my part, she returns to the paper, mumbling, "You can always have it shaved off, you know. Nonsense!" She adds, becoming very cross-eyed, as she tries to make out the small print, "Go on, I'm listening."

Dr. Wichita is good for me. "Why don't you give up?" she keeps telling me. It's the first thing anyone told me that makes sense. "Why don't you simply give up?"

Sometimes I still wonder if one day I will be reborn as a proper child. But then my feet, rubbing against each other, feel large and calloused.

Dr. Wichita says, "Are you still at it?"

Most of the time now I just stare at her, or out the window at the leaves trembling. She makes telephone calls, files her nails, writes out bills.

"Are you going to sleep there?" she asks. Sometimes I do.

"Maybe I'm cured," I say.

"Maybe you are."

I am wheeled out in the courtyard, when the weather is nice.

THE SHARKS

WHEN THE boy closed his eyes the sea rushed up under his lids and rose over his head, a warm green sea, glass clear; his face was in the water, his eyes wide open looking down the bottomless blue past his pale frog legs. Each time the sharks came. First one then a second and a third, they came at him from several sides and from below, white and faceless, their killing jaws cut askew in their undersides. Sometimes he saw the blades of their tailfins a little way off bearing toward him straight and torpedo swift. His fear was white and cold as the killers. He didn't dare to turn and flee, as it was for his legs he feared most. He would have offered his throat or heart, but he knew the shark would chew off his legs. Sometimes he fought fiercely with his fists, pretending that the shark's teeth only grazed his thigh; he played the hero and rode the huge fish like a dolphin plunging his scout knife in his side. But more sharks came, excited by the blood, and swarmed about him. Exhausted, he finally closed his eyes and, floating limp, suffered them to take huge chunks out of him. After all it was only a dream. But he awoke feeling weak and his legs hurt at the places where the sharks had bitten him.

They came every night as soon as he closed his eyes. It was useless to make himself stare with wide-open eyes to try to keep awake. It never worked. Even while he felt the strain of keeping his lids from falling, sleep had already grabbed him from behind and turned his eyeballs into his head where the noon sun flooded the peaceful sea, dissipating all threat of darkness. Without the least awareness of a change of scene he would splash about in the sun-spangled water unsuspecting, until suddenly, looking down, he saw their white bulk, the saw-toothed jaws open toward him. Then they killed him surely. He awoke feeling that he had actually been dead a few minutes. The sharks were less terrible when he closed his eyes deliberately and waited for them to come.

But now having just been startled awake at the point where the sharks were tearing him limb by limb, he was too weak with pain and fright to face them again right away. He wanted his mother.

He sat up in bed. The sheets lay twisted about him, gray and fluid. Terror lurked in every crease. He sought the reassurance of the familiar objects of his room, but they had all allied themselves with the night against him. The fringed lampshade, his table and chair, assumed the shapes of the creatures of his dream. The floor had an eerie wet sheen. Mustering all his courage he crept out of bed and made his way across the room stepping warily on the linoleum, his eyes avoiding the black hole of the window and the half-open closet door, careful not to brush against the furniture, afraid to touch anything before he put on the light. He had to brace himself to turn the light-switch which was also enchanted. Snapped in the electric glare, the objects became lifeless once more, reduced to mere surfaces.

He decided to go upstairs to his mother. When he opened the door to the hall he could hear her voice as if she were quarreling with someone. He stood at the foot of the stairs listening. He heard her groan and the little shrieks of breaking threads like a sheet being ripped. She was crying and when she raised her voice he heard strange words. His mother slept alone in the big bed upstairs since his father left the house. His father was gone on a long trip, his mother told him. Whenever he asked her when his father was coming back, she looked away from him and said, maybe Christmas. His mother was pacing in the room upstairs, talking. Although he only heard her voice he was sure someone must be with her; his father. He must have come in secretly at night, for the boy often heard his mother plead with him and reproach him. He pictured his father standing silently in his light gray hat and coat, smoking cigarettes that he crushed with his heel on the floor. Sometimes he thought he heard another voice speak in a strangled whisper and a man's footsteps coming down the stairs and the front door slam. Thinking of the man who was with his mother he was afraid to go upstairs.

He felt cold and sleepy and he went back to bed to wait till the man would leave. He closed his eyes trying to think of the present his father would bring him for Christmas. A real Indian headdress with eagle feathers. A live monkey. The monkey's eyes started to glow strangely like the burning tip of a cigarette in the dark. The boy tried to think of something else; he imagined a whole toyshop with little cars, trucks, and trains. The toys began to float around bobbing up and down as if the shelves and counters had turned into water. He sat up rigidly in bed to resist the wave of his dream which always flung him to the sharks and stared hard into the darkness.

Slowly the night thinned and the first pallor of dawn filled the window frame. He sat motionless listening for footsteps down the stairs. He continued looking hard, not allowing himself to blink. Then he saw his father's face appear in the window. His father climbed through the window like a burglar, his light gray suit creased and dirty. I mustn't be afraid, the boy thought. It's only my father. "Daddy, did you bring me a present?" he asked. His father did not smile. He pulled out a gun from his trouser pocket and fixed it at him. It's a game, the boy thought, and raised his hand his fingers crooked in position to pull the trigger aiming at his father. He felt a stream of bullets tear through his chest and throat but he held his ground. It's a toy gun! he wanted to say, but only blood bubbled up his throat. His eyes grew dim but he felt no pain. He saw the blurred shape of his father retreating through the window and heard the window banged shut. He seemed to be looking through a fogged glass. He took a step forward and stumbled against the windowpane. On the other side of the glass there was water with swaying weeds and darting fish. The house was under the sea surrounded by water. The sharks came swarming up to the window, their enormous white bulk flattening against the glass. They turned so that he saw their bloated silver bellies and upside-down moon-shaped mouths with the saw-edged teeth showing. And the boy saw his father in the water, holding a package, kicking with his hands and feet, a burning cigarette in his mouth. His father was swimming with the sharks before the window, he seemed to be motioning to the boy to open to him. But the boy was afraid the sharks would come in if he raised the window to let him in. He saw his father shaking his fist under the water. He went back to bed and drew the covers over his head. He could hear his father trying all the windows in the house. He pretended to be asleep.

He crept out of bed when he heard his mother in the kitchen. It was still dark. She stood in her white nightgown, barefoot, cracking eggs into a big frying pan with her eyes shut.

"But it's still night," the boy said.

She turned toward him without opening her eyes and smiled, her teeth unusually long and beautiful like carved ivory. "Get yourself a bowl and eat your cereal," she said.

She continued breaking eggs on the edge of the pan. For whom was she making all those eggs? the boy wondered. The eggs crashed into the hot fat with a shriek. He couldn't find a bowl or the cereal box but he didn't say anything; he looked into the night through the kitchen window. He saw two tired eyes. He was outside looking in at his mother who was stirring something in a large cauldron. He thought he saw a hairless tail. Then the face of his baby sister bobbed up. His mother was giving her a bath. But she seemed dead, her flesh came crumbling off the bone, gray and flaky. His mother smiled the same long-toothed smile.

He screamed. It was silent in the house. He went out into the hall and listened under the stairs. His mother was no longer pacing. The man must have left. He tiptoed up the stairs into her room and creeping under the sheet beside her nestled his face in her shoulder and slept.

One morning the boy found his mother dead. He had gone to her in the middle of the night; he tried to wake her in the morning tapping her cheek but she didn't stir. It was dark in the room, the shades were drawn, but he thought he caught a glance of her eye. He went downstairs. He decided he would surprise her by dressing himself. His mother had forgotten to put out the clean shirt and pants she wanted him to wear that day. For a while he sat disconsolate on the edge of his bed listening to his sister make little gurgling sounds in the next room. After a while he started to put on the crumpled shirt and pants that lay in a heap beside his bed from the day before. The baby's crooning grew louder and more plaintive. It turned into a whine. While he was lacing his shoes he heard the alarm of the electric clock upstairs ringing for a long time until the minute hand passed the point on which it was set. He went upstairs into his mother's room, banging the door against the wall. He made the shades ride up with a roar flooding the room with light. His mother lay with her eyes open but she wasn't awake. When he pulled her arm her hand dropped. That afternoon they came and took her away.

Now if he died in his sleep he could no longer seek refuge near his mother's body because she lay in a coffin buried in the earth. His father never returned bringing him a present. Perhaps he also lay in a coffin somewhere. The boy and his sister went to live with an aunt in a big city. His aunt was old. She wore dentures which she kept in a glass of water on her night table. He embraced her stiffly. He didn't ever want to lie in a coffin. He was afraid of being buried alive.

When the sharks came at night he no longer tried to flee or fight them. He called to them and offered his limbs and bore the pain bravely until he swooned away. They were beautiful sharks now, velvet black with fringed flippers, they weaved slowly through the water, their bodies turning like scarves, their snouts were soft, and he could feel their lips caressing him before they sunk their teeth in his thigh.

A FATAL DISEASE

DERBY left the doctor's office after his yearly routine checkup dazed and depressed. Outside it was a brilliant winter day. But even though his eyes blinked mechanically as they adjusted to the brightness after the doctor's heavily shuttered consulting room, Derby took no notice of the clear blue day. For some minutes he stood hesitating near a bus stop at the street corner, but when he saw the bus approach, walked away.

He had walked several blocks along a straight avenue lined with gray apartment buildings. But where was he going? He stopped to look at his watch. It was 2:17. He had over an hour and a half to fill, he reflected uneasily, till his next engagement at 4:10. One hour and thirty-three minutes exactly, not counting the twenty minutes it would take him to get there. He contemplated this stretch of time with vague anxiety.

When he left home that morning he had planned to attend to a number of errands in the downtown area after his visit to the doctor. He had promised his son to buy him cartridges for a special kind of toy gun which only one store carried; his wife had asked him to pick up an order of party napkins at a downtown store; he had to look up a reference in the public library and stop by his publisher to approve the cover for his new volume of essays. The doctor had kept him waiting almost two hours, however, and now Derby was doubtful whether he could cram all this business in an hour, for it would take him twenty minutes to get downtown, and even while he was considering how to spend the time, time was passing.

He might have enough time to settle his business at the library and with the publisher, and perhaps one more item: the cartridges for his son which he had promised for over two weeks. But his wife needed the party napkins by tomorrow evening. So in any event he would have to make another trip the following day. This being so, it seemed more reasonable to do all his errands tomorrow in a single trip rather than have to go twice. The sensible thing would be to take the bus to the university and spend the free hour reading in his office. But this he immediately rejected. At this moment everything connected with his work, especially the desk heaped with student papers and mail, filled him with disgust. He decided to take a stroll through the park.

Every time Derby went for a medical checkup he secretly hoped that the doctor would discover that he suffered from a fatal disease and had at most one year to live. The thought that his end was imminent always gave him a sudden sense of release and new vitality. He would be free at last, free from all obligation—of which the most oppressive to him was to decide, plan and make arrangements for the future. Suddenly he could breathe and for a brief moment tasted a wild and delicious freedom he never experienced otherwise, unless in the most distant, irrevocable past, as a small boy running through the fields. Subsequent considerations of what he would do with this freedom for a whole year or even for a single day inevitably bewildered and depressed him. Would he make some last effort toward happiness or trust that year? Would he simply continue as before, or leave everything, his work and his family, and go off alone to some distant place? Could he bear to confront himself now? Was it not too late? The initial sense of liberation soon dissipated into dread. Suppose that year he would go through the same kind of endless dying as all the other years, only more intense, more unmitigated, more horrible because it would be final.

But the doctor found him in satisfactory condition. His complaints could be traced to nothing more serious than a nervous stomach and insufficient air and exercise. There was the slightest suspicion of a tumor in the rectum but it was no cause for alarm; the doctor advised him to come back in a few weeks for an X-ray. Aside from that Dr. Beeswax suggested that Derby go on a bland diet to remedy his watery stool and try to fit in at least an hour of physical activity like bowling or judo in his weekly schedule.

As Derby stood at the entrance of the park the brilliance of the sky struck him. He looked up through the still bare branches and remembered that it was almost spring. The wind was freezing, still it was a beautiful day. The beauty had something remote. He was aware that he could not enter into its depth. At the same time it had a different quality from the picture-postcard flatness the world usually had for him.

Walking along the path he shut his eyes and turned his face toward the sun. Perhaps he did not feel as badly as he had imagined for the past year and the doctor was right. He tried to draw assurance from the doctor's diagnosis. But although he enjoyed the sun on his face, he could not dismiss the dull pain in his stomach and sense of nausea, or ignore the pressure on his chest. He was tired. Every breath he drew seemed to involve an effort—almost a decision. Every now and then he caught himself holding his breath for a prolonged period as if he were underwater.

He sank down on a bench and smoked. It was a fine day but he wasn't enjoying his walk. His watch showed 2:29. He still had over an hour. If he turned back and took a bus downtown he might still have time to settle one or two errands. Buy the cartridges for his son, and perhaps pick up the napkins. He would attend to his own affairs some other time since he didn't feel up to deciding about the cover for his book or hunting up the quotation he needed in the public library. He did not feel like going downtown but he hated to disappoint his son. The boy's first question when he ran to the door to greet him would be whether he got him the cartridges. Derby couldn't think about his son without a sense of uneasiness bordering on guilt. The boy's future weighed on him oppressively. Was the new private school right for him? He was already thirteen years old but he had no serious interests. Wasn't he too old to go around, bang bang, with a toy gun? Was it his fault for not forbidding him to play with guns in the first place? He would have to speak with the school psychiatrist about him. But now he had promised him the cartridges.

He was cold sitting on the bench. The sensible thing, he told himself again, would be to proceed to his office and spend the hour before his class looking over mid-term papers. He rose and started walking back uncertainly. He stopped as he reached the playground. The knowledge that in an hour he would be in class lecturing to some fifty students taking notes filled him with despair. He remained standing with his hands on the wire fence.

He looked at his watch. It was 2:40. He still had an hour. An hour, an hour, an empty stretch of time when he had nothing specific to do.

He watched a group of boys coming along the path their ice skates slung over their shoulder, jostling each other. It was 3:29. If he was going to cross the park and take a bus to arrive a few minutes before his class started he had better be on his way. But he lit another cigarette and did not move.

Perhaps, Derby thought, he had a fatal disease and the doctor simply thought it best not to tell him. [He had the] numb thought of dying slowly without knowing it, without anyone caring or acknowledging it. And so it would go on for years till one day the thread went completely slack, the choice would no longer be his and in a matter of hours he would die drugged on some operation table. It was the death most men died, and he too unless he did something about it.

He knew that he was free to choose the time of his death. Strictly speaking this freedom was restricted to the present instant: he was free to die *now*. In the past he was content to derive a general reassurance from this knowledge. What he felt now was not a greater urgency to act upon it but rather a sense of hopelessness about ever feeling that the time had come. His act would lack necessity a year hence as it did this very moment.

Suppose he set it quite arbitrarily, a week from today, as he made a professional appointment, or reservations for a trip. Would he meet it with the same indifference? Would he perform it as a matter of business. If it is decided, he thought, why not now, this minute? But the more desperately he longed to end it all, the less will he could summon to plan and carry out the act of self-destruction. He resented having to work out the details. Time to breathe, think things over. Come to a decision perhaps. He began walking slowly across the park. The thought that by the time he reached the other side of the park he might be an entirely different man with a different future was at once exhilarating and frightening. Who knows, he thought, I might simply not appear at my class today, or go home for dinner. Who knows what I might do—But what would ultimately decide him to take one course or another? The part of him that had ideas very often did not get together with the part that had to execute them.

As he strolled idly by the pond watching the ducks, the idea gained on him that he had to come to a decision. Did he really have to? The nature of the decision was not clear. He tried to find momentary peace looking at the line formed by the ducks but the voice within him nagged: to avoid making a decision also amounts to a kind of decision. But what am I to decide about? he thought irritably, whether I'm going to meet my class in fifty minutes or what I'm going to do after that, or in a week? But first he would have to decide whether he would make a decision within the next hour or by the end of the day or the week. When would he make his great decision?

He felt so tired. It didn't seem the right moment to make any important decision. He sank down on a bench again and smoked. If the doctor had at least advised him to take a few weeks' rest in the country or disengage himself from some of the many obligations that weighed on him. But the doctor suggested nothing of the kind. He inquired about Derby's work with such fervent interest and admiration that he felt suspicious as well as resentful. Was this part of the doctor's bedside manner, his effort to boost the patient's morale? Or was Dr. Beeswax genuinely interested in those ideas which have for a long time now ceased to matter to Derby. They spent a half an hour discussing a fine point in Derby's last book review although the waiting room was crowded with patients. Derby recalled in particular a girl with a running sore on her eye which she kept daubing and a tremulous old man whose head was bandaged with pink tape. Did Dr. Beeswax philosophize with all his patients, or was he singled out because he taught at a college? Just then it struck Derby that the doctor drew him out on his ideas at such length that he forgot to mention to him a number of the symptoms that worried him, like the pressure on his chest, his headaches and dizzy spells. Also he meant to ask the doctor to renew his prescription of sleeping pills, which of course he forgot as well, distracted by the conversation and silenced by the doctor praising his blood pressure and finding him in such blossoming health. He was most annoyed by the doctor questioning him minutely about his son, how he was adjusting to the new school, whether he wouldn't do well to consult a psychiatrist. Derby was offended by this intimacy. Perhaps Beeswax wasn't a serious doctor after all, or at least did not take him seriously as a patient. He barely examined him, he didn't even bother to take a chest X-ray. And the business with the suspected tumor, why didn't he look into it then and there or send him to a specialist? Why was he so vague? A slight suspicion: Didn't all grave diseases begin that way? He recalled a colleague of his, a young man who died recently from skin cancer. At first he was told it was a perfectly harmless irritation. Of course he couldn't trust Beeswax.

He rose and started to walk. Once more he indulged his fantasy which relieved him precisely because the burden of setting a term to his life and executing the sentence was not his, nor the responsibility. But can I leave it up to chance? he asked himself.

As an act of choice his death lost its sense of necessity. A sudden loathing rose in him against his former train of thought. Wasn't it stupid, contemptible and sneaky besides to run out on his family? Yet it was clear to Derby even as his doubts rose that the moment had come: if he set the date it was now or never. Whatever he resolved this moment—or some subsequent moment—involved a purely arbitrary act of will. Thus he would will himself in a taxi that took him to his class, thus he could equally well will himself to do what is required to die. The senselessness of it all troubled him. Yet every moment of his life was a relinquishing of sense. The arbitrary, gratuitous act whereby he would end his life which was lacking in a single moment of necessity would thus be a negation of a negation and an affirmation of the sense of necessity which was denied to him both in the act of living and dying.

But Derby was still not sure whether he was entirely resolved. Would something accidental, of which he could not conceive now, decide him for or against ending his life in the next half hour?

It was almost four o'clock when he reached the park exit. He leaped into a taxi and told the driver to hurry to the university. For a moment he felt saved. He had wasted an hour and a half in morbid brooding. It was a hideous idea and the professor in him smiled at himself. But Derby smiled back coldly.

DR. ROMBACH'S DAUGHTER

THEY LIVED in an old two-story frame house, Dr. Rombach and his daughter, Marianna. Dr. Rombach was a psychoanalyst of Viennese origin, a heavy-set man, somewhat hunch-shouldered, with jutting eyebrows. His chin sunk on his chest, he scrutinized the world out of deep-set, melancholy eyes.

There was no psychoanalyst in Brighton before Dr. Rombach arrived and set up his practice, first in a modest midtown hotel, and after a year, in the house he bought on Wilbur Street.

Dr. Rombach received his patients at his home. Except for his visits to the State Hospital every Thursday afternoon he hardly ever left the house. Occasionally he was seen standing on the front porch inspecting the condition of the boards.

Dr. Rombach's daughter was a gawky girl tall for her thirteen years with entranced eyes that seemed all the more oblivious to the world as she was always running. Her schoolbooks hugged to her chest, her unbuttoned coat flapping about her and her hair flying in her face, Marianna Rombach raced down Wilbur Street. Sometimes she would come to a sudden halt and remain standing, arrested, her glazed eyes fixed on some revery; or she would unexpectedly dart sideways into the street when the warning horn would freeze her in her tracks like a startled hare. Summer or winter she went bare-legged in a pair of worn ballet slippers, the hem always showing under her outgrown overcoat.

Dr. Rombach rose at a quarter to seven every morning to allow himself ample time for the orderly and meticulous performance of his washing, shaving, dressing, breakfast and toilet ceremonies before the arrival of the first patient at nine o'clock. At eight o'clock he came into Marianna's bedroom, raised the shades approximately three inches below the center window frame, announced to her the time and went downstairs to prepare his breakfast.

Although Marianna was awake listening to her father wash and dress since the alarm rang at a quarter to seven, she always remained in bed until her father's second call at half past eight in order to keep out of his way. Dr. Rombach liked to make and eat his breakfast alone; also he reserved for himself the use of the bathroom from a quarter to seven to eight and from half past eight to a quarter to nine. After Marianna heard the lock of the bathroom click, she threw on her clothes and grabbing her schoolbooks bolted out of the house.

A dilapidated trembling negress with bloodshot eyes came daily for three hours to clean the house and prepare a warm lunch for the doctor. She came five days a week and on Fridays made a roast duck or a meatloaf for the weekend. Besides the patients, the maid and the delivery men nobody ever entered the house.

On her way home from school Marianna always stopped at the corner drugstore to check the time, so as to be sure that she wouldn't be approaching the house just when a patient was coming or leaving. Her father had impressed upon her since she was a small child that she must not be seen by the patients, or leave any of her personal effects, her coat, books or hairbrush, in sight of his clients. Such negligence, the doctor warned, meant that a good part of the session was wasted on the patient commenting on the disorderliness of the analyst's daughter. Marianna was as careful to avoid seeing a patient as to be seen by one. If she happened to be sitting by the window when the patient's car turned in the driveway, she would duck behind the armchair rather than risk catching a glimpse of him or her coming up the porch steps. And since the patient might arrive early or late she always bowed her head as she approached the house and entered swiftly without looking right or left.

Home from school, Marianna settled down in a corner of the

living room, downstairs. She sat perfectly still and waited. Thoughts did not always come. Sometimes she sat for hours with nothing in her head. When her emptiness oppressed her she tried to pass the time paging through the dictionary or covering a sheet of paper with random words. She preferred to stay downstairs rather than go to her room which was on the same floor as her father's office.

Between patients Dr. Rombach came creaking down the stairs to sort the day's mail, make telephone calls, put out a suit for the cleaner, the money for the grocer, munch some chocolate and give a few minutes to his daughter. At five o'clock every day he went through the house from room to room winding up the clocks.

"Aren't you daydreaming?" he asked when he found his daughter staring at the wall with a glazed look. Marianna insisted that her mind was quite blank. Dr. Rombach, however, was not satisfied.

"You are repressing!" he contested. "At your stage of development it is normal for a girl to have sexual fantasies."

Marianna acknowledged her father's remark in silence.

"Your coldness and indifference toward me," Dr. Rombach observed, smiling, as Marianna stiffened when he twisted her face around toward him to kiss her cheek, "is simply a compensatory mechanism in overcoming your strong oedipal attachment to me."

The doorbell rang, announcing the arrival of the 5:10 patient.

"He is five minutes early, as usual," Dr. Rombach observed, pursing his mouth significantly.

"It is interesting," he continued, "that you still repress certain feelings even after I have explained to you their mechanism." And before proceeding upstairs, he recalled to her instances of her possessiveness toward him between the ages of three and eight.

Marianna took everything her father said to heart. But she could not actually remember wanting to kiss him on the mouth, or asking, when her mother died, whether she could have her bedroom. What she remembered, was her father telling her these things before. She had difficulty remembering herself as a child. In the last years her thighs had thickened and her breasts had began to swell; her body no longer felt like her own but some cumbersome burden she had to drag around. She made herself run as she used to as a child in a last effort to defy the weight of her body and flee into motion. But the sensation of her breasts jostling and sagging against her side filled her with despair.

Marianna was sitting in the living room with a notebook in her lap, holding a pencil poised midair when Dr. Rombach pushed the sliding doors apart and passed through on his way to the telephone table to cross out the grocery order he just saw delivered at the foot of the stairs.

"What were you thinking right now?" He turned on her suddenly.

Marianna looked up. She saw her father cross out the grocery list, crumple the slip of paper and drop it in the wastepaper basket.

"It must be something very important," her father said slyly, "if you can't say it."

Marianna was trying to think of something to say. "I was just thinking that you're coming into the room as you came into the room."

"Were you irritated?" Dr. Rombach asked. "Admit that you were a little irritated. It's perfectly understandable—an old man getting a bit sloppy! You're tired of seeing me come in, hour after hour. You'd like to see a young man walk in, who is interested in you as a sexual partner—make up to you a little. And you are perfectly right to feel that way," he added and sat on the arm of the chair, fondling her. "What is a father's love after all?" Then, in a serious tone: "You must not repress these natural drives out of irrational guilt feelings arising from your Oedipal attachment to me. Of course, you're a growing girl, your glands are beginning to work, your breasts are developing—" he studied her breasts, "they could be a little, well, shapelier. Don't you wear a brassiere?"

Marianna shook her head.

"Stand up and let me look at you," he ordered.

"No," Marianna muttered.

"Bashfulness," her father proclaimed, "is only a hidden form of exhibitionism. Acknowledge that you are in reality eager to display your femininity before your father, and you won't blush."

Just then the six o'clock patient rang. Dr. Rombach went to answer the door.

Marianna tried to remember what she was thinking before her father came in and interrupted. The page of the notebook before her was blank. She was trying to think of something to write in it. A beautiful phrase. She looked around the room but she did not see anything that wanted to be put into words. Then she listened. There was the whirr of a lawnmower and the noise of cars passing along the street. *Blank* was the only thing she could think of. The color of blankness? It had no color. Blank was a bad word, it belonged to the mind and to the page. The heart could never be blank, though it might be empty, or void. There were better words than blank. Vacant conjured rooms, deserted houses. Blank was a flat word, flat as a page. Void had depth; it was dark, or a foggy white. Empty pertained most to the heart. Marianna was not sure that she had a heart.

Every evening at a quarter past seven Marianna prepared for her father a pair of wieners with baked beans, which he ate in the kitchen reading the afternoon paper while Marianna went back to the dining room to do her homework. Sometimes he called out across the pantry and read aloud to her a news item from the crime and accident column which illustrated his conviction that all mankind was insane or served to point out how careful one must be.

When the 8:30 patient arrived, Marianna went to the kitchen and while washing the dishes nibbled on some bread and leftover beans. Food was something she did not like to think about. Her father had made her see everything she ate, wore or used in terms of his labor. The groceries represented so many hours of his work, listening to people with sick minds. But this wasn't all. Food tasted queer in her mouth. The smell of cooking food revolted her. She used to care for fruit, but lately even apples had a strong, fleshy taste.

Her father gave her $2.50 a week to buy herself lunch at the school cafeteria. But Marianna welcomed the opportunity to go without food and save the money. Eating only made her feel more heavy, and she enjoyed the slight faintness produced by an empty stomach. She bought cigarettes with the lunch money. Smoking had always fascinated her. Already as a child she dreamed of living off smoke. Children who smoked stopped growing, she had heard people say. For some years now, she had, every so often, smoked a few cigarettes she stole from her father, but it failed to arrest her growth. On her twelfth birthday she resolved to make it into a serious discipline. She made herself smoke first five, then ten cigarettes a day. After a while it became easy. She could hardly wait for the morning classes to be over so that she might satisfy her craving.

Every day she spent the lunch recess in a deserted back alley, smoking under the fire escapes. Sometimes she missed the afternoon session and went down to the creek where in the winter she could wander across the fields and smoke freely without fear of meeting anyone. She was happiest when she was completely absorbed in the physical sensation of the smoke filling her body. She sucked it in deeply and held it, till she felt a faint tremor start in the pit of her stomach and a sweet numbness spread through her limbs.

After she had been smoking for a year Marianna felt like a different person. Dreams and cravings for things she had as a child left her. Now she only wanted a feeling of increasing lightness. She longed to be light and diffuse like smoke.

When she finished drying the dishes Marianna went out on the back porch, smoked three cigarettes with avid haste and, hearing the rumble of footsteps upstairs, returned to the dining room to do her arithmetic.

After the last patient left, Dr. Rombach puttered around upstairs for a while, aired his consulting room, attended to his correspondence and accounts, wrote out the memo for the following day, took his evening bath, and before retiring, came downstairs to enjoy a small snack followed by a whiskey and soda. Usually he settled down with his drink at the dining room table where his daughter was studying and told her about his most interesting cases while Marianna sat frozen to the chair, staring fixedly at her book. She had a trick of tensing the muscles behind her ears and producing a kind of whirring sound which partially drowned out his voice.

Sensing his daughter's inattention Dr. Rombach would look through the pile of books on the table and, seizing on any volume which was not pure science, read a sentence from a page opened at random and exclaim with irritation, "What do these people really know about human life? What clinical data do they have?"

Midway through his whiskey Dr. Rombach would turn to investigating his daughter's mind. His interest, he assured her, in order to impress upon her the importance of giving an honest reply, was strictly scientific.

Was she afraid of mice? Insects? Did she ever dream that she walked out on the street naked? That she lost all her teeth? That she was a man? What were her feelings toward him? Did she have suicidal fantasies? Look forward to motherhood? Would she be able to resign herself to spinsterhood? What was her principal aim in life? Could she fall in love with a negro? A cripple? Was she happy?

Marianna had difficulty answering most of her father's questions. She was not sure how she felt about anything. Was she capable of real feeling? But Dr. Rombach never pressed his daughter. When her answer wasn't forthcoming he would provide it himself and proceed to the next question.

"Are you happy?" he asked with more than scientific concern. "I have a feeling that you can't really be happy."

"I am happy," Marianna insisted with quiet defiance.

"Can you explain your happiness to me," he demanded, more irritated than pleased by her reply.

Marianna knew that she must not speak to her father about her love for certain things. He interrupted her silence with his own view of happiness. Dr. Rombach was happy when everything was in order.

"Pleasure," he set forth, "is simply the removal of tension. Every stimulus is basically a source of pain." But Marianna wasn't listening.

When he began to feel the effect of the whiskey, Dr. Rombach would yawn, declare mankind a mistake and shuffle off to bed.

Marianna sat motionless for a long time after her father went upstairs, listening to the thud of his slippers, the creak of the bed, the five-minute radio news broadcast and finally, the click of the light being turned off. She sat still and waited. After a while she became aware of the breathing of the house, the throbbing of the frigidaire, the concerted ticking of the clocks, and every so often a strange noise as of something cracking inside the walls.

Sometime between three and four in the morning, Dr. Rombach left his bed to go to the bathroom. When he saw light in the hall he went downstairs for inspection. Perceiving her father in the doorway, Marianna sitting under the hundred-watt light bulb had the scared look of a doe surprised in the thicket. She quickly turned the page she had been writing on, face down.

"You're still up!" Dr. Rombach lisped, his mouth kneading without his dentures.

"I'm working," Marianna blurted without thinking.

"What are you working on?" Dr. Rombach demanded. "I always see you work late into the night. You're not still working on your homework?"

"No," Marianna confessed.

"What are you working on then?"

Marianna continued staring. She did not know herself what she was doing. She simply liked to stay up late at night. She could spend hours just paging through the dictionary. Sometimes she copied down words and arranged them in groups. Marianna loved words. Words were her only means of getting hold of things. The things remained outside and apart from her. The blue she saw, the sadness and shame she felt, the quivering moth on the lampshade, they eluded her. But the words, *blue*, *sadness*, *shame*, *moth*, belonged to her. The word *blue* was more than the blue of the sky or a piece of blue velvet. Everything blue was captured in the word *blue*. The world was like a wall. Its objects were turned away from her until she named them. Then the sky allowed her to enter. She called things by their names and they came to her like animals. Sometimes she fed them. Sometimes they offered themselves to her as food. Sometimes they sat on her heart and devoured her.

Dr. Rombach was annoyed at his daughter keeping such late hours.

"Well," he demanded, "are you writing something?"

"I'll show it to you when it's finished," she said weakly.

"But what is it?" he pursued irritably. "I am afraid you're wasting your time. Are you sure you have talent? Most people who think they are artists are merely neurotics. Take your mother for example—"

"I am not writing anything," Marianna cut in sharply, "I am just writing."

Dr. Rombach made a face and squashed out his cigarette.

"Don't forget to put out all the lights when you go to bed," he reminded her.

After her father left the room, Marianna promptly resumed her meditation. She turned over the page on which she had written, "leaf, leaves. Scarf, scarves. Grief, grieve," and saw forms progressing from repose to number and movement.

When the paling night deepened into blue, Marianna tiptoed off to bed, a quiet joy, light as the foreboding of day on her lips.

One Monday afternoon after the six o'clock patient left, Dr. Rombach came into Marianna's room, pulled down the shades, screwed back the top on the ink bottle, peered over his daughter's shoulder to see what she was reading, went to the door, then stopped and turned to her saying, "Can I have your attention for a moment?"

She raised her eyes reluctantly from the book.

Dr. Rombach cleared his throat. "Tomorrow between two and five in the afternoon I would like to have privacy in the house," he announced. "Is that possible?"

"I'll go to the public library," Marianna said promptly.

"I think you are old enough to understand," her father went on, "that I am still a virile man and sometimes I need sexual gratification. I will not ask this often of you, and if at any time the hours are inconvenient you will let me know. I think once every two weeks or ten days, once a week at most—no," he corrected himself, "ten days at most I will need to have privacy in the house."

"That's all right," Marianna said.

"Where did you say you'll go tomorrow?"

"To the public library. I wanted to get some books anyway."

"You can take a taxi. I'll give you the money."

"I don't need a taxi. I'll go straight from school. There is a bus that goes to the library."

"It might rain." Dr. Rombach said and put a dollar bill under the ink bottle. "From two to five. Will you remember?"

"Yes," Marianna promised.

"I'll remind you again tomorrow morning," Dr. Rombach said on his way out.

Coming up the stairs late that night Marianna glanced at the note on the bannister her father wrote for himself to remind him of his chores the following day. "Put out brown pants and money for the cleaner; order groceries. Call plumber for leak in toilet. Call M.P. to confirm appointment for two. Tell Mrs. Green to finish cleaning by one."

Marianna felt sad for both of them. For M.P. as well as for her father.

That Tuesday evening, while warming up the remains of the roast duck, Dr. Rombach questioned his daughter.

"Did you experience any jealousy toward this person?" he began. "Do you wonder what we do together? You don't have to answer that. You can't help it, of course. Does it upset you? Do you resent it? Did you think about it while you were in the library?"

Marianna felt progressively cornered by his questions. She thought for a moment. Sitting on the bus she had wondered if the woman was his patient. For how else would he have met her? The idea of woman patients who came to lie on her father's couch being potential sexual objects disturbed her.

"Is she a patient?" Marianna asked.

"No. I met her socially. No, it was at a faculty tea," he corrected himself.

In the weeks that followed Marianna spent many afternoons at the public library.

After a time Dr. Rombach made a slight alteration in his schedule. "I will need privacy Sunday afternoon for about two hours," he informed his daughter, "but you don't have to leave the house. I only need the upstairs and we may come down for a few minutes to the kitchen, so you can stay in the living room but keep the doors closed. And if you have to go to the bathroom use the toilet in the basement; only be sure to put out the light afterwards."

Marianna's sense of propriety, however, nevertheless bade her to leave the house while her father was having his sexual gratification. Since the library was closed Sundays, she went roaming about the streets.

"I would introduce you to this person," Dr. Rombach remarked one Sunday to his daughter as she stood in her coat about to leave twenty minutes before two. "She is a very attractive and cultivated woman, but she has legitimate reasons to prefer to keep our relations secret for the time being."

Late one evening as he was finishing his whiskey, Dr. Rombach asked his daughter: "How would you feel about it if I would marry again?"

Marianna thought it odd that her father should ask her approval.

"Well," he continued, "I have thought it over. Since a growing girl needs a mother and since I am still a virile man, and furthermore, since I don't want to be left alone when I'm old—after all, one day you'll leave me," he peered at her over the rim of his spectacles, "won't you? I have thought about remarrying. But only with your agreement. I will arrange for you to meet this person in a week or so.

You will think it over carefully, because I don't want any difficulties afterwards."

"I want to emphasize," he concluded, "it is only a possibility I am considering."

Next Sunday noon while Marianna was warming up the meatloaf, Dr. Rombach briefed his daughter on the procedure for the afternoon: "I expect Mrs. Picnic at two. We will go upstairs for a while. I want you to stay in the living room. Around three we will come down together and I will introduce you to her. Her name is May Picnic. Miss May—I mean Mrs. May Picnic," he corrected himself. "Is everything clear?"

Marianna nodded, and having served her father went to the dining room, leaving him with the Sunday papers. She closed her eyes and tried to concentrate on certain words but the crackling of the newspaper disturbed her. She thought of going upstairs to her room, but she did not want to be there when her father's girlfriend arrived or risk meeting them on the stairs. She stood around idly listening to her father flap the pages, thrust the paper in the waste basket and move about the kitchen and the pantry. After a while he came in.

"She is three minutes late," he announced, looking sharply at the clock on the mantel. They waited in silence.

At exactly seven minutes after two the doorbell rang.

"We will be down at three o'clock," Dr. Rombach said on his way to the front door.

Marianna hastily withdrew to the kitchen with a book. She read, forming the words silently with her lips and tried to keep her mind from straying. Not a sound came from upstairs till she heard them coming down the stairs. She waited till her father called for her and went slowly into the living room.

"Marianna, I would like you to meet Miss May Picnic," he said overcoming a sudden hoarseness. "Mrs. May Picnic," he corrected himself, and taking Marianna's arm showed her a large white box on the telephone table.

"Mrs. Picnic brought this cake—"

"Do you think you could find us a plate?" she chimed in, joining them. "I hope you like danish pastry."

"I told you I don't eat any kind of pastry," Dr. Rombach said.

"But I asked your daughter, Herman," Marianna heard on her way to the kitchen.

Marianna was surprised by May Picnic. She expected her to be dark and buxom, with ponderous breasts and a bright voluptuous mouth. She imagined she would look somewhat like a former psychoanalyst friend of her father, a certain Dr. Lora Hirsch, with whom they often had their meals when they lived in a hotel in New York. She remembered being overwhelmed by Lora's fragrance, the glitter of her smile and pearl button earrings. She always wore tight, dressy suits with a strong sheen which showed off her well-developed breasts. Her look, under heavily mascaraed eyes, was provocative.

May Picnic had little in common with her father's former girlfriend. May was small, blond and fragile, almost drab except for the twinkle in her blue eyes. Her light hair was drawn back in a bun. She wore a tailored suit with a striped blouse and underneath her chest looked rather flat.

May came into the kitchen to assist Marianna, but she had already filled the plate and they returned to the living room, May praising her artistic arrangement. In her high heels she barely reached Marianna's height.

May chattered on like a little girl, and although Marianna's father was continually urging her to sit, she kept flitting about the room to look at a painting or piece of woodwork, to pass the plate of pastry which was still full around once more, or lift the window shades—why did he keep them down on a perfectly gorgeous day! She teased her father about his choice of furniture; but she found it suited him perfectly. Dr. Rombach pointed out her habit of drawing close to people and touching their arm when she spoke to them, explaining the motivation behind her strategy. May responded with a peal of laughter and winked at Marianna who blushed in turn pleased and embarrassed.

"We must have a talk," she said to Marianna, as she was about to leave. She took Marianna's hand in hers and looked intently into her face. "Will you come and see me at my place? Come tomorrow. I'll be expecting you after school."

Marianna promised she would come.

"Ah, it's good to be alone!" Dr. Rombach exclaimed after May Picnic left. "She talks too much, don't you think? Well, how about my baked beans?"

"She is a poor girl," her father went on, forking his beans while Marianna watched the toast. "Her husband left her a few years ago. She earns a living of a sort teaching art history. She is only an instructor. Women have it hard. Going on forty. She'll be attractive to men for another five years maybe, and then..." Her father made the sound of air escaping from a balloon. "Women have it tough, you see."

Marianna was late to school next morning. She took so long making up her mind what to wear since she was going to see May Picnic. Everything she tried on looked wrong. Finally she decided on a black dress that was a little too large and, at least, didn't make her look fat. She had been up most of the night looking through her notebooks and trying to put some of her most beautiful words together in a poem to show to May Picnic.

May Picnic lived in a small furnished apartment in a residential downtown hotel. She received Marianna warmly, ushering her in, her arm hooked in hers.

"This is only temporary," she laughed, apologizing for the furnishings which were not to her taste.

May Picnic loved beautiful things, she told Marianna while they were having tea. She talked about different styles of furniture, about paintings and clothes. Marianna sat rigidly and listened, without quite knowing what to make of May Picnic's fluttery gestures and swift, breathless chatter. May said she had a lovely face, it reminded her of a painting and started playing around with her hair, pulling it back with combs. Marianna wondered if she should show May her poems. When she looked in the mirror she didn't like herself with her hair pulled back, but she did not say anything.

"We must go shopping next time," May said as Marianna was leaving. "I'll speak to your father about buying you a new winter coat and some becoming dresses."

Marianna didn't understand why May showed so much interest in her. She felt she ought to tell May that she didn't really care about dresses, but she wanted May to like her. When she was at the door she pulled out a folded paper from her pocket and offered it to May.

"It's just something I wrote," she mumbled.

"Marianna, I didn't know you wrote poetry," May said softly as she opened the page. "May I really read it? Wait," she said, "let me give you something." She went in the other room and in a minute returned with a blue and yellow silk scarf and draped it around Marianna's neck.

That evening Marianna sat with her father while he was having his supper. She felt like talking about May Picnic.

Dr. Rombach did not seem to be impressed.

"I want you to know," he said after a while, raising his eyes from the newspaper, "that I have no intentions of marrying her."

"I hope you understand," Dr. Rombach said Saturday evening when Marianna came in showing off a new winter coat, "why she takes an interest in you?"

Marianna shrugged her shoulder. She liked the coat; it was gray flannel with silver buttons and she was happy with May's scarf around her neck.

"Look," Dr. Rombach went on, "she would very much like me to marry her, and well, it's understandable that she should try to win your affection. I don't mean to say that her behavior toward you is merely hypocritical; there might be an element of genuine fondness. But I want you to see what is behind it and not be deceived. Also, you should know that I am not taken in by these strategies."

Dr. Rombach asked to have privacy the coming Sunday afternoon.

"You can stay in the living room with the doors closed," he instructed Marianna.

"We'll come down around five and have dinner together."

Marianna wandered through the streets Sunday afternoon and returning somewhat early sat on the backporch steps and smoked. She didn't understand why it pained her to think that upstairs her father was alone with May Picnic. She had decided that she really liked May, and she wasn't jealous. But to think of her upstairs with her father made her want to cry. After a while she heard her father bring May to the front door. She left without seeing Marianna.

"Oh, here you are," her father said entering the kitchen. "May had to go home. She asked me to tell you how sorry she was that she didn't have a chance to see you. She'll call you tomorrow evening or Tuesday."

May Picnic called Tuesday afternoon. She asked Marianna to come over to see her Wednesday after school.

In the evening Marianna reported to her father her telephone conversation with May at his request. Dr. Rombach acknowledged her account while cutting his wieners, then proceeded to read aloud from the local newspaper how a mother accidentally electrocuted her child when the toaster fell into the kitchen sink, where she was bathing the baby.

"By the way," he added as he rose wiping his mouth, "I think perhaps you ought to know that I have stopped seeing May privately. I am afraid I raised expectations I couldn't fulfill. Anyway, I think it is better so. I have told her this. She took it very courageously. Don't be surprised, however, if her interest in you will not be as intense as before. She might simply drop you. You must be prepared for that. We are still friends, but she was beginning to fall in love with me and I found this a burden. I explained this to her and she understood. In any case, I think she is going back to the West Coast."

It was raining when Marianna came out of school Wednesday afternoon. May received her warmly but somewhat of a rush. She was getting ready to go out for dinner, "…with a brain surgeon, isn't it exciting!" She was lining her eyes.

"Do take off your coat," May insisted. "I have a minute. I am so sorry I have to go out." She excused herself while she went to the bathroom to put on her stockings. "Oh, and your poems! May I keep them? I wanted to talk to you about them. When can we? I am leaving at the end of this week you know."

Marianna still stood in her dripping coat. She felt May wanted her to leave before the man came to pick her up.

"How is your father?" May called gayly from the bathroom.

"I have to go," Marianna said.

May rushed out of the bathroom and squeezed her arm.

"Will you call me tomorrow? We must see each other again."

Marianna understood that she meant goodbye.

When she reached the house the last patient had just left. Dr. Rombach was airing his office. Marianna remained standing before the front porch steps. After a while Dr. Rombach came out on the porch to pin a letter for the mailman on the mailbox.

"Oh," he said. "It's you. Why don't you come in?"

MEDEA

THE REFLECTION in the mirror was blurred: a dim white shape, the face in darkness.

First Isabel Marston buttoned the front of her wedding gown, then the long tight sleeves. The house was still. Beads of moisture formed on her scalp as her fingers worked twisting the heads through the tiny satin loops. There were sixty buttons. She skipped none; her hand did not cramp. Done, she reached for the knife on top of the dresser. Damp heat steamed up her back and through her dense hair.

She went out into the lit hall, bare feet kicking the long skirt aside, moved noiselessly over carpet and wood; she stopped only to listen. The house was still. Only the telephone lying off the hook signaled bleating faintly.

Barefoot, knife in hand, she followed the streak of light from the hall across the dark bedroom, stepping carefully along the floor strewn with toys.

A faint flare from the window diffused grayly over the humped shapes of the two children lying on their cots. One stirred. She stopped, head raised in the breathing dark. The small one in the crib by the window made some sucking sounds, drew up his knees. She stood holding her breath, eyes and ears straining, then moved on, knife in hand, stepping carefully.

The older boy lay huddled to the wall, back curved, the bunched sheet between his legs. Her foot sliding forward pushed a toy: it started off, grinding noisily hit against the leg of a chair; stopped. The boy sighed; a slender white arm rose slowly. He sighed again.

She took a long step, drawing close, stood leaning over him as he stretched turning on his back, slowly like a swimmer, she watched him turn.

He looked up. A brief, blank look, her hand clamped down over his eyes. He let out a long blabbering wail. Knife poised, she held him by the temples. His arms flew up; a sudden scream rose from the other bed.

She brought her knees down on his struggling arms, knife raised, the face twisting in her hand, she struck, the blade missing the throat as his chin pressed down. Blood gurgled from the cut mouth. Short, shrill shrieks of fright ripped the dark. She clutched him by the hair, pulled back the head and struck. The blade slashed the bared throat. Sudden blood spurted, vaulting, a tall bright jet shot high and splashed her breast. Dark blood, slower, gushed filling the trench of the wound, ran down his side. His head fell back, lay still.

For a stunned instant she stared at the cut stalk, blood seeping through her skirt, screams, raw as the rent flesh swelled in the dark. The wet handle of the knife stuck to her hand.

She drew away. A dark pool had gathered in her lap, soaked through the folds of satin to her skin. As she rose it ran down her legs over her foot. Stepping heavily she moved toward the blurred white shape jumping up and down, the mouth screaming in the dark.

The hand clutching the knife had grown numb, but at the root of the arms force was gathering, a current streaming from under the shoulder blades lifted the arms. Sore and tingling the arms rose. One hand grabbed the child's waving arm and pulled; he tottered, lurched forward against her, the small fingers digging in her breast and arms. She struck blindly, driving the blade in his back, his side, between the ribs, stabbed at the hidden root of his cries; his face pressed against her shoulder, the small fingers clinging to her skin, she stabbed blindly at the buried heart.

Limp, the silent mouth gutted with blood, still he held her. One by one she unbent the tiny cramped fingers and drew away.

The floor littered with spectral objects was rising; she pressed it down, bare feet sticking to the boards, pressed down hard against the rising ground and followed the band of light out into the hall.

Isabel Marston sat down on the landing and waited. The blood hardened on the front of her dress. The dry blood pulled on the skin. In the silence she sat and waited. She was still waiting when the first morning light showed under the drawn shades. The house was still; only her breath rode up and down in short, hoarse jerks, as if someone else were panting inside her.

2

Isabel Marston stood motionless, arms folded, staring dully at the barred window while the two men seated themselves.

Dr. Seidler, dark, thickset, heavy jowled, pulled a thin folder from his briefcase and set it on the table before depositing his bulk in the chair.

"Please sit," he murmured.

She lowered herself slowly in the chair.

Dr. Willis, a slight freckled man with worried blue eyes, sat his chin sunk on his chest, twirling a strand of hair.

"Mrs. Marston," Dr. Seidler began and dropped his eyes on the open folder, "you are charged with the slaying of your two children, Richard, aged nine, and Malcolm, aged four, on the night of the fifteenth of August." He raised his dark, ash-ringed eyes.

"Yes. I killed them."

"Mrs. Marston, were you aware of what you were doing?"

"Yes."

Dr. Seidler pressed the tips of his spread fingers together forming a cage.

"Mrs. Marston, why did you do it?" His mouth shaped the words large as though she were deaf. "Do you know why you killed them?"

She was silent. Only her lids flicked.

"Did you act on a sudden impulse?"

"No."

"You had been planning to kill them for some time?"

"Yes."

"Since when?"

"I don't know."

"You don't remember? Was it a few days? Weeks? Months?" She did not answer.

"Mrs. Marston," he leaned forward heavily, "do you feel any repentance or horror for having killed them?"

Her eyes widened. "Everyone must feel horror," she said tonelessly.

"But you are not sorry that you killed them?"

She stared, silent, her mouth set resolutely.

"You are not sorry?" Dr. Seidler repeated.

"No." She stared at him steadily till he dropped his eyes.

"How old are you Mrs. Marston?" Dr. Willis asked, lifting his chin suddenly.

"Thirty-two."

"How many years have you been married?"

"Ten."

"Any other children beside Richard and Malcolm?"

"I lost a child last spring. In the sixth month."

"You wanted more children?"

"Yes."

"What is your husband's occupation?"

"An art dealer."

"Where was your husband the night you killed your children?"

"I don't know. We weren't living together."

"Had you jointly agreed to separate?"

"He left me. He was living with another woman." She spoke with her head turned to the side, the lips barely moving.

"Since when was your husband living with another woman?" Dr. Willis asked.

"I don't know. I was in Rome expecting our third child."

"What were you doing in Rome, Mrs. Marston?"

"My husband was looking for Etruscan objects; so we took a house in Rome last winter."

"Was he living with you then?"

"Yes. We were expecting our third child."

"Where were you and your husband living before you went to Rome?"

"Different places. We have been traveling ever since we were married. Alexandria. Crete. Istanbul. I don't remember all the places."

"It must have been hard on you having to move around so much with the children."

She looked down on her hands.

"And you were expecting your third child—"

"We would have been settled by then," her hand rose to her mouth. "He promised to arrange things so he wouldn't have to travel. By September, he said."

"Here in the States?" His worried eyes blinked probing her fixed look of incomprehension.

"He didn't know then. He left for New York in April."

"Why didn't he take you with him?"

"It was only for a short trip, he said. Two weeks. A month at most."

"But he did not return as he promised?"

"He needed more time to settle his business, he wrote."

"Did you press him to return?"

"No. I believed he was arranging things for us. He kept writing things were developing. Then I had to go to the hospital."

"When was that?"

"May."

"And when did you join your husband in New York?"

"June. The fifteenth."

"Did you leave Rome because you began to suspect something?"

"No."

"He had never been unfaithful to you before?"

"I had no suspicions when I left. He was my husband and I wanted to be with him. Then I arrived and found out that he had lied to me about this trip. Perhaps lied about the others."

"How did you find out, Mrs. Marston?" Dr. Seidler asked.

"He made no secret of it. They were always together. He said she was useful to him professionally among other things. He didn't see anything wrong with it."

"But you Mrs. Marston resented his having an affair with this woman?"

"I asked him what he intended to do. 'About what?' he asked. I told him: 'About the woman. About us. About everything.' He didn't see that there was anything to decide. He was in the midst of important negotiations and couldn't be bothered. I told him: 'Then I must decide.' 'It's your problem, isn't it?' he said." She spoke rapidly in a low voice.

"And what did you decide, Mrs. Marston?"

"He never had time to talk. He was always leaving. Then he stopped talking to me. He only came to see the children. He had keys. I latched the door. He rang and shook the door on the chain till the children screamed to let him in. Then he wanted a divorce. My consent to a divorce. He threatened to take away my children. To deprive me of custody—"

"On what grounds, Mrs. Marston?" Dr. Seidler asked.

"He said I was crazy. Demented. He said it before the children."

"Were you crazy, Mrs. Marston?" Dr. Willis asked sympathetically.

"My behavior wasn't civilized, he said. He had deceived me, lied to me, scorned me. He had broken my life and I didn't take a sensible attitude. I wasn't friendly to his mistress. Then he claimed I drove him out of the house. Because I was crazy."

"Mrs. Marston," Dr. Willis pursued, "can you think of any particular act your husband held against you as evidence that you were crazy?"

"He said I tried to put the house on fire and kill the children."

"Did you?"

"No. I was just burning papers. It made a lot of smoke. One of the children woke up and got frightened and told him."

"What did you burn?"

"Letters we had written each other. Pictures. Things I had kept over ten years."

"Why did you burn them?"

"He made everything we lived together a lie. Meaningless."

"Where did you burn these things?"

"In the kitchen. On the tile floor. Nothing caught fire. Only the legs of a chair were burnt. He made a big thing out of it."

"When did this happen?"

"Some weeks ago. I don't remember exactly."

"Mrs. Marston," Dr. Seidler asked, "What financial agreement did you make with your husband when he left you?"

"None. I would accept none."

"But he offered to provide for you?"

"Yes. But I wouldn't accept money. Not from his hands."

"How did you manage?"

"I managed," she said coldly. "I had some antique jewels he left with me in Rome. I sold them."

"Didn't they belong to your husband, Mrs. Marston," Dr. Willis asked, "part of his business?"

"I helped to smuggle them out of Greece three years ago. But say I stole them. What difference does it make?"

"How long could you have managed on that?"

She did not answer.

"Mrs. Marston," Dr. Seidler asked, "why didn't you sue your husband for a divorce. Did you consider that at all? It was he who wronged you, after all. You could have taken him to court and made him pay."

"Pay?" she murmured. "Pay, for breaking my life? For making the lives of my children futile and ugly? There is no money that could pay for that."

"Still," Dr. Seidler pursued, "you could have made it very unpleasant for him. No man likes to be dragged through scandal, litigation—"

"How? Drag him through dirt when all his dirt reflects on me! No," she said softly, "I'd rather drag him down with me to hell. It was I who was made ridiculous. I who was dishonored. I, not he. He wasn't ashamed. He and his mistress went around to dinners and parties having a good time. He didn't think he had done anything wrong. Other men had done what he did and other women had accepted it.

I was alone screaming at a wall, What have I done wrong that I'm left here with these two children after ten years of loving him—there never was another man in my life, I wouldn't have been able to look my children in the eye. And now to degrade myself one step further by taking it to court, making it public."

"He was guilty of adultery. Any court would have granted you a settlement entirely in your favor. Were you aware at the time of your legal rights?"

"What could I gain by a legal settlement? Cut him out of my life on a piece of paper, and he walks away, free to live another life as if nothing happened, as if there never had been anything between us."

"A legal settlement would have made you equally free. You would have been just as free to start a new life."

"I know all about the kind of freedom a woman with two children after ten years of marriage can have. I have seen those women—they're all over the world. They are lucky if they find a man to marry them. Anybody. They're lucky if they find anyone even to sleep with them. I have seen how those women live; both the ones that parade themselves and the ones that never go out of the house. I have listened to these women and seen what happens with their children.

"No.

"A man does what he does and walks away. It's not the same thing for a woman. She belongs to the children she conceived in bed with him: her body, her breasts, her heart, her hands belong to them. He walks away and I'm left with the monthly payments for raising the children he denied. And to have to look at him when he comes around to visit them, once a week, once a month, once a year, or ever again. To have to look at the children. Hear their voices every morning; and to have to answer their questions: 'What are we going to do today?,' 'What should we put on?,' 'What are we going to have for breakfast? For lunch? For supper?,' 'When is Daddy coming again?' To have to look at them every day and not understand why they are there, why I must look at them. Look at them and not see them, but always something else. Him. The nights I loved him, the day I married him, the first time I looked at him, and so on, further back, see only incoherence and the horror."

She looked up.

"If I offered a sum of money to compensate for the lives I have taken, would any court accept such a payment? No. No court would. Nor would I for what he did to my life."

"So you made him pay with your children's lives," Dr. Seidler said gravely.

"They were mine. My children. I brought them into the world."

"Do you believe that gives you the right to kill them? A special right," Dr. Willis asked, "the fact that you brought them into the world?"

"Yes," she said simply, "I do."

"Mrs. Marston, you have killed your children out of sheer vengefulness, do you deny it?" Dr. Seidler asked.

"You don't understand," she said, shaking her head slowly, "Nothing touched him. My life was in his hands. I could not even plead, it mattered so little to him; less than one of those rare objects he'd risk everything for, not because he wanted it to keep and enjoy but only for the prestige of the acquisition and the profit he'd make in reselling it. He bought only to sell. And I mattered to him even less. He wouldn't even see what he had done to me. He couldn't see."

"You killed the children to make him understand how deeply he wronged you?"

"No. Not to make him understand. He saw what I did, saw their bodies; but he did not understand any more than I understood. I did not do it to make him understand, but to confound him as I was confounded."

"You wanted to make him suffer as he had made you suffer."

"It was the only way I had to his heart. He left me no other way."

"Mrs. Marston," Dr. Willis asked, "do you feel absolutely no repentance, or—" he hunched his shoulders, "fear of judgment?"

"Judgment has been passed. What the courts decide to do with me is utterly irrelevant."

"Did you pass judgment, Mrs. Marston? You alone?"

She was silent.

"Did a voice command you to do it?"

"Yes."

"Was it your voice or somebody else's?"

"Nobody's. A voice. A judgment."

"What did the voice say to you?"

"*You will kill them. When they are asleep, you will take the knife from the kitchen drawer and kill them.*" She spoke slowly, a trace of sadness in her voice.

"It was not your own voice?"

"I was crying. The voice was quiet and firm. I kept saying, *no*. For a long time I said, *no, I can't*. It was difficult to accept. But that night, when the voice said, *you will do it now*, I didn't say no. I was silent. Then it was simple."

"When exactly did you first hear the voice?" Dr. Willis asked.

"The morning of the day I married Lance Marston."

"But that was before you had children—"

"I was putting on my wedding gown; I was buttoning the front of the dress when I heard the voice."

"What did it say to you then?"

"*If he breaks trust, there will be blood.*"

"Did it say anything else?"

"No. Just that. *If he breaks trust, there will be blood.*"

"And when did you hear the voice again?"

"When I realized that everything was over."

"Did it tell you to kill the children then?"

"It just said, *blood, blood.*"

"Did you ever think of killing your husband's mistress?"

"No. She is nothing to me."

"Of killing your husband?"

"Yes, but I couldn't."

"Why couldn't you?"

"Because of the children. I couldn't kill their father."

"Were you afraid of your children?" Dr. Willis asked. "Were you afraid of their judgment?"

She was silent. Her lids rolled down.

"What did you do all day on the fifteenth of August?" Dr. Seidler asked.

"Nothing. It was like all the other days."

"You got up and made breakfast for the children?"

"No. He came in the morning. They had breakfast with him."

"Did you see your husband?"

"I was in bed when I heard the doorbell ring. He kept ringing and banging and rattling on the chain."

"Why didn't you open the door?"

"I couldn't stand the way he looked at me."

"Did the children let him in?"

"Yes. I heard them running to the door and greeting him."

"Were the children fond of your husband?"

"Yes. They saw so little of him. When he came he always brought them presents and played with them."

"Around what time did he come?"

"I don't know. I lay with my eyes closed. They made a lot of noise, tearing open packages, laughing and shrieking. He brought them a toy tank that made an awful grinding noise. Then all of a sudden he was banging on my door. I said, 'Don't come in.' But he burst in the door, the children after him. I said, 'Get out!' and pulled the sheet over my face. He told me I was not reasonable. He tried to rip the sheet off my face. I was ashamed before the children."

"What did your husband want?"

"To talk about the papers. The divorce. To sign the papers."

"How long did he stay?"

"They left before lunch."

"What did you do the rest of the day?"

"We went out. I had promised to take them rowing in the park. We went shopping. Then we came home."

"You spoke to no one else that day?"

"My husband called in the evening. He said he would bring the papers again tomorrow. He wanted to know if I would sign. I said I would. I would sign."

"Had you any intention of signing the next day?"

She did not answer.

"What did you do after you put the children to bed?"

"I cleaned up in the kitchen."

"What were you thinking about?"

"Nothing. I washed the dishes. Wiped the table. Mopped the floor."

"When did you get the knife?"

"Later. I cleaned up downstairs. The living room. The stairs. It was past midnight."

"What did you do after you got the knife?"

"I went to my room. I dressed."

"Why did you have to dress, Mrs. Marston, in the middle of the night?"

"I put on my wedding gown."

"Why?"

"To get blood on it."

"Why?"

"Because it was betrayed. Then I would be strong and pure again. As on the day I first put it on."

"What did you do after you killed them?"

"I hid them."

"But your husband saw their bodies."

"I hid them afterwards. I wanted him to see so that their blood would stick to his eyes."

"Why didn't you want other people to see their bodies?"

"No," Isabel Marston said, "no one else will ever look at them or touch their bodies or visit their graves."

"What did you do with their bodies, Mrs. Marston?"

"I told you. I hid them. All three bodies are hidden with me."

"Did you bury the children somewhere?"

"I won't tell you. They are my children. It does not concern anyone else."

"We would only like to understand—"

"I have nothing more to say."

Isabel Marston rose abruptly and went to the window which was a darkening red now.

3

The cell had no window. Isabel Marston stared at the three dim bars of light on the wall. She lay motionless on a narrow iron cot and listened. When she heard a noise she pulled the rough gray blanket over her head.

The questioning went on for many more days. But Isabel Marston had nothing more to say. Others answered for her; they offered explanations and arguments. She was silent. Their judgment did not concern her. She had finished.

She had finished with them. Now she was preparing her flight. Under the dark blanket her mouth moved, shaping words carefully. Sometimes she let out a scream.

She had to be careful. They were still looking for the children. She heard footsteps, muted voices. Suddenly there would be heads turning toward her. She made their faces warp and dissolve as they came close, like reflections in turgid water. She had outwitted them. The children were inside her, all three, three hearts beating.

She lay in the dark with her mouth open, a child panted inside her. The small girl was panting. The two boys lay quiet on each side. If they made a noise, she screamed like a madwoman to cover their cries. In a little while she would join them and they would stop crying for her; they would all be safe in the big house. She had to be careful while she prepared her flight.

The house was there, all ready for her; she had only to enter. But something weighed her down, an enormous rock, a mountain of sheer granite; she felt its weight in her back and her arms. Someone lay crushed under that rock. It was not the children. The children were safe with her. It was not she. She looked at her hands clutching the edge of the blanket, she unbent her fingers one by one. It was not she: someone connected with her, a part of herself. It did not matter. The rock was so heavy no one would ever be able to lift it and see who was under it. She let go. She left it. She became light. She was free.

Inside her there was space, more space than she had ever known, wide meadows, forests, streams, and it was all hers. The sun too was inside, her own sun, it made everything shine like gold.

The children were happy in the big house. Now they had all the room they needed, room to play, room for their pets, their toys and for all the things they liked to collect, seeds, shells, stones, birds' eggs, bones, butterflies and sticks, they could bring everything inside the house. There was room for everything she wanted to keep for her children, for all the linen and dresses and jewels she was keeping for her daughter. They played all day in the sun. The dress she wore was not white or red or black. It was gold.

The others could not enter inside her space. She had deceived them: for them she was like dead, a bound mummy in a coffin. Once in a hundred years they were allowed to raise the lid and look at her.

"I am complete," she told them, because they brought her gifts. She looked at their tawdry offerings, tin plates and cups, a faded towel.

"I am complete," she said. She did not tell them that all their wealth was inside her.

"I am complete," Isabel Marston told them when they bared her face. More she would not say.

No one ever found her children's slain bodies.

EASTER VISIT

HESTER stands in the door. Hester my cousin. I sit bent over my desk studying a map and don't raise my eyes. I feel her eyes all over the room. Her gaze flits from my sleeve to the washbowl, across the bedspread, and back to my hand. It circles around my temples like a drunken bee, grazes my ear, and alights on my lip. I am afraid if I move it will sting me in the eye.

She walks so lightly that I am not aware of her standing at my elbow, until I see the thin, freckled hand place a saucer of milk before me. I am sure the milk is poisoned, but I close my eyes and gulp it down quickly. When I open them she is gone.

Hester stands at the foot of my bed. My cousin Hester, wrapped in a sheet. She calls me by my name, but I do not answer. I lie naked on top of the blankets, my eyes wide open in the dark. She holds the sheet drawn gravely over her head, and her mouth spreads in a wide involuntary smile.

She skirts my bed, feeling her way lightly along my leg. Then runs her palm across my loin, furtively like a child touching the marble balls of a statue. I hold my breath while her hand moves up my side. Just as she is about to slide in my armpit, I grab her wrist and pull. Her naked body glides over mine; she hugs me between her knees and flips from side to side. I dig my fingers in her scalp. Her hair is damp at the roots like wild grass that grows in swamps. Her hair is all colors like wild grass at the end of winter when the ice is beginning to thaw, when the frozen ground cracks into puddles, and the water seeps through one's soles. I twist her hair between my knuckles; she pulls herself up till her mouth lies open on mine and dives after my tongue.

"Your tongue is rooted like a snail," she says, after we have done. "It will die if I tear it out." And once more her limbs hug my ribs and thighs and twine like the tentacles of an amorous tropical squid.

We sway entangled, quiver and clasp, then close like the two valves of a calm.

Hester wakes up first. She sits up holding her head.

"I've never been so alone," she cries.

We meet in the street. Hester looks weird with makeup. Her face looks painted on like a clown's or like an African spirit mask. Her mouth slides past the lipstick, and her pale eyebrows grow all wild, and skip over the thin black line she has drawn across them.

Cars race past before and behind us. Planes roar over our heads. Mobs of people, hunched under umbrellas, push against us. I throw my coat over her head, grab her arm and we run.

Tonight we do not need to make love. We lie on the rug with only our fingertips touching and talk till daybreak.

"I want to throw my life away," Hester says. "I wish I had it to throw away a hundred times." She tells me how. All the hundred ways.

But when we go to sleep, our parts fit together like pieces in a Chinese puzzle.

We have tied ourselves into a hundred and one different knots. But Hester will not find peace until she has pulled my veins apart and wrapped herself in my entrails.

"You're all smooth and hard like a marble statue," she complains. "You're all sealed up."

I say nothing. I lie and gaze quietly at her breasts while her trembling fingers run across my mouth.

"You should have a cunt," she whispers, and tumbles over me like a waterfall, caressing me wildly. I hold her firmly. My palms, supporting her haunches, press against the flat bone that rises from her back, and I slip her on like a ring.

Hester wants to offer our bodies to a bird of prey in whose belly our substances would at last be indissolubly mingled.

"Your eyes are green like oysters," she hisses behind clenched teeth. And sets to work with the tip of her tongue to gouge them out.

"Nothing more can come of this," I keep telling her. "It's a good thing you're leaving soon." But Hester isn't listening.

"Water me!" she gasps. Her head rolls off the bed, and I pee in her ear.

We sit on the floor huddled under a towel after a shower, and try to imagine ourselves a month from now.

"I shall be sitting in an igloo in the Arctic," I say, "drawing maps for the navy, in thick fur-lined gloves and boots, my back itching under six sweaters and chilblains on my nose."

"I shall be sitting on the back porch steps in Virginia," Hester says, "with a basket of wash in my lap, wondering what to do next; iron the shirts or bathe the baby, or put Eddie on the pot or the roast in the oven, or feed the cat."

And we laugh till Hester stops my mouth with a kiss.

"We're being silly," she murmurs tearfully, and cradles my head in her arms.

Hester leaves in another day. Her impending departure does not seem to affect our mood. Perhaps we cannot believe in anything beyond the present. And certain of our doom, we walk to it poised like actors in a play who know on which line the curtain comes down.

We spend our last evening on the tower of the Empire State Building. Hester presses her body against the railing, bends over and leans out as far as she can. I follow her. The wind whips her hair in my eyes; as our heads hang in midair, we kiss.

THE GOLD CHAIN

ROSALIE was long dead and buried. Rosalie and her child rested with the earth. And slowly like all the others who were laid inside the earth, she rose up in the branches, rose all the way along the worm's path through the apple into the appleseed. Rosalie crawled away with nine snails and forty-nine caterpillars; she flew up scattering in a swarm of little white butterflies. Rosalie walked with the wind. Only a little pile of gold remained still glittering in the dark earth. Rosalie rolled with the creek and turned with the whirlpool. She turned and she turned.

A child stood waving a stick in a field at the edge of the forest. He lashed the tall grass with shouts of joy. Stamping and leaping he beat the ground and stabbed at the sky. Before him stood the forest like a dreadful bride, all still and white under a hoary shroud wound by billions of tiny blind worms.

It rained on Rosalie's wedding day. Her bridegroom was very shy and delicate as a child; he had gentle oldish eyes. His face was smooth except for a small dark beard on his chin, and for a wedding present he gave Rosalie a long gold chain that once belonged to his dead grandmother. Sylvanus Thrush stood waiting for her before the train station under a black umbrella with a package in brown wrapping paper under his arm. Rosalie ran all the way from home, leaping over the big puddles so her stockings wouldn't get splashed.

—Quick! he said, put on your dress, the train is leaving in a few minutes.

—Where shall I put it on? Rosalie asked.

—Why, in the lady's powder room. Where else?

Rosalie stood before the mirror in the lady's powder room pulling at the hem of her dress. The skirt was just a bit too short. Rosalie had such knobby knees she hated for them to show. She tugged at the hem trying to make it stretch over her knee, but as soon as she let go it rode up higher than it was before. Rosalie scowled at herself in the mirror and left the room.

After the wedding they strolled through the crowd in the square. Vendors came selling toys and balloons, candy, flowers and drinks. There was a man playing the fiddle with a monkey on a chain. The monkey jumped around to the music making cartwheels and summersaults and people began to dance.

—Oh look, Sylvanus! Rosalie cried clutching his hand, can we dance too?

—Why, yes, Rosalie, if you like, Sylvanus said, and putting his trembling hand on the small of her back he stepped once to the left and once to the right.

Sylvanus turned her slowly, he hopped like a sparrow and grinned foolishly. Every now and then Rosalie broke away and turned by herself, she turned very fast till she was dizzy and fell into his arms. Everybody was dancing, children and couples, even old people, some hobbling on crutches. It had grown quite dark now, the streetlights went on and the rain started again in a soft drizzle. The crowd had dispersed and they were hurrying down narrow, deserted streets.

—Watch your step! Sylvanus kept saying.

Rosalie felt something sway under her. She looked down and saw a sudden glint of water. Above her head all the stars throbbed in the naked sky. They were crossing the gangplank of a ship. There was a dining room inside. They sat down and Sylvanus ordered a big meal. Rosalie ate everything to the last crumb of her pie. The ship did not seem to be moving. She looked out the porthole and saw the shore-lights as close as they were before. Sylvanus stood up.

—Come now, Rosalie, he said, or we'll miss the last bus home.

Rosalie got up, then suddenly turned pale.

—Oh Sylvanus, she whispered, can you put your coat around me? I'm afraid I have stained the seat of my dress.

—Why, so you have, Sylvanus laughed softly and wrapped his coat around her shoulder.

It was near midnight when they got off the bus. They had to walk some time before they reached the house; not a single window along the whole street was lit. At last they were inside.

Rosalie stood with her head bent before the bed.

—I am so sorry it happened on our wedding night, she said.

Sylvanus worked all week. Next Sunday morning when Rosalie heard his footsteps coming up the stairs she ran out to meet him. She threw her arms around his neck, she kissed him and squeezed him and pulled him in the door.

—Let me rest a little, my dear, Sylvanus said. And as soon as he sank into the armchair he fell asleep. Dusk was setting in and Sylvanus still sat slumped in the armchair snoring softly; only the whites of his eyes showed between the lids. Rosalie set the soup on the table loudly. Sylvanus woke up with a snort, rubbed his eyes and came to eat.

After the meal Rosalie went into the other room and put on her nightgown. After a while she came out and stood in the door barefoot with her hair loose.

—I'm all right now, Sylvanus, Rosalie said.

—I am so glad, Sylvanus said. He rose and his small mouth touched the tip of her chin. Goodnight now, Rosalie. Sleep well. And he went and lay down on the couch in his clothes.

When Sylvanus came in to say goodbye to Rosalie the next morning, he found her sitting up in bed playing with her gold chain. She poured the links from hand to hand as if she were weighing the gold.

—Till next Sunday, he said, and blew her a kiss.

—Did you remember to leave some money in the pocket of my white dress? she asked, still playing with her chain.

—Have you spent the month's allowance I gave you last time, Rosalie? Sylvanus asked.

Rosalie just played with her chain.

—On what, Rosalie? Soft drinks and games and ice cream on market day? He laughed and put some silver coins in her palm.

Rosalie decided to buy Sylvanus something nice he could wear at home instead of the shabby gray suit he wore for work. She loitered a long time before the old clothes dealer's stand. She rummaged through a box of bright feathers. She turned every dress on the rack. She wasn't going to buy anything for herself: she just wanted to look. A pale flame-colored dress caught her eye. It was the color Rosalie had always dreamed of, just that shade of red!

—How much is it? she asked the woman.

—You can't wear that, she said, shaking her head.

Rosalie remembered that she came to buy a present for Sylvanus. There was a big box with a jumble of things. She pulled out a little red jacket with gold buttons and a pair of blue silk pants; she pulled out a Turk's hat with black fringes. He'll look like a prince in that! she thought.

—How much? Rosalie asked.

The woman looked from the corner of her eye and gave her a lopsided smile. It cost next to nothing. Rosalie gave her a paper bill and put the change in her pocket. She was saving up for that red dress. On her way home she bought some blue thread because the pants had a lot of holes and tears.

Rosalie sewed half the night. She was up early heating water for a bath.

—How shall I go about it now? she wondered. Give him his present first and his bath last? Or bathe him first? But he will want to sleep after his bath and then I won't see him in his nice new clothes. But if I dress him first, he won't want to get undressed again and I will have heated all that water for nothing. In any case he'll want to sleep. In any case, whichever I'll do, I'll have to undress him first.

Rosalie ran down the stairs to meet Sylvanus and threw her arms around his neck.

—Come quick, Sylvanus, she urged, pulling him up the stairs and into the room, I have something for you! When they were in she tore off his coat and grabbing his foot began to tug at the shoe. Sylvanus hopping on one foot laughed protesting.

—Rosalie, you dear, dear child—I'm quite used to sleeping in my clothes—but if you wish—

Rosalie pulled off his jacket, she pulled off his shoes and socks; she began to unbutton his shirt when Sylvanus caught her hands.

—What are you doing, Rosalie! he gasped.

—I'm going to give you a bath Sylvanus, she said, I've got the water all ready in the tub—

—Oh no, Rosalie, what are you thinking of—

—Yes. Yes. Yes. She pleaded as she unbuttoned his shirt.

—But why, Rosalie? he asked holding on to his pants.

—Because you're my husband, Rosalie said and unhooked his suspenders, I have a right to it.

Sylvanus dropped his hands and looking at the ground said,

—It's as you please, Rosalie. I suppose you have. In another minute he stood in his drawers which were many sizes too large for him and hung down to his knees. Rosalie drew in her breath and started unfastening the safety pin that held up his drawers. But Sylvanus clutched her hand.

—I can't. I can't, he cried, his eyes glazed with tears, please don't do it, Rosalie.

Rosalie stepped back. She felt tears filling her throat.

—If you're really so shy, she said and her voice broke, I guess I love you all the more. Then she went and got the clothes she'd bought and showed them to him.

—Please put them on, she begged, holding the blue silk pants for him to step in. Sylvanus sighed. He looked at the pants and he didn't seem pleased.

—Oh please, Sylvanus, Rosalie begged, stroking his leg.

—Oh I'll do it to please you, Sylvanus said crossly. But you do make me feel silly.

Rosalie dressed him up. Jumping and squealing with glee she pulled his feet through the blue silk pants, pulled his arms through the sleeves of the red jacket, buttoned the gold buttons and pressed the Turk's hat with the black fringe down over his head. She danced around him, clapping her hands and laughing. She laughed so hard she had to hold her ribs and squat. Sylvanus stood blinking, a miserable look on his face. Rosalie caught him in her arms.

—Oh Sylvanus, what am I going to do with you! she cried, and squeezed him so tight that he croaked like a frog.

—May I take them off now? Sylvanus asked when she let go.

—All right, Rosalie said, Get ready for your bath. You can undress in the bathroom if you like. But I insist on washing your back. The next time you can wash mine.

—I guess you won't give me peace till I do, Sylvanus said and went.

Sylvanus sat in the tub, his face very pink looking down on his scrawny chest. The water had turned a thick soapy gray, hiding the submerged part of his body.

I've washed all but my back, Rosalie, Sylvanus said.

Rosalie washed his back; she took long caressing him up and down with her palm. Then she wrapped him in a towel and helped him out of the tub.

—Why do you weep, my dear? Sylvanus asked.

—For happiness, Rosalie sighed and twined her arm around him. Come lie on the couch and I'll rub you down.

And Rosalie rubbed him up and down, she squatted over him, her knees straddling his slight waist, she bounced up and down and she rubbed, while Sylvanus squirmed and kicked, giggling helplessly.

—Oh please—don't tickle—Rosalie! Stop tormenting me!—he

howled and thrashed about wildly clutching the towel around him while Rosalie's little fingers sneaked under the edges and crept all over him. Sylvanus lay doubled up in stitches, his chin clamped between his knees; Rosalie rolled him around, she poked her finger in his ears, his eyes, his mouth, his nose, she poked him down the spine, but when she reached a certain spot Sylvanus croaked—No, no, Rosalie—dirty, dirty! and tossed her off the couch. Rosalie got on her knees, she grabbed his foot and tickled it and licked his sole.

—Stop! Sylvanus sobbed, I can't stand it—you'll kill me!

Rosalie sat back on her heels and crossed her arms with a grin. Sylvanus lay panting, his eyes closed, his streaming face which was very red a minute ago had suddenly turned gray. The towel had slipped off. Rosalie looked at him nude. She saw the skin rolling over his ribs as he gasped for air, she saw the heart skipping under his skin like in a newborn chick and she saw a little red thumb pointing in the air between his thighs.

—Cover me, Sylvanus moaned weakly. Rosalie took his hand that dangled over the side of the bed and tugged it as if she were tolling a bell.

Sylvanus opened his eyes, his face haggard.

—What is it Rosalie? he brought out feebly. What is it you want of me?

—Nothing, Rosalie said and let go of his hand. Nothing, Sylvanus. And she crouched on the floor beside him, hugging her knees, and rocked slowly back and forth on her heels.

Next morning when Sylvanus was leaving for work Rosalie followed him to the door.

—I wish you wouldn't go away for so long, she complained. We have never spent more than a day together.

—It's like this, Rosalie, Sylvanus explained. I must be away and work all week if I'm to spend Sunday with you. I must be away and work a fortnight if I'm to spend Saturday with you as well. And I must be away and work a month if I'm to stay a whole week with you. So you have your choice.

Rosalie hung her head.

—I guess I'd rather you worked two weeks and stayed with me two days in a row.

—It's as you please, Rosalie, Sylvanus said and left.

Rosalie had time on her hands. She sat on the windowsill winding her chain around her middle finger. She tried to sing but her voice was so faint it died in the middle of the phrase.

—I'll make myself a new dress, she thought and cut up a sheet and ruined it and cried.

Rosalie had long, long hair. It reached all the way down to the end of her spine. She wore it in a single braid, but now she opened it and sat combing it strand by strand. She filled the tub with water, knelt down and tossed her head, watching her hair float and sink. Rosalie took long washing her hair. Then she sat naked on the bed letting it dry. She looked down on her bush; it was reddish like her hair and very curly. The scissors with which she had cut the sheet still lay open on her bed. She took them and clipped her bush very short. So most of the day passed.

Sylvanus slept most of Saturday. And when he embraced Rosalie before she went to bed he could feel the short stiff bristles prick him through her thin nightgown.

—What have you done, Rosalie? he asked.

Rosalie's face turned hot.

—I was clipping the ends of my hair, she said, and I'm afraid— Sylvanus, I want a baby!

—No, that's out of the question, Sylvanus said firmly. But I thought we might move into another house with lots of sun so that you can grow potted plants.

Rosalie came in after Sylvanus lay down on the couch Sunday night; she rose in the middle of the night and stood at his feet.

—Sylvanus, she called softly.

—What is it? he mumbled half in his sleep. Rosalie slipped off her nightgown.

—Sylvanus, she called, look—

Sylvanus blinked. He drew in his breath and closed his eyes. Rosalie kept calling his name in a small voice like a bird. She called and called till her voice broke.

Sylvanus sat up holding his hands before his eyes.

—What is it you want, Rosalie? What is it you want of me?

—I want you to give me a baby, she said in a singsong voice. Sylvanus sank back.

—Don't ask that of me, he groaned. Ask me anything but that.

—Well, then, Rosalie said in the same singsong voice, I want you to buy me a new dress. And lifting her nightgown from the floor she tied it in a knot and went back to bed.

Next morning when Sylvanus stood at the door ready to leave, Rosalie said to him:

—This time I'd rather you work a month and stay with me a week.

—It's as you please, Rosalie, Sylvanus smiled.

—And you better give me the money for the dress you promised before you leave.

—Why, of course, Rosalie, he said and handed her a paper bill.

Rosalie stuck the money under the band of her sleeve and turned sharply on her heels.

—Won't you give me a little kiss for it? Sylvanus asked, smiling foolishly.

—A month from now, maybe, Rosalie said, and closed the door in his face.

Saturday morning Rosalie went to the market, she went straight to the old clothes stand and took the flame-colored dress off the rack.

—How much is it? she asked.

—I told you it's not your size, the woman said.

—It's for someone else, Rosalie lied, and I want to know the price. The woman named the sum, looking down on her hands.

—Here! Rosalie said between her teeth and handed her all the money she had. Fold it up nicely and put it in my basket.

Rosalie turned in front of the mirror in her new dress. It was just a bit loose on her.

—That's so I'll fill it out, she said and went out on a stroll.

It was Sunday and there was nobody on the street. When she got home she took her old white dress from the closet and tore it into dusting rags.

Saturday morning Rosalie went out in her red dress, the basket on her arm. She walked with her chin thrust out, swinging so her skirt swished and the gold chain bounced on her belly. Boys sat on the curb and teased her as she passed. Men stood before the stalls and turned around. Some laughed; some simply stared; some teased like the boys.

—Where are you going in that red dress, Rosalie?

—Tell us, where's the ball?

—Why are you carrying that empty basket?

—Watch out you don't trip on your chain!

They threw nutshells, bruised grapes and tin coins in her basket. They came up close to touch her skirt and snatched at her chain. Rosalie walked on swishing her skirt and grinned. When she came to the end of the market she walked on out into the fields.

In the evening she passed through the market on her way home. Boys sat on the curb and teased. Men turned to look at her. Some laughed, some simply stared, some teased like the boys.

—What were you doing in that red dress out in the fields?

—Rosalie makes love by herself in the bulrushes!

—Take me with you next time!

—Haven't you filled that basket yet? You better hurry, the market's closing!

Rosalie lay down in the tall grass and dreamed. She dreamed of rain. The rain drove down like a hundred thousand lances piercing her with long silver points. She dreamed of lightning and tall silver blades of grass rising up around her. She dreamed of thin slanting whips of rain lashing her across the face, swift, dark and silver. She dreamed of rain drizzling down like fine silver from the moon and covering her.

Someone was coming. Rosalie shut her eyes tight and breathed in deep. A man was coming through the tall grass. He stepped out from between the trees, a man tall as a tree, tall and straight as a tree trunk from his armpits down to his heels, came striding through the tall grass parting it with his thighs. Rosalie shut her eyes and breathed in deep.

When she opened her eyes the sun was sliding down the sky.

Next Saturday Rosalie walked through the market in her red dress holding the gold chain in her fist. And when she passed a group of young men she dropped the chain on the ground and walked on.

She walked out into the fields and lay down in the grass. She dreamed of rain pouring down till it filled the creek and the creek swelled into a river rolling over the fields.

Someone was coming. Rosalie shut her eyes tight and breathed in deep. A man was striding toward her through the tall grass; Rosalie did not look. He lay down beside her. When her hand reached out it touched his naked skin. He took her hand, he turned up her palm and filled it with the chain. Rosalie kept her eyes shut tight, thinking, If I look it's sin; but if I keep my eyes shut it's like it happened in my sleep.

—Put it around my head, she whispered. She clasped her hands behind his neck while he hung the chain and drew him down over her.

They rocked embraced from side to side. Rosalie laughed. Her face lay pressed against his chest and when she opened her eyes for an instant it was all dark. Rosalie moaned; her thighs clasped his sides and her belly rose. She lay with her head thrust back, she opened her eyes for an instant and saw nothing but sky. A bee hummed around her head; it settled in her hair and tapped on her scalp. Rosalie tossed her head from side to side. The bee got caught in her hair, it stung her in the ear. Rosalie did not cry out. She was breathing in deeply, sucking in the bee's sting with the whole expanse of sky till all space was inside her. Then Rosalie cried out. She shrieked like a bird shot in flight. Like a shot bird she came plummeting down through space turning faster and faster till she dropped to the ground and lay still. For a long time Rosalie lay still and unknowing. Then she felt the man moving around her, slowly moving away. She stretched out her hand blindly and touched his knee.

—Take the chain, she said and lifting it from her head held it out to him. Take it and come and meet me here two weeks from today.

The man took the chain from her hand. He kissed her eyelids.

—No, no, Rosalie whispered. If I look it's sin. And she rolled over on her belly, her face to the ground while he strode away.

Rosalie waited till after dark when the market closed. Then she got up and started walking slowly back home. Her skirt clung to her and her thighs stuck together as she stumbled through the fields.

Sylvanus came slowly up the stairs, stopping at every fifth step to catch his breath. Rosalie wasn't waiting for him on the landing or in the doorway. Sylvanus went in but she was not in the room.

—Rosalie, he called, and looked in the kitchen and in the bathroom, but she wasn't there. He called her name again but she did not answer. Sylvanus opened the bedroom door and saw Rosalie lying on the bed in a red dress, her hair open and her arms wreathed around her head.

—Are you asleep, Rosalie, he asked and tiptoed closer. Rosalie lay, her eyes wide open, staring into space and smiling.

—That's a very lovely dress you bought for yourself, Rosalie, he said and sat down on the edge of the bed. Very lovely indeed. Still she did not look at him.

—Rosalie, you promised me a little kiss when I came back, Sylvanus said timidly.

—Well, come and take it, she said.

Sylvanus bent down over her, when his beard touched her chin, she pulled him down by the ears and kissed him on the mouth so it hurt.

Sylvanus winced and drew back.

—Rosalie, you've bit me! he cried. Look, there is blood on my mouth.

Rosalie stepped out of bed and walked up and down before the window, making her skirt swish. Sylvanus stood staring at her, a handkerchief pressed to his mouth.

—What has gotten into you, Rosalie? he asked weakly.

Rosalie lifted her skirt and sat on the windowsill.

—If you won't give me a baby, she said, grinning, someone else will!

—Oh, no! Oh, no, Rosalie!

—Oh, yes! Oh, yes! she cried and hid her face in her hands so Sylvanus couldn't tell whether she was weeping or laughing. Sylvanus watched Rosalie as she rocked back and forth. He saw a white streak of flesh open down her side where the seam of her dress split, and he trembled.

—All right, Rosalie, he said breathing hard, have your will. I suppose you have a right to it. I'll do it, Rosalie—

And he came toward her, his eyes moist and his mouth drawn in a foolish smile.

Rosalie stepped down from the sill, she narrowed her eyes and thrust out her chin.

—You've kept me waiting seven weeks, she said between her teeth, I suppose I have a right to keep you waiting seven days. Anyway, I'm too sleepy now. And she lay down on the bed.

Sylvanus went out and curled up on the couch in his clothes; but he couldn't sleep.

All that week Sylvanus made the soup, Rosalie stayed in bed, or went out walking. Saturday morning he prepared a bath for Rosalie. He waited before the bathroom door till she said he could come in. Sylvanus gaped at Rosalie lying naked in the tub. He opened his mouth to say, O, and she threw the wet sponge in his face.

Sylvanus went out in the hall; he paced up and down on the landing, cracking his knuckles and biting his lip. When he went in Rosalie was sitting on the couch in her red dress sewing up the split seam. Sylvanus came up to her softly. He squatted down on the floor.

—I have a little present I'd like to give you tonight, Rosalie—

—What is it?

—I can't show you till you're in bed.

—Is it big?

—It's only about the size of my finger but if you take good care of it, it will grow till it's as big as a watermelon, Sylvanus said and laughed.

—Where will I keep it? Rosalie asked somberly.

—Under your heart.

—Won't it be too heavy?

—When it'll grow too heavy it will roll down on your lap.

—And I'll cut it open and eat it?

—No, Rosalie, that's not what I mean, Sylvanus moaned.

—Then you had better give it to someone else, Rosalie said and stalked off to bed, shutting the door behind her.

Sylvanus tiptoed into the bedroom in the middle of the night, but Rosalie was not in bed. She sat on the windowsill in her red dress holding her head.

—Don't cry, Rosalie, Sylvanus said. Lie down and close your eyes. I'm going to give you a baby tonight.

Rosalie lifted her head, her mouth was set in a sneer. She stepped down and crossed her arms.

—I'm not going to lie down or close my eyes, she said in a high singsong voice. I'm going to stand right here with my eyes open, looking hard. And if you want to give me a baby, you must pull down your pants and get down on all fours barking like a dog and try to take me from behind.

—Why do you ask this of me, Rosalie? Sylvanus whimpered.

—It's the way I've seen dogs do it, she said, and I wouldn't know how otherwise.

Sylvanus cracked his knuckles.

—Very well, Rosalie, if you insist. His eyes glittered, his small mouth was drawn in a smirk. He unhooked his suspenders and began to unbutton his pants; but Rosalie bolted to the door.

—Not here, out in the fields! Out in the fields! she cried as she ran out and down the stairs with Sylvanus after her, clutching his pants.

—I can't run so fast! Sylvanus gasped, but Rosalie went on running zigzag down the dark street. She darted between two houses into the fields behind.

—Where are you, Rosalie? Oh, Rosalie, have pity! she heard Sylvanus wheezing in the distance.

—Who will have pity on me! she laughed rushing through the grass. She ran till her knees buckled and she fell panting to the ground.

Sylvanus tripped and hurt his hip running in the fields. He caught a chill in the wet grass.

—I can't move, Rosalie, he moaned feebly and coughed.

Rosalie sat in a chair winding a ball of white wool.

—I'm so sorry Sylvanus, she said sweetly without lifting her eyes. But I'm afraid you must go out and work so that I and my baby will have something to eat.

And Sylvanus struggled into his coat and limped out of the house holding his side.

Rosalie went to the place where she gave away her chain a fortnight ago. She lay down in the grass and waited.

Someone was coming. She heard someone whistling in the distance. He was coming toward her whistling as he cut across the tall grass. Rosalie called out to him and closed her eyes. When she felt him close she reached out and touched the chain that dangled from his neck as he bent over her. Her hand moved to caress his face but he grabbed her wrist, pinned down her arms and crushed her under his weight. Rosalie wondered why he was so different this time. She started pleading with him, but he clamped a rough hand over her mouth. When his frenzy was spent he got up and left.

In a little while he came back. Rosalie was still crying. He came softly now. He stroked her hair, blew on her tear-stained cheek; he tickled her with the chain. And when she laughed he drew her to him gently. They embraced and the wonderful thing was that tall as she imagined him their two bodies fitted mouth to mouth, groin to groin, the tips of their outstretched hands touching. Rosalie cried out in bliss as on the very first time.

—Don't leave me, she pleaded when she felt him drawing away. She lay all limp in the grass and her voice was so weak she was afraid he didn't hear. But in a little while he was back. Her hands stretched out to clasp his neck; she caught her finger on the chain. But this time he came on her wildly again. He bit her and pinched her and flung her about till Rosalie screamed. When he had spent his frenzy he got up and left.

Rosalie lay in the grass shaking and crying. In another minute she wanted him again.

—Come back, she cried. Do what you want with me! She heard the man laugh not far away.

—Come, she begged. Come!

He was coming. Rosalie lay very still on her back, her arms crossed over her eyes; only her knees trembled. She felt the tip of his shoe against her bare leg. He pulled up her skirt, he threw it over her head, he forced her legs apart. Rosalie submitted, crying softly; he held her pinned down under his knees. Then he twisted her arm till she rolled over on her belly and took her from behind. Rosalie howled with pain. He rode her till she had no more strength to cry and left her whimpering on the ground.

—Give me back my chain! she sobbed. But he was gone.

Sylvanus winced when she told him she lost the chain.

—I lost it the night you gave me the baby, she lied. I've gone back a dozen times looking for it. Maybe someone took it.

Sylvanus looked at the ground and wrung his hands weakly. He was very thin now. His beard had turned all gray and he barely spoke at all. He still worked all week. When he came home Sunday Rosalie put him to bed; she fed him and washed him and nursed him all day.

I suppose if I sent him to work for a month I'd never see him again, she thought vaguely. She felt her belly. But it was still very small.

Rosalie lay awake at nights grieving. She missed her chain. Her hands stroked the sheet, they stroked the hard iron frame of the bed; they stroked anything they touched. She went out in the fields to the place where she had met her moody lover; she waited till long after sunset but he did not come. She went again the following Saturday and the Saturday after that and waited in vain.

Rosalie grieved that he took her chain and did not come to meet her. Night after night she paced her room; she opened the door to the stairway and listened, but he did not come. She wanted her chain.

—He stole it! He took the most precious thing I had! She swore and raged through the night. Then she softened, she calmed. When she lay down she thought of the chain lying against his skin and it soothed her to sleep.

Rosalie's belly grew and her breasts swelled out. She had to let out the seams of her dress. But Sylvanus was growing thinner all the time. His legs shriveled up, he had to use crutches. His face had shrunk to the size of a child's and his beard turned completely white. By the time Rosalie was eight months with child he was so wasted that she could easily carry him in her arms. She nursed him patiently, but Sylvanus only cried and complained.

—You want to starve me to death, he whined, when she brought him his soup, or you wouldn't bring me things you know I cannot eat.

—Are you trying to smother me! he groaned when she covered him with blankets.

—You're killing me, he whimpered when she opened the window to air his room.

—Drown me and get it over with, he rasped when she gave him his bath, since that's what's on your mind.

One bleak morning in March two workmen brought in Sylvanus covered with snow and laid him on the couch.

—What do you bring him to me for? Rosalie asked. Go and bury him.

—I'm sorry, ma'am, one of the men said, but he isn't quite dead. See his left lid twitch?

Sylvanus Thrush lay on the couch with his eyes closed for another week. Only his left eyelid twitched continually.

—Maybe there is a flea under it trying to get out, Rosalie thought and smelled him. She bent over close. Sylvanus opened his eyes: two dull gray balls rolled out from between the crumpled lids and lay in his wasted face big with reproach. He did not speak.

For another week Sylvanus lay on the couch, his eyes fixed on the wall. Rosalie paced the small room holding her bulging side. The baby thrashed about and kicked inside her belly. She wondered if he was going to break through the skin and her palms pressed down hard.

Rosalie bent over Sylvanus to see if he was dead. She looked at length in his glazed staring eyes. Then she saw his lips begin to move. They parted and pursed around a little hole in the middle. After a while a sound came out.

—Why? Sylvanus asked.

Rosalie looked at him indifferently.

—Why? Why? the mouth of Sylvanus Thrush said. And the eyeballs in his wasted face swelled and stood up as far as they could and said, Why have you done this to me?

Rosalie turned away. The mouth of Sylvanus Thrush kept saying, Why? Why? Why? It wouldn't stop. Rosalie clapped her hands to her ears to drown out the voice. A pain shot up her spine and Rosalie clutched her waist. It was silent in the room. The mouth of Sylvanus had stopped. She walked over to the couch. Sylvanus Thrush lay on his back, his knees drawn to his chin, stiff as a dead puppy. There was a gray film over his eyeballs and his mouth was rigidly pursed around the little dark hole in the middle.

Then Rosalie took a long needle and pierced his throat, just to make sure.

Sylvanus Thrush was dead.

—Ai! Rosalie cried. A pain flashed up her sides and down her thighs. She felt something inside her burst and come running down between her legs.

—Ai! Ai! Ai! she wailed and squatted down on the floor holding her haunches.

—Where did you get that baby, Rosalie? the boys jeered as she passed through the market.

—Do you want it? Rosalie asked without raising her eyes.

—Does he come with the basket?

—Can you make another one with a nose like this?

—With ears like this?

—With six toes?

Rosalie hastened her steps.

—What are you going to do with that baby?

Rosalie pulled the blanket over the baby's face and, her head lowered, pushed her way through the crowd. She walked out into the fields, she walked all the way to the edge of the forest. Then she put down the basket and lay down. The morning sun shone bright. She hid her face in her arm and tried to sleep.

—Hello, Rosalie! a man's voice called. Haven't you missed your chain?

He walked up to her. His shirt was open in the front. Rosalie saw the gold links gleam between the dark hairs, she saw his teeth white and straight in his jaw, but she did not move.

He lifted the chain over his head and held it out to her.

—Here, he said, don't you want it?

Rosalie stood motionless her head bent. The man laughed and hung the chain around her neck. Rosalie caught his hand.

—I don't know who you are, she said, but you're the father of my child.

—Maybe I am and maybe I'm not, he said, looking down on his shoes.

—You had my chain, she said. It was you who took it. You gave me this baby.

—Maybe and maybe not! The man laughed and prodded the chain with his thumb. That chain got around, you know! There were five fellows took turns with you. One the first time and four the second time. So how can anybody be sure?

The man was gone. Rosalie crouched in the grass crying.

—Well, at least I got my chain back, she laughed to herself, and a baby.

She awoke dazed, the sun right over her head, pointing a long light-spoke through the leaves. Rosalie reached into the basket for an apple, and instead touched a living child.

—Ai! she cried and rolled over her face to the ground. She heard the child whimper, a long muffled wail. Rosalie sat up on her knees, her face covered with earth, and crouched over the basket. The blanket had slipped over his head. She watched his feet kick and listened to him wail. When he grew more quiet she uncovered his head and saw he had a man's face, and the queer sad smile of an old man on his face. He opened his mouth and the voice of Sylvanus Thrush came out of him, his old, sick voice, whimpering, Why? Then Rosalie took off her gold chain and slipped it over the infant's head, she wound it around his neck twice and thrice then pulled on the chain and wound it a fourth time and a fifth, pulling harder, she wound it around his neck till she used up the length of the chain. She heard a voice calling from all around, now close, now far, a voice faintly taunting.

—What are you doing out in the fields Rosalie?

Rosalie let go of the chain.

—Nothing, she said, and sat back on her heels.

Rosalie looked into the forest, she looked for a tree with a man's head. But instead she saw the flat face of a child leering at her, big as the full moon on a summer night.

—Serves you right! he laughed and leaped about, showing his shimmering transparent limbs—Girl, girl, crazy girl!

Rosalie took the chain off the baby's head and ran after the child swinging the chain at him. She swung the chain in the air chasing him down the field, she swung it at his leering face in the trees, while he leaped about laughing and taunting.

—Look at her run, that wild thing! She will run and run swinging her crazy chain till it gets caught on a live branch, then she'll jump trying to get it clear till her chin gets caught in the loop. Then she'll begin to turn, she'll turn in a circle till she steps off the ground and her neck goes crack!

He was leaping about so fast all she could see was that he was silvery, for his shape kept changing as he moved about. When he leaped up high he thinned out to the length of a grown man but when he bounced against the ground he flattened into a round, silvery blob.

—Crazy, crazy, Rosalie! The child's jeers clanged like a bell, so loud they must have heard it in town.

Rosalie ran after him, she ran into the forest hooting and screeching and swinging her gold chain as she ran.

But the child was more cunning than she. He ducked down in the grass and let her rush past headlong into the dark tangled woods. When he was sure she was out of earshot he stood up and laughed and laughed.

A wind rose from the east and rushed over the grass and on through the trees. The wind strode across the field and through the forest like a man and was gone. The grass stood up tall and the only sound was the small sounds of living things foraging between the blades. The child listened to the sighing of the grasses as they bowed and the groans of the branches bending and here and there a sudden *crack*!— as when a dead twig broke.

SWAN

HIGH UP in a circular room she lay stone-still in deathlike sleep as the years passed, Griselda Sigismund, the name entered by her father, admitted to the county insane asylum at the age of nineteen; hair: black; eyes: black; sex: female—"virgin," written in her father's hand; distinguishing marks: a brown mole on the inside of her left thigh.

Nineteen years old she came with her father, Sigmund Sigismund, then head of the asylum. It was not the first time they saw her inside the institution walls. Some years before she had come often with her father and the two walked arm in arm down the lanes of the asylum garden, the girl silent, her black eyes darting all around while the father spoke in his rasping toneless voice, pointing out to her one inmate after another and explaining their maladies.

The time Dr. Sigismund spent visiting his patients in the building she waited for him in the garden. Uncurious of the inmates she could amuse herself for hours looking for things in the grass, or writing on the prescription pads her father left with her.

"Humanity is mad. Mad," Dr. Sigismund always said, coming out of the building to his daughter, who would continue smiling at a little white worm poised on her finger. Nothing her father said applied to her or to him.

Sigmund Sigismund was a big man with an imposing head, bald but for a thick fringe of hair that stuck out from under his collar. His look from under jutting eyebrows was at once mistrustful and insinuating, and the dark line of his mouth turned up at one corner and down at the other. His daughter resembled him. She had his large frame, long lips and heavy-lidded eyes; but she was slender around the waist, her hair curled down over her shoulders, and her expression was her own. No one had ever heard Dr. Sigismund mention Griselda's mother. He arrived alone with his daughter when he was appointed head of the asylum. To her he had sometimes spoken of his marriage as his "one mistake."

"And yet," he would add, looking her over with pleasure, "what would I have in this world if it were not for that one mistake!"

Those who watched them stroll arm in arm up and down the graveled lanes of the asylum garden wondered why Dr. Sigismund brought his daughter with him. Was it simply to have her at his side? For he eyed her very fondly. Was it the child's whim? It was known he could not resist her wishes. Or was it, as some of the inmates whispered, to pick her future husband from among them? Some members of the staff believed he was grooming her to become his successor, for he had not found any of them worthy of carrying on his work.

After a while she stopped coming with her father and for a number of years the old man came alone. His daughter had married, he told them, a healer like himself, and they assumed she had gone to live somewhere else, since Dr. Sigismund was the only healer in the county.

Then one day they came together again, father and daughter. She had changed. She walked slowly now, her eyes on the ground or staring glazed into nowhere. Her hands hung inert while her father leaned an arm on her shoulder. She sank down on a bench and would not even raise her eyes to look at the inmates her father pointed out to her. To the questioning glances cast at him the doctor replied, "Marriage annulled."

Then the clock on the tower struck four—the hour the doctor usually made his rounds with the patients who were confined in their cell—but this time his daughter did not wait for him in the garden. Rising, Griselda accompanied her father into the building. Together they entered and walked down the long hall with two attendants behind them, stopping briefly before each cell. She would look through the small round opening in each door, till they reached the last cell where a man stood against the wall, his arms outspread, stark naked save for a hood over his head.

"Him," she said, staring fixedly through the round hole.

"Not him," the doctor whispered, and pleaded with her in a subdued voice.

"Him," she said again loudly. "Tell them to unlock the door."

And the doctor told them to open the door.

At that moment both attendants were convinced that Griselda Sigismund would succeed to her father's post and this was her maiden voyage. For besides Dr. Sigismund and the male nurse who gave him his daily injection, no one had ever entered the man's cell. The doctor looked grieved and bent with age when he gave the instruction. His hand reached out to touch his daughter's arm—too late. Griselda walked in without looking at her father, she walked in and closed the door behind her.

Dr. Sigismund told the attendants to leave and remained before the door, his head turned to the side, one eye pressed to the hole. Around midnight he drew the lid over the opening and retired to his office in the building. At his desk he made several attempts to write, but his hand shook so violently that he could only produce jagged scrawls.

"They must be left undisturbed. Totally undisturbed," were his orders the next morning.

Now the members of the staff as well were certain that Griselda Sigismund would succeed to her father's post.

For three days the girl remained alone with the patient. On the third day the doctor told the attendants to look in the cell.

"She is a big girl," he told them. "As strong as a man. Still, she is a girl." And his voice rose.

The record in the institution files is silent as to what happened between those two. It states only the condition in which they were found, the man dead, hung by a tough silk hose, and the girl prostrate on the ground before him. It mentions strange bruises and toothmarks on his body and that there was blood in his hair which had turned white. It states that the man expired and the girl fell unconscious at about the same time. More it did not say.

Clutching the pen in his fist like a knife, Dr. Sigismund committed his daughter and a few weeks later committed himself.

"White she dreamed him, then silver," Griselda Sigismund wrote, "and went barefoot. For she would not put on her father's shoes. She would not. They were the only people in the world, the sorcerer and his daughter. But he promised her a husband. Out of dirt and spittle and memories of dead men he drew lewd pictures on the wall."

Many years ago in her father's house she wrote these things on scraps of paper torn from his prescription pad. In those days Dr. Sigismund still saw patients at his home, but two afternoons a week he spent at the asylum and left his daughter at home. He returned late in the evening and, stopping every so often to rest his bad leg, approached the house which stood three stories high and isolated at the end of the road.

As usual the lights were on.

"What can that girl be doing in all the ten rooms?" the doctor asked himself, leaning on his stick.

For when he was at home she scarcely left her room or her featherbed for that matter.

"She must be dancing through the house," he chortled.

By the time he walked through the front door, his daughter had retreated to her top floor room under the eaves. As usual the house was in riotous disorder, no piece of furniture in its place, the carpets pushed against the wall, all the chest drawers flung open. She had left dirty cups, melon rinds, nutshells, and clumps of weeds lying about, besides stray articles of clothing both his and hers, and removed the clocks he kept in every room and hid them in a closet smothered by a pillow. As usual innumerable scraps of paper were strewn about, some still floating down the stairwell, sheets torn from this prescription pads, on which she had scribbled words strange, incoherent, sometimes foul, often illegible.

"Lovely he hung and silver," he read aloud, and wondered if she meant him.

"Would not wear men's shoes," he read, and said, "but she puts on my dressing gown and leaves it on the floor."

"Put fire to the bed," he read, and laughed, "she is still in love with me."

"She saw her father in a coffin," he read on, "the empty eyes, wasted face. Watched them nail down the lid. Beautiful she rose from her bed—"and still picking up the loose scraps and glancing at a phrase here and there, "she does it only to spite me," he muttered, laboring up the stairs toward her room. "Like her stammer and blushing and false pregnancy symptoms, only to vex me. Wants a man. That's what she wants," he mumbled, banging on her door.

"Hush," he heard her low voice, "I am busy."

"Busy!" he wheezed hoarsely, catching his breath. "I shall wait for you in my room. Must speak to you. Something important. Don't be long."

In his consulting room where he also slept, there hung on the wall facing his bed a portrait of his daughter made when she was ten years old by a patient of his, Larssen, whom he had committed that same day. It showed her in a riding habit holding a toy whip, her long black hair curling like angry serpents down her shoulders and starting breasts. The artist accentuated her strong jaw, the heavy sensual mouth, the eyes mocking and disdainful, the thick ivory pallor of her skin.

"Cruel," he said, speaking to her picture. "Your eyes are loveless and cruel."

"I told him about you," he announced to Griselda when she entered. "Told him everything." Dr. Sigismund broke off, swallowed, then exclaimed, "Poor Larssen! It was too much for him. Had to commit him this afternoon. I am afraid he shall never be able to marry you. That's how it stands with Larssen."

"Larssen?" she asked vaguely.

"The eleven o'clock patient. The man who painted your picture," and he pointed at it.

"It's the twelve o'clock patient I was thinking of anyway," she shrugged.

"Ah, the one with the bandaged head, that's an interesting case—" he began, but his daughter was already out of the room.

"Cruel," he said to the portrait. "Her eyes are loveless and cruel."

Up in her room under the eaves, Griselda Sigismund continued writing:

"The one she dreamed and loved in secret, he snatched away. Her father, the old sorcerer, bewitched him and locked him in a cell. He would not even let her look at him unless she put on his shoes. But she would not wear men's shoes. She would not.

"'You're dreaming,' he said, when he lay down beside her, so that she did not cry out or protest. But as soon as he was asleep she stole the key which was in his shoe and set fire to the bed.

"She watched him burn. Watched the thick yellow smoke curl from his body, turn brown, then black. And the last giant cinderflake drop and crumble. Beautiful she rose from her bed—"

The record in the asylum files gives the several opinions of the doctors as to whether it was more plausible to suppose that the patient died by his own hands or by hers, considering his former and her subsequent condition. Dr. Sigismund registered the conviction that the man was already dead when his daughter entered the cell, which was in conflict, however, with the medical findings. The record further states that all efforts to revive the girl over a period of years had failed.

"Barefoot she ran up the winding stairs and pushed the key in the lock," she wrote years ago, when she lived in her father's house. "The first night she lay on his cold body and sang over him. The second night looked all night long in his silver eyes," Griselda Sigismund wrote in the middle of the night.

Her father was calling her. She came slowly from her room, scattering the scraps of paper as she came down the stairs to his room.

"A false step!" he groaned. He stood on one foot, hugging his calf. Silently, with her secretive smile that was not for him, she began unlacing his boot.

"You need a big man, Griselda, a very big man," Dr. Sigismund murmured, eyeing his twelve-year-old daughter uneasily. "And you can't marry me, you know."

Griselda continued unlacing her father's boot and smiled complacently. She had all his patients to choose from.

"Now, if you're thinking of the one o'clock patient," he began, and both corners of his mouth turned down.

"I could be happy with a little man," she protested. "I mean, he would amuse me," she added quickly, not to offend her father whose large foot lay in her lap.

"But you want him to give you a child, and that is not so simple," the doctor said, frowning at his daughter, who had risen and stood tall, her head slightly titled before her portrait on the wall. Her face was paler and her features softer than the lines of the portrait. The child in the picture looked him straight in the eye, mocking and flirtatious, over the shoulder of the girl whose eyes were not looking at him at all.

"I have worked over thirty years with all sorts of cases," he went on, "and it's not a simple matter at all!" he said with his little chortle to the picture of the child, for the girl had left the room and returned to write under the eaves.

According to the records, Dr. Sigismund died a little less than a month after committing himself. Every day, till the day he died, the father came and sat with his daughter. Leaning over her, his eyes shut, one large hand on her forehead, he sat with her through the long evenings. A week before his death he behaved strangely, roaming the corridors at night in his institution gown. He staggered between the two walls, as if he were inside a lurching ship. Some members of the staff felt he should be deprived of the key to his daughter's room. But before a decision was reached, he was found one morning, slumped over her bed, killed by a stroke.

The asylum record further states that several months after Griselda Sigismund was brought to her cell, her belly began to swell. And, that some nine months after the date of her admission, she was delivered of a child. The record does not say, for the child's protection, to whom he was entrusted. Father unknown, the record states.

"For three days he suffered her caresses, her tears flowing over his frozen stare, and her mouth watering his mouth," Griselda Sigismund wrote many years ago, lying on her featherbed in the house at the end of the road.

"For three days suffered her song echoing in his skull, her voice now soft, now shrill, then howling desolately. But on the third day he rose and without even looking at her, loosed the sash from her waist, took the sash without ever touching her body or feeling its heat, and looped it and hung himself. She watched him swing, and saw his emblem rise hard like a bird's beak. Once more she shrieked. Then gathered the drops of silver in her palm and danced wildly."

Griselda Sigismund wrote, and flung the loose sheets swirling out the window.

From that window she had watched her father's patients walk up to the front door since she was a small child. Through a spy glass, she had watched them come and go, both the men and the women. The women, as well as the men, she observed carefully, whether they were large, with ample breasts.

One day her father announced he would never marry again.

"I have looked over the wide world and not found a woman equal to me," Dr. Sigismund sighed, eyeing his big girl uneasily.

Then Griselda watched the men only. Sometimes she let out a sudden bird shriek, or dropped a handful of feathers out the window, as one approached to cause him to look up that she might have a full view of his face.

So she had watched them from her window year after year while she was growing, and saw their number dwindle. One after another her father had them committed. By her fifteenth year, patients no longer came to the house.

Dr. Sigismund spent all day in the asylum, leaving his daughter alone in the house. But when he observed that her breasts were ripening, and noted her pallor, and saw her full lips half parted, he began to take her with him on visiting days.

Season after season father and daughter walked up the path and looked around: he for a mother for her who lacked one; she for a son for him who wanted one. And down the path they walked and looked around: he for a father to replace him; and she for a daughter to fill her place. Arm in arm they walked, wishing only to please one another. But each time the father pointed encouragingly, the daughter frowned and looked away; and each time the daughter's eyes lit up and she looked inquiringly at her father, he made a disparaging gesture and the corners of his mouth turned down.

When they passed the main building, the doctor raised his eyes to a certain window and sighed.

"Poor Larssen! Imagine if you had married him!"

Griselda split a leaf lengthwise, and smiled her secretive smile.

So it went on season after season. But Griselda stopped looking at the men. As her father pointed to his favorite cases, her eyes darted all around at the frozen branches, the drifting snow, the sun a pale silver on the December sky.

"No, you cannot marry a tree," Dr. Sigismund said to his daughter, when she laid fresh sheets on his bed.

"No, you cannot marry snow," her father told her sternly, the second time she laid fresh sheets on his bed that night.

"No, no, Griselda," he said, "you cannot marry the sun, or the moon, or any planet."

It was the third time she lay fresh sheets on her father's bed that night. Dr. Sigismund, pale and perspiring after his enema, lay down on the made bed. His haggard face now resembled the life-size pencil drawing of an old woman, his mother, which hung above his bed. Beside it hung the portrait of a bearded man, leaning forward pointing a finger. The man with the black beard and piercing eyes was not Sigmund Sigismund's carnal father, but his master, the world-renowned hypnotist, Hosea Garfinkel. A small snapshot of Sigismund, the elder, wearing skullcap and prayer shawl, was tucked in a corner between the glass and frame of the mother's picture.

Griselda was struck by her father's resemblance to his mother. Yet she could not conceive of her father as a woman, even when she transferred her grandmother's wig on his head and imagined her lace blouse over his hairy chest. She was about to rise to inspect her grandfather's picture from close up, but her father's hand pressed down on hers, which lay on his abdomen where he had placed it.

"Where are you going?" he asked with sudden ferocity. "Don't tell me you're going to bed. I know you're up till dawn writing foul phrases about me. I'm hungry. Go and prepare some hot sausage and beans."

She rose, suppressing a smile. Sigmund Sigismund watched her walk to the door. He was a big man, but his housecoat fitted her.

"Wait," he called after her, and asked her to come near.

"I am old," he said, "and will die soon. Do you remember everything I have taught you?" he asked, drawing her down to the bed.

And once more Sigmund Sigismund instructed his daughter at length. Sitting beside him, her hand in his, she listened to him speak of the germ cell of which he and she were ephemeral carriers. Of love and death. Of man and woman, and how their bodies were made to fit to each other.

"You are in love with me," he said. "But you will get over it. Before the end of the month, you shall have a husband."

"No," she said on her way out. "I won't. Never."

Sigmund Sigismund finished the plate of sausage and black beans his daughter brought to him, and, rising from his bed, went to the cupboard and returned with a bottle of peach brandy and two tumblers.

"No," she said. "Not for me."

"Only on the sly, eh?" he snickered, inspecting the level of the brandy. "Go, then. Write foul things about me. I'll drink alone."

"Wait," he called, when she was at the door, and asked her to come near.

His hand reached down, lifting the hem of his dressing gown which she wore. Griselda drew back.

"Don't be silly," he said irritably. "I want to see your mole. We must have it removed," he muttered, after studying it at length.

Then, pushing up his pajama pants, he displayed a great bearded mole just above his knee.

"This," he whispered confidentially to his daughter, "mustn't be disturbed."

"Wait," he called after her, for she had started toward the door. "Put on my slippers. It's cold."

"No," she stammered, leaving. "I won't. Never."

Sigmund Sigismund downed the remaining half of the peach brandy, and stood in the middle of the room, contemplating the picture of his master.

"Curious, how alcohol has absolutely no effect on me," he remarked to Hosea Garfinkel, then gave a small grunt as his rear hit the floor.

"Poor Garfinkel," he sighed. "I wonder if he's still alive in that foul rat-ridden cell in Roumania? Sometimes they live over a hundred when they're catatonic."

Sigmund Sigismund heard someone sneeze. He brought his eyes to focus on his mother's picture. She had a man's face. Then he noticed that his father in the small snapshot was winking at him. Just then, the clock struck four, the hour when Dr. Sigismund permitted himself to yield to what he knew were morbid, delusional states.

His father, in the small snapshot, sneezed again.

"God bless me!" he said, and sneezed again, and blessed himself the third time.

Dr. Sigismund watched him climb down from the picture. Very cautiously, using his hooked stick like a monkey tail, he lighted on the brass orb on the bedpost. Then he spread his prayer shawl like bat wings, and glided into his son's lap.

"What do you think, Papa?" Dr. Sigismund asked his father, pleased with himself for hallucinating so realistically. He was pointing at his daughter in the picture on the opposite side of the wall. "How do you like her?" he asked.

Once again the little old man spread his prayer shawl, and, flapping his arms, streaked across the room. When he struck the child's picture, he clung to it. There he remained, his arms outspread, stuck to the canvas, till Sigmund Sigismund's lids dropped and he fell asleep.

"Lovely he hung and silver. She danced around him barefoot, his silver seed on her tongue," Griselda Sigismund wrote, when her father called her name the third time.

He stood waiting for her on the landing, dressed in Hosea Garfinkel's black satin coat with a collar of raven feathers, which he wore only for the highest occasions.

"Come, daughter, and meet your bridegroom," he intoned, ushering her into his bedroom.

Griselda Sigismund looked around the room. She looked before her and behind her; she looked to the right and saw the picture of herself as a child; she looked to the left and saw her father's huge bed empty and the two portraits above the bed. She turned around once again; then she heard someone sneeze, and saw a little man. He had just landed on his feet, as if he had dropped from the wall. He wore a skullcap and an institution gown, with a fringed prayer shawl over it, and had merry slanted eyes.

"Rabbi Isaak Wunder," Dr. Sigismund whispered to his daughter, his flushed face close to hers. "An incurable, but perfectly harmless, case."

The little man stood for a while looking wise, and stroking his thin white beard. Then he pulled a silver rattle from his pocket and shook it gleefully, jumping from one foot to the other.

Dr. Sigismund watched his daughter blush, then put her hand to her mouth to suppress a thin giggle. Then he watched Isaak Wunder sweep Griselda in his arms; squatting, he pulled the big girl in his lap, and kissed her with a sidelong winking look for his approval.

Sigmund Sigismund cleared his throat, and married them quickly. While he blessed them, Rabbi Wunder also raised his hands in a blessing gesture.

Then they all three lived together in the big house, and Isaak Wunder made merry with both father and daughter. They indulged his every whim. She cooked for him all kosher delicacies, and he provided him with the women he needed to make him happy—fat Hottentot women and little red-haired girls with a hair lip.

Isaak Wunder had a merry time. He complained to the father about the daughter, and to the daughter about the father.

"A stupid old ogre," he conceded to her.

"Mad, like her poor mother," he granted him. And the two men commiserated with each other over tumblers of peach brandy.

For almost three years the three were living together, and the father continued to bribe him fearing he might leave his daughter, while the daughter continued to humor him fearing to be left alone once again with her father.

When Dr. Sigismund asked his daughter, "Where are the children?" Griselda looked at the wall.

"Griselda," he called, as she started walking to the door, "do you love your husband?"

"He amuses me," she said, without turning, and was gone.

Isaak Wunder had a gift for mimicry. In an instant he could change into any man, woman, or beast; only his little winking look betrayed Isaak Wunder. He made merry turning himself into a mouse, a butterfly, a harlot, an inquisitor, into Dr. Sigismund, and sometimes into Griselda herself.

But when Griselda said, "Now turn into my husband," Isaak Wunder simply sneezed. His nose twitched, the whites of his eyes between the slanty lids turned a watery pink, and he sneezed with mounting abandon, till Griselda pulled him by the beard and spat at him.

Isaak Wunder went to Sigmund Sigismund, and complained about his daughter.

"She is insane!" he said, throwing up his arms with a compassionate wink at the doctor. "You yourself have always said she was insane. Then have her committed. I insist."

"A grave decision," Dr. Sigismund murmured.

"Better do it quick," he said, circling around the room, "before she runs away. She's threatened to—"

"You ask me to make a very grave decision," Sigmund Sigismund groaned.

"We could still visit her every day," Isaak Wunder smiled, and poured two tumblers of peach brandy.

"Give me one more day to think it over," Sigmund Sigismund whispered, emptying the tumbler in one gulp.

Dr. Sigismund was on his way home from the asylum the evening of the following day.

"Can't commit her yet," he muttered to himself, while he paused to give his bad foot a rest. "She must have a child first. A little granddaughter," he chortled. "Then, perhaps—" he mused, and walked on.

"Why can't he give her a child," he muttered, as he paused once again a little way from the house. "Perhaps, under hypnosis. Or is it because of her titled womb?" He walked on.

Coming up the front steps, Dr. Sigismund heard loud groans. Inside he found his daughter stretched out on his bed, eating a melon.

"Isaak," he cried. "Where is Isaak? What have you done with him?"

"Upstairs," she mumbled, her mouth full, "giving birth."

"Then why aren't you with him?" he exclaimed, and rushing off pulled himself up the stairs to his daughter's room.

Isaak Wunder lay on Griselda's featherbed and glared at his father-in-law indignantly. Two great lumps had risen on the top of his head.

"Your fault," he said.

"The tumors will disappear," Dr. Sigismund promised. "Am I a healer for nothing?" he roared.

Then with one hand raised over Isaak Wunder's head and his eyes fixed on his, he spoke in a monotonous voice till the tumors subsided. But in a little while, another two lumps started to grow from under his armpits. Once more Dr. Sigismund's healing art made them shrink; but immediately they reappeared, this time on his most vulnerable part. Isaak Wunder's lids dropped as he fainted, and the doctor decided to operate.

"Help," he called to his daughter. "Quick! Some towels." Griselda came slowly up the stairs.

"You killed him," he sobbed when she appeared in the door, towel in the hand. "Dead," he said. "Dead. Dead. All dead."

Griselda shut her eyes and did not breathe, while her father placed the lumps of flesh on the towel in her outstretched hands.

Once again, father and daughter were alone in the big house.

"If only one of the children had lived," Dr. Sigismund sighed, limping from room to room to wind his many clocks.

Griselda paced up and down the narrow strip of grass beside the house, her eyes on the ground. When she found a snail, she tore it from its shell. Watching her from his study window, Dr. Sigismund noted the ripeness of her body and sighed uneasily.

"Impossible," he muttered. "A husband. She must have a husband."

He pleaded with her to come with him once more to the asylum, and she could choose any man she wished. Yes, any man. She was no longer writing on scraps of paper, torn from her father's prescription pad, as she used to many years ago. She looked for things in the grass. Griselda Sigismund went to the asylum with her father.

"...and swooned the instant she swallowed his seed," Griselda Sigismund wrote, years ago in her room under the eaves.

"Fired by a silent shot she soared off, pure speed and light, growing immense with distance till she struck the side of the sky. There she hung fixed and did not fall.

"High up in a deserted tower she lay in a deathlike trance," Griselda Sigismund wrote about the sorcerer's daughter. "And while she slept the seed took root in her body and flowered into a man. He touched her face but she did not wake. He kissed her lips, still she did not stir. He called her Swan because she glided white and silent over the lakes of the sky. And Swan, who was once the sorcerer's daughter, looked up at him and saw his face, and she remembered the silver eyes and recognized him. Her lips parted to speak, but no sound came from her mouth.

"Together they departed, a man riding a great swan up the stream, deep in the night they rode up the fast currents of mountain springs, till they vanished into the source.

"And since that time swans are mute."

Griselda wrote, and, rising from her featherbed, tossed the last slip of paper out the window. She watched it rise for an instant, then glide away on a spring breeze.

THE LAST DANCE

DEATH came to Mary Ann in the guise of a lover. He came to her in the night, and kissed her in her sleep. Night after night he came to her, till Mary Ann said to him, "The next time I want you to come when I'm awake. I want you to kiss me for real and take me with you."

One day, as Mary Ann walked out of the house on her way to school, she found him waiting for her by the garden gate all pale and lovely in the morning. Mary Ann ran into his arms and lifted her face up to his.

"If I kiss you now," he said smiling, "you will die. And if I take you, it's forever. Do you still want to come with me?"

Mary Ann considered. "I want to be your bride, Death," she said after a while. "But I am too little. Will you wait for me till I grow up?"

"I'll wait," Death said. "But you must pledge yourself to me."

Mary Ann pledged herself to Death. Their wedding was to take place on her fourteenth birthday.

But when she turned fourteen, she persuaded her bridegroom to postpone it for another few years.

"I'm barely a woman yet," she pleaded. "Look how small my breasts are! I want to learn how to dance first, and look like a real lady for our wedding!"

"It's as you like, Mary Ann," Death said.

At seventeen Mary Ann married a divinity student.

"He will prepare me for you," she explained to Death. "You must be patient, dear. We mustn't rush things. Our wedding is too important a matter. In ten years I shall surely be ready."

But when Death came to her ten years later, she was so busy with her household and children he couldn't bring himself to disturb her, but waited around the house. One day he caught her alone in the garden.

"I cannot wait any longer," he said. "I must have you now or never. I love you, and I have been faithful to you all these years. But now I feel you're playing with me."

"A little more time," Mary Ann pleaded. "After all, we shall be together for all eternity, and with my husband, you know, it's just a thing of a few years."

"Are you happy with him then?"

"How could I be happy with him!" Mary Ann said, stroking his cheek. "When he kisses me I close my eyes, but I always wake up afterward; so we have to keep on doing it over and over again, and that spoils it, of course. You're the only one whose kiss shall put me to sleep forever. You're the only one I love. But wait just a little longer."

"Why, what have you to do that's so important?"

"Nothing important to do," Mary Ann smiled. "But we planted a pear tree some years ago, and this summer it will bear fruit. I am curious what it will taste like."

"But you've eaten pears before," Death said.

"But not from this tree," replied Mary Ann. "I must taste a pear from this tree before I can come to you."

That spring Mary Ann and her husband had a quarrel, and by the time the pears were ripe to eat, they still hadn't finished fighting. Death watched her bite into the pear. Mary Ann made a face. It was a gritty pear.

"You see," Death said, "you could have spared yourself this. Come now. And don't tell me you have to stay for your children's sake!"

"It's not that," Mary Ann said. "But you see, I'd like just a little more time to set things right. If I came now you might think that I'm simply running away, whereas I want you to know that I come out of love and no other reason than that I love you. Give me just another year."

"And then you'll be wanting to stay on another year to bring your daughter to her first dance, and another five years to see your son turn into a man. You'll be curious to see how you look with your hair all white, or you'll tell me you simply have to take a trip to the moon before you come to me. Always your insatiable curiosity! I am beginning to think you're the kind of woman that wants to be raped. But I am a shy and gentle lover."

"I know," she said. "That's what I love about you."

"I am not going to make any more rendezvous with you, Mary Ann," he said. "When you want me, call and I shall come. But do not wait too long. I am delicate, and if you grow too heavy I shall not be able to carry you off. You have remained remarkably light for your years. But you're too greedy. If you stay around till you've had your fill, it might be too late." And with that he left her.

That year brought nothing good to Mary Ann. Nor the next. She had only troubles to contend with. But she was determined to put her house in order. "Anyway," she said to herself, "I can't have Death see me with my face all swollen like this."

There came a time when Mary Ann was so lost to her misery that she even forgot about her lover. One night as she lay sleepless, a stunned moth fell on her pillow. It had a white face painted on its wings with the saddest eyes and a smiling mouth. Mary Ann was moved by its fragile beauty, and she remembered Death and called for him.

Death came. He was very thin now, but more handsome than ever.

"Now," Mary Ann said. "Take me now, this minute."

"But you're much too heavy," he said. "Your tears alone weigh more than I can carry. And with all the grief hoarded in your heart, I'm afraid I couldn't even lift you. No," he said sadly, "you'll have to wait now and take your turn with my brother, the henchman."

"No," Mary Ann pleaded, "it's you I want. My life has never meant much to me, you know that. It's only your kiss I crave. Is there nothing I can do to get rid of all this weight?"

"If you were truly happy for a single instant," Death said, "that would make you light again. But you would have to call me that same moment, before you had time to grow heavy again. I see little hope for you," he said. "First of all, your chances of happiness are slight.

And even if you should find it, would you have the strength to re-nounce it the very same moment?"

Mary Ann looked at Death with a baffled look. For she had never known true happiness and she did not understand what he meant.

"I must leave you now," Death said. "Be careful the next time you call; for if you are heavy like this, my brother, the henchman, will come in my place, and there's no pleading with him because he is a big, ugly brute who just raises his hatchet and brings it down on your head."

"Wait," Mary Ann said. "The conditions you have set are impossible. You alone can make me truly happy."

"Because you have answered well," Death said, "I will give you one more chance. Sunday, in a week, you will go to the midsummer masked ball. I will be there in disguise. Many will ask you to dance, but if you accept to dance with anyone else but me, I'll not take you, but send my henchman brother to dispose of you when and as he pleases."

Mary Ann put on a white dress for the ball. "I shall surely recognize him," she said to herself, "for my heart always beats a certain way in his presence."

One by one the men came up to Mary Ann and asked her for a dance. They were dressed in gaudy costumes, some like fantastic beasts, some like princes, pirates, angels, and devils, some like clowns; there was even one dressed like a skeleton. But Mary Ann saw through their disguises. None made her heart beat that certain way, and she refused them one after another. It was already past midnight, many of the couples had left, and still Mary Ann had not danced.

The musicians were announcing the last dance. Mary Ann looked over the ballroom. Had Death deceived her? Just then she saw a gaunt figure standing by the door on the other side of the ballroom. She had not noticed him till now because his dress was so similar to the livery of the footmen and waiters, only much shabbier and ill fitting. Unlike the servants, however, he had a sack over his head like a hangman's hood tied around his neck.

"That must be him!" Mary Ann thought, and her heart was beating slowly, very slowly, but hard like a hammer against her side.

She walked up to him, her eyes lowered to the ground. All she could see were his large feet placed wide apart. He wore boots, but the leather was split in places showing a discolored toenail and calloused skin.

"Let's dance," she said.

"I don't know how," he said, in a muffled voice.

Mary Ann looked up. The sack over his head was spattered like a butcher's apron. He seemed to be smiling at her with two mouths, the rows of tiny pointed teeth just barely visible in the eye slits.

"Dance, dance with me!" Mary Ann pleaded.

He raised one arm and moved it around her waist slowly like a robot. He raised his other arm and brought the hand down heavily on her shoulder. He wore white gloves, but the leather was split in places showing a claw and tufts of blond fur.

"Dance, dance with me!" she pleaded, and he began to turn her around, slowly at first, then faster. The lights in the crystal chandeliers dimmed then lit up red. He flung her about to the left and to the right, and whirled her around with mounting fury. The violins kept playing the same note faster and faster. His claw ripped her side, and he shook her till all her memories fell out.

"Death, speak to me," Mary Ann pleaded. "Let me feel your kiss that I should know it's you."

She wanted to tear off his hood and press her lips on his, but she was growing smaller and smaller or he was growing taller and taller, so that she couldn't even reach his shoulder with her outstretched hand. He took her by the heels and slapped her against the wall like a fish. Still Mary Ann didn't lose hope.

"I've never known true happiness," she thought. All her life she had been waiting for the kiss of death, and now she was curious to find out.

But her partner had long ago ripped up her face; she had no mouth anymore. All that remained was a lot of bones, and the insides that the butcher was still whirling around. And when the last spark of life flew out of her, he dug a hole in the ground, stuffed her in, and kicked some earth over it with the side of his boot.

OTHER NEW YORK REVIEW CLASSICS

For a complete list of titles, visit www.nyrb.com.

HANNAH ARENDT Rahel Varnhagen: The Life of a Jewish Woman
POLINA BARSKOVA Living Pictures
DINO BUZZATI A Love Affair
DINO BUZZATI The Stronghold
CAMILO JOSÉ CELA The Hive
EILEEN CHANG Written on Water
FRANÇOIS-RENÉ DE CHATEAUBRIAND Memoirs from Beyond the Grave, 1800–1815
LUCILLE CLIFTON Generations: A Memoir
COLETTE Chéri *and* The End of Chéri
E. E. CUMMINGS The Enormous Room
JÓZEF CZAPSKI Memories of Starobielsk: Essays Between Art and History
HEIMITO VON DODERER The Strudlhof Steps
FERIT EDGÜ The Wounded Age *and* Eastern Tales
ROSS FELD Guston in Time: Remembering Philip Guston
BEPPE FENOGLIO A Private Affair
WILLIAM GADDIS The Letters of William Gaddis
NATALIA GINZBURG Family *and* Borghesia
JEAN GIONO The Open Road
VASILY GROSSMAN The People Immortal
MARTIN A. HANSEN The Liar
ELIZABETH HARDWICK The Uncollected Essays of Elizabeth Hardwick
ERNST JÜNGER On the Marble Cliffs
MOLLY KEANE Good Behaviour
PAUL LAFARGUE The Right to Be Lazy
JEAN-PATRICK MANCHETTE The N'Gustro Affair
THOMAS MANN Reflections of a Nonpolitical Man
MAXIM OSIPOV Kilometer 101
KONSTANTIN PAUSTOVSKY The Story of a Life
MARCEL PROUST Swann's Way
ALEXANDER PUSHKIN Peter the Great's African: Experiments in Prose
RUMI Gold; translated by Haleh Liza Gafori
FELIX SALTEN Bambi; or, Life in the Forest
ANNA SEGHERS The Dead Girls' Class Trip
VICTOR SERGE Last Times
ELIZABETH SEWELL The Orphic Voice
ANTON SHAMMAS Arabesques
CLAUDE SIMON The Flanders Road
WILLIAM GARDNER SMITH The Stone Face
VLADIMIR SOROKIN Telluria
JEAN STAFFORD Boston Adventure
GEORGE R. STEWART Storm
ADALBERT STIFTER Motley Stones
ITALO SVEVO A Very Old Man
MAGDA SZABÓ The Fawn
SUSAN TAUBES Divorcing
ELIZABETH TAYLOR Mrs Palfrey at the Claremont
TEFFI Other Worlds: Peasants, Pilgrims, Spirits, Saints
YŪKO TSUSHIMA Woman Running in the Mountains
IVAN TURGENEV Fathers and Children
ROBERT WALSER Little Snow Landscape
EDITH WHARTON Ghosts: Selected and with a Preface by the Author